THE PECULIAR BOARS OF MALLOY

The PECULIAR BOARS of MALLOY

DOUG CRANDELL

SWITCHGRASS BOOKS   NORTHERN ILLINOIS UNIVERSITY PRESS   DeKalb

Library of Congress Cataloging-in-Publication Data
Crandell, Doug.
The peculiar boars of Malloy/ Doug Crandell.
   p.   cm.
ISBN: 9780875806334 (pbk.: acid-free paper)
I. Title
PS3603.R377P432010
813'.6--dc22
2010001724

A portion of this novel was awarded the Sherwood Anderson Grant in
Fiction for a novel in progress. Portions have appeared in the *Indiana Review,*
the *Nebraska Review,* and *Night Train.*

For Maggie, Luke, and Jake

There are extraordinary similarities between the Midwest in America and Europe in that there is this sense of vast, open sky and loneliness and cold.

—*Ajay Naidu*

ACKNOWLEDGMENTS

Writing a novel is a lot like taking a trip without any luggage, money, or sense of direction. You sit down and try to travel to an unknown but necessary destination by sheer grace. In other words, you'd be stranded without the help of others, and, to that end, I'm forever grateful to a number of people who have made the trip with me.

The Sherwood Anderson Foundation provided a fiction fellowship that not only helped me pay my bills, but also provided me with a much needed boost of confidence. This novel never would have been written without their gracious support.

The folks at Switchgrass Books have helped me shape the book into its best form, and for that I'd like to thank Sara Hoerdeman and Tracy Schoenle for their insightful edits and patient support.

To all of my family—Kennedy, Walker, Jennifer, and Nancy— I'd like to say thank you for helping me laugh, eat, love, and relax. Finally, I often find myself praying for help with writing, and I'm humbled to report that in my darkest moments, when the journey seems all but lost, I'm blessed with typing just one more word, and there's light again.

PROLOGUE

My pint-sized dad told everyone that we'd started using artificial insemination because it was scientific, but they knew the reason I had to smear greasy, man-made pheromones on the rear of a metal dummy sow and then wait until one of the boars mounted it to manually collect his seed: It had to do with the gay boars we'd bought from the Conner farm off Highway 31 in the southern part of the state, where I now fly a jalopy of a crop duster, spraying herbicide over fields of high corn and blooming soybeans. It's a remote view I appreciate even more after tromping around on the mucky ground below during all of adolescence. From the sky, the few farms that remain seem more like raised bumps on a topographical relief map than crumbling homesteads. As a kid, I longed to live in the sky, hoping from there our mother could be seen. When our dad got all revved up, fibbing to compensate for his littleness, it was easy to see how our mother could've run off. Back then, Ronald and I used to imagine where she was, how she might be wearing her hair, and if she ever thought of us.

Our aunt Lee was our mother and gently instructed us that our real mother's ambition was to be famous. It didn't matter for what. We knew she could draw. At one point, just out of high school, our mother won a contest for a self-portrait. Every Christmas after she'd left us, without fail, we'd get hand-drawn cards, one for Ronald and one for me. They were excellent. I kept all of mine in a cigar box in my underwear drawer, but Ronald refused to keep his, so I'd dig them out of the trash and put his with mine. Even now, after all that's happened and Ronald and I are full grown, I go out of my way and fly over her newly built house and try to see right down through the big roof. I wonder if she's inside doodling or drawing and if a couple of them might be caricatures of us.

To understand a man, they say, you must look to his father, and if that's true, a story of him from when he was a teenager might help. My small father was on his first airplane flight, en route from Indianapolis, Indiana, to Sioux City, Iowa, as part of a regional hog judging contest sponsored by the Future Farmers of America. He was sixteen, and more than anything in his young life he wanted desperately to do well in the area he'd decided to concentrate all his agri-energies: the crossbred gilt class. The fact that the handlers of these estrus-ready females used lipstick to highlight the vulva of the animal for competition—while merely a side note—is enough to make me wish I had never grown up having been made privy to such things, but I have been, and so have a whole host of people my age in the Midwest. More than a handful of middle-aged teachers in Fort Wayne know how to tell if a sow is receptive to a boar; the fortyish grocery store manager in Terre Haute can recognize a cow in heat. It's a curse we carry with us, those who are long of the farm.

Anyway, it had been a tough sophomore year for Gerald Bancroft in that he'd been subjected to a number of humiliating practical jokes, which includes yet another story I must tell before getting too far into the airplane fiasco. Please forgive me for straying, but ever since my mother gave a skinny, bumbling pig farmer two healthy boys and then moved on, my memories include only the antics of a silly, failed father. The part of my memory where a mother grows is as vacant and queer as the sound of wind coursing under the wings of my little two-seater when I spray the buggy fields of foreclosing farms. When I search for memories of her, I only hear the sound of air rushing past.

Aunt Lee said our dad had always been teased and in high school had once been forcibly stripped of his clothes and entirely swaddled in Saran Wrap, with the only openings being a mouth hole and two slits for his eyes. She said that some tough-neck boys propped him up just inside the girls' locker room showers so that when the gossiping girls came in, the first sight they saw was a naked twig in see-through mummy wrap. To make matters worse, the jocks at his school convinced the athletic director and the principal that they'd overheard the little sicko purposely planning the caper with a friend so that he could get his jollies. They even made up a story that my dad had supposedly told them: "They'll think some of the football players did it to me." He was suspended, and his Presbyterian parents were humiliated. When word got around that little Jerry had purposely wrapped himself in plastic in order to sneak a peek at the naked girls entering the showers, he got a reputation for being both a bit desperate and a tad creepy, a view of him that made living and farming in the cold, northern part of Indiana something of a proverbial challenge. Strike one.

Now back to the airplane troubles.

During the flight aboard a small Wabash Airlines plane owned by a Midwestern steel mill proprietor named Ralph Tannerfield, my father became thirsty. Since this was a relatively short flight, and due to the fact that Wabash Airlines was struggling to pay even its pilots, there was no meal or beverage service. My father, pimply faced and all of eighty pounds, repeatedly asked the vo-ag teacher, Mr. Swatz, if he could get a drink. Irritated by my father's incessant nagging for a drink of which there was no source, Mr. Swatz said loudly—so the others clad in their blue-and-gold corduroy FFA jackets could hear— "Bancroft, why don't you just go get a quench out of the bathroom spigot. I'm not gonna tell you again, boy—there just isn't anything.

Just wait until we land in Sioux City." My father took his teacher's errant advice and went to the small bathroom, closed the door behind him, locking out the uproarious laughter of his peers (who had started the school year by hearing about his alleged perversity surrounding the girls' locker room), and proceeded to gingerly put his lips to the sink faucet. Now, it should be said that what happened next could never in a million years have been predicted by Jerry Bancroft, or anybody for that matter—except for possibly the maintenance personnel of Wabash Airlines, who in their logs stated that they'd been consistently having trouble with air getting trapped inside the onboard water hulls. Years after first hearing the story, I had to read the logs myself, looking for an explanation beyond mere genetics or some ordered family curse. In the reports, the maintenance men had cited "unusual water line burps just after fill" and "excessive vacuum forces in water lines during tap use."

Once Jerry's tongue was suctioned up into the water faucet, it became almost impossible for him to scream for help. He may have kicked the floor or basin with his mini-sized feet, but it wouldn't have produced much in the way of sounding an alarm. With nearly two hours left in the flight—and the rest of the cabin's future sodbusters and pig breeders headlong into preparing for the big showdown in Sioux City—my dad was at the mercy of someone else's intestinal pressures or weak bladder.

Near the end of the flight, during last call to roam freely around the cabin, Mr. Swatz headed to the restroom. When he tried to push the door inward, though, there was resistance—small, yes, but all the same there seemed to be something blocking his entry. Mr. Swatz called the stewardess, and, as they say, the rest is history. The story around the county remains that Gerald Bancroft spent the majority of his time in Sioux City, Iowa, in an emergency room where attendants tried mightily to reduce the swelling of his purple tongue and provide some relief for his severely bruised lips. But he was determined to get to the hog judging competition, and to his credit he figured out how to get from one side of a foreign town to the other in time to partake partially in what he hoped would be his forte. Still, he was mocked by the swarm of other high school farmer boys from all points east of the Mississippi as he tried in vain to make himself understood to the judges. I often imagine him trying to vocalize his specific observations to an elderly ring judge, how he must've sounded trying to talk about a gilt's teat alignment or the irregularities of her vulva protrusions that might lead to difficult birthing, all the while his fat tongue garbling every word as the bewildered judge gave up and moved on to a kid who could at least articulate what he'd seen.

Aunt Lee said when her young brother returned home from the trip that fateful year, he became the butt of endless jokes that fishtailed out of control and grew legendary with the farmers around the county. I guess, in a way, it was the start of something that would eventually get televised. Just four years later he met our mother, had my brother and me, and saw his wife run off with another man. I have dreams of him, even now, in which he is hanging on a nail in a cinder-block room under the tight constraint of the Saran Wrap, his mouth smooshed flat and black and blue, whispering words through the slit. At night I wake up and try to make out what he is saying. I always think he's whispering: "Fly me around some, Lance. I want to see it all, too." But I can't be sure, because there's also a loud round of laughter rumbling through the scenes. And sometimes it's not even him up there on the wall trapped in plastic—it's me, and I can never hear myself in dreams.

Part
ONE

CHAPTER ONE

Bill and Leroy stood by the sire run our dad had cobbled together using warped wood from one of our many crumbling sheds. Bill and Leroy smoked cigarette after cigarette, cracking vile jokes and laughing like donkeys. The ground at their feet was useless marl, ugly soil that didn't give way to something more fertile until the precipice frontage dropped off into a river valley of dark black loam some three-quarters of a mile away. But that lush plat of earth wasn't ours, couldn't be—we were the Bancrofts, unlikely to own anything of much value.

We had a shoal of empty outbuildings, a grange only partially worked. Even the fly-ridden carrion of our bygone livestock when sold to the stink-wagon were priced lower than our neighbors; the drive down our long lane, said the owner of the fertilizer company, cost him more gas than most. It was agreed around the county that our greatest asset was our matriarch, Aunt Lee. Some said all three of the Bancroft males were her peons, certainly nothing more, most likely less. Still, she believed her nephews were bright boys with healthy futures, and she tried hard to help her brother look good in front of us.

From the house, a slap of the screen door accented Aunt Lee's parading glide down the concrete steps. She carried an etched glass platter of what amounted to homemade Egg McMuffins above her head as she sidled up to where the men were standing. They all held Styrofoam cups of coffee between their calloused and cracked fingers as they leaned on the fence, waiting for the livestock truck to deliver the boars. They wore insulated coveralls with corduroy collars and brass zippers. One back pocket usually encased a matted red hanky that they'd pull out at what seemed to be precise intervals, blowing their bulbous noses as if they were trying to loosen up their brains. In a row on the fence, they appeared to me as a string of woolly bears that had recently been taught the trick of drinking from a cup. My dad stood near them, trying to imitate their postures; he was fidgeting with his pants, a nervous habit that sometimes could be mistaken for attempting to touch his privates in public. My brother, Ronald, busied himself with spreading sheaves of straw around the pen—a chore he'd been dragging out for nearly an hour. Ronald loved animals more than people, and he wanted the boars' new home to be cozy, but he also took his time on a chore to simply avoid our father. As he shook the sections of straw loose, he made certain to create the exact coverage of bedding he'd no doubt read of in the volumes of veterinarian books he kept at his bedside. Ronald was handsome, and, at twenty-one, with the love of animals defining him, and his clear blue eyes peering out from under a mop of thick roan hair, he was able to do what was right without fearing the possibility of rejection. I wished my eyes were his color, not the dull brown that reminded me of cow pies. Later, even after his left eye had been damaged by a flying shard of metal from a power takeoff while he was on call at a Holstein farm, he was still attractive, like a new crossbreed no one had ever thought of mixing. The tan fleck on his blue iris looked like another pupil, penetrating and mysterious.

"Okay, fellas. I had Lee here put together some breakfast sandwiches for us." As he pointed toward the plate of food, my dad again rearranged his britches and smiled at Aunt Lee, grateful for her playing along with his little stint of show-and-tell. "Help yourselves, now. Eat up."

She swallowed her pride and didn't roll her eyes. "Eat them while they're hot, men," she said, smiling slightly at her brother, who was a good six inches shorter than she. One time, when we were just kids, we went to see Kenny Rogers's *Six Pack,* and the ticket taker thought our dad was just one of Aunt Lee's boys, the oldest.

When the platter was nearly empty, Aunt Lee made sure to bring Ronald and me the two biggest sandwiches. She turned to leave. "I've got wash to do and the books to keep." If the men weren't around, we'd have gotten big wet kisses on our cheeks; instead she just patted us lightly on the forearms before she made her way back toward the house that always smelled of her blessed bleach.

We heard the truck before we saw it grinding over the brow of the last hill, which was a scrub knoll that had succumbed to thistle weeds. My dad set his cup down on top of one of the newly erected creosote poles, straightened his yellow seed corn hat securely down over his dinky forehead, and gave the midsection of his jeans another upward tug. He cleared his throat and said proudly, "Well, here they are, fellas." He asked the men to step aside to free up the area around the rusty gate. Leroy flashed a quick, knowing wink at his brother, Bill—a gesture that made me blush with the knowledge that they were mocking my dad. They'd been friends of his all their lives, but it seemed they hung around more for the laughs than out of any real sense of loyalty. You couldn't blame them, though—our dad never failed to turn an everyday task into a legendary blunder. It was as if his specific role in the world was to make things worse; he couldn't help it. But still, a young son often sees his life as a man in his father's daily routines, and as he stumbled and nearly fell over a piece of lumber, it was hard not to feel sick. I watched him as he wiped mud from his hand onto his coveralls.

"Leroy, will you give me a hand here?" My dad and Leroy drug the cobbled pine chute from the side of the barn around to the open pen. As he stooped over to make sure the chute was placed just right, the label on his white briefs rested flat on the small of his thin back. It'd been blacked out with a permanent marker to hide any indication of the small size: a boy's 14/16.

To open the truck's slender portal, the driver yanked the weighted jute rope down to his crotch like he was ringing a church bell. The boars' noses, two black nostrils enmeshed inside swirls of pink, twitched and sniffed at the new air wafting up in their direction. First one, then the other took cautious steps in a hesitant trip down the steeply inclined chute. Once inside the pen, their legs quivered from trying to become accustomed to the solid ground beneath them.

I held my breath. My dad wanted this debut to make him a man's man, something I wasn't sure could ever be accomplished. If he could only start his herd off right, then he'd get the respect of all the farmers in the tri-county area. He'd saved for nearly ten years for this day, selling scrap copper tubing and working as an auctioneer's assistant each autumn. The boars were impressive. Their bodies were magnificent, rangy, and toned. The breeder had oiled their coats with a spray-on sheen used for shows, and they glistened in the early morning sun like newly minted coins. The bristly hairs on their broad backs stood erect in the breeze as they turned up their snouts to take in the exotic smells. My dad looked as if he wanted to hug them. It reminded me of the time two years earlier when Aunt Lee had come home from surgery to remove a cyst on an ovary. He gave us all hugs that day until Aunt Lee told him to knock it off, that she'd keep right on living just to spite him. He hadn't hugged us since we were little. His embrace was weak, faint enough that if you closed your eyes, it'd feel as if someone had draped a towel around your shoulders.

"Well, looky there, Jer, ya got ya a fine set of screwers. Just look at the nuts on those bastards, would ya. Hell, they'll hump anything that even begins to oink."

When Bill had finished with his compliments, Leroy took over. "That's goddang right, Jer. Them sons a bitches will have you running fence just to keep them from screwing all the sows from here to Madison County."

The boars went to the trough and sniffed its empty insides before getting spooked by Ronald. He was closing the barn door to keep rain from wetting the bales of straw he'd been using to bed the three sick piglets he'd nursed through a nasty case of cholera. Ronald loved farming for one reason: the animals. Several times I'd spied on him as he picked up a tiny pig after docking its tail or giving it a shot of Terramycin, and he'd held it out right in front of his face and rubbed its nose on his like an Eskimo, talking to it in a methodical voice of reassurance. In those moments, he was what I felt my dad should have been: a man who could see past his own needs, a man who was authentic in his desires, a father who'd not embarrass me by being the county's primo laughingstock. Ronald was three years older than me but tried to father me, using his brotherhood like a vaccine.

My dad cinched his belt tighter and put out the cigarette he'd been smoking for the benefit of the men. The truth was that he wanted badly to be able to chew Skoal or Red Man like the guys at the grain elevator, but he always ended up swallowing the juice rather than spitting it out. Chewing tobacco gave him the runs. This severe allergy was not diagnosed early enough to prevent him from having an embarrassing accident at the county fair shortly after he'd graduated from high school. Aunt Lee said it was an awful sight—the way he looked all covered in a brown slime as the ambulance attendants in plastic smocks lifted his nearly lifeless body onto the stretcher.

With the cigarette ground conspicuously into the dirt outside the pen, Dad threw a scrawny leg over the fence and almost lost his balance. He peered over his shoulder at the clapboard as if it was the cause of his mishap. Inside the pen with his new prized possessions, he said, "Yeah, you're damn right, boys. These babies are gonna make them gilts of mine . . ." He paused, trying to mimic the style of speech Bill and Leroy had used. "Crazy. These bastards are sure gonna make 'em crazy."

Bill and Leroy clambered upon the fence with their armpits resting on the top rung in order to get a better view of the hogs. Ronald motioned to me, and we both ambled over to the fence ourselves, taking our places. It was a ritual of sorts, a type of farmer's ceremony. We'd traveled with my father all over the countryside to the farms of friends and neighbors to inspect everything from newly hung barn siding to brand-spanking-new farm implements and even the occasional aboveground pool or cable TV. Out there on the tundra of the country's flyover area, Reaganomics was giving way to Farm Aid as people who desperately needed a new tractor decided to go in debt on account of their kids, a generation that wanted cable as badly as their peers in Boston or San Diego. On those trips to neighboring farms, my father was always courteous and sincere with his compliments. But on our drives back, in the battered pickup truck we'd bought at an auction, he'd have a look of reverie in his black eyes, as if he were practicing in his head for the day when it would be his turn to display the wares of agri-success. This was the day he'd dreamed of for nearly a decade. It was small in comparison to what others had achieved, and something about that scared me, gave me goose bumps on my arms.

"Well, boys, what do ya think? Don't your dad got himself a fine set of boars here?" When Leroy was finished, he used his head to motion downward into the pen where my father stood surveying the entire scene: new boars, brawny men, observant sons, and a makeshift enclosure. A satisfied smile spread across his apple-red face as the rain fell in even bigger drops, splattering audibly at his dinky feet. For a moment I felt relief—my dad now had something to be proud of, something tangible he could use as a diversion when he was being teased. I imagined him in the grain elevator with other farmers, bragging on and on about his boars, just like the real men there did.

The boars began to nuzzle noses as the drizzle picked up. With gentle ruts, the slightly bigger boar worked his head down along the body of the other, using his snout to root and sniff the belly of his companion. We all watched, engrossed by the docile maneuvers. My father beamed, his usually sandy face ruddy and aglow.

"Looks like they're gonna get along just fine, Jer. Ya know, I had a pair once that nearly shredded each other to death. They thought there weren't gonna be enough breeding to go 'round, I suspect." Bill slapped Ronald's back and said, "You boys get to doin' that down there at Goldie's Saloon, too, don't ya? 'Specially when one of the Bidwell girls comes a-strutting in, huh?" Ronald shrugged his shoulders, shot his eyes at me. Bill and Leroy were drunks and instigators but also successful owners of a used farm machinery business. They always had time on their hands and were willing to spend it around our father.

When the boar reached the rear of the other, he flared his nostrils and inhaled the air beneath his buddy's curlicue tail. His body vibrated a bit as the long pink corkscrew that was his penis began to unsheathe itself, augering in and out of its casing with each breath he drew in. There was something tender in the way the two interacted, but I pretended to be looking toward the house, acting as if Aunt Lee might be calling me.

My dad didn't notice the commotion at first. He was preoccupied with rearranging the straw bedding and placing vitamin pellets around the mounds of crushed corn that sat like beehives in the two freshly coated troughs he'd painted with silver spray paint the week before. Seeing him primping the lot some more gave me hope that he'd start behaving like the fathers of our friends and we could live inconspicuously, out of the limelight of ridicule.

"Uh, Jer? You sure you told that breeder that you wanted straight boars? These boys here look like they might be a smudge closer than what you might want," said Leroy, looking toward Bill. "I mean if the idea is for them to sire, that is." Leroy was smiling wide as he tattled on the pigs. The fence rattled with the deep, jolly laughter of Bill. Ronald and I snickered.

My dad swung himself around, golden straw flying in all directions. "What's that, Leroy?" Dad's eyes lit upon the boar's slithering penis just as the boar mounted his mate. The boar on the bottom stood very still, ears back and tail hoisted up like an antenna. My dad was shocked at first and stood as still as the boar getting the loving, but when it dawned on him what his teeny eyes were seeing, he jumped toward them, purse-faced. "Shoo! Shoo! Get off of there, now. Shoo, shoo!" He sounded like Aunt Lee when she scolded one of the many raccoons that filched sweet corn from her garden. I felt doom well up in me. Here it was again: a goofy Jerry tale everyone in the county would be telling before dark.

"Oh, I think he's a-getting off all right, Jer. Ain't no problem there," said Bill. The fence shook with laughter again. Dad grabbed the top boar by the ears and tried to pull him off, but with the rain falling harder now, forming sepia puddles in the pen, he only managed to lose his footing.

"Stop it," said Ronald. "Leave them alone."

The boars were huge—over four hundred pounds—and no match for Jerry Bancroft. He slid under the bottom boar's belly. Leroy laughed so hard, he had to hold his distended stomach. Bill was able to curb his laughter some and hopped the fence to help my dad out from beneath the boars. Ronald looked sick. My thought was to climb in and help, but I resisted. I didn't want to be any closer to my dad than I was.

Red-faced, holding back laughter, Bill thrust his arm down to my father, who was now lying faceup and squinting to keep the rain and mud from his eyes. "Let me give you a hand, Jer." Bill helped my dad squirm out from underneath the boars, but he still lay on his back in the pen. Our dad yanked his arm away from Bill like a child throwing a tantrum and was about to turn to get up when the top boar dismounted, landing nearly on top of his head. The full length of the boar's penis slapped my dad in the face, leaving a sticky, clear residue splattered across his hairless chin. He screamed and leaped to his feet, spitting and wiping the area around his mouth with the cuff of his shirt. Ronald climbed down slowly from the fence. I wanted to run and hide in the barn somewhere. I thought of the statistic our ag teacher had given us in husbandry class: there were over two million hogs on the planet at any given time. My father had managed to find the two that were capable of mocking him as well as any human could.

"What . . . what the hell? I . . . I think that . . . that it came on me. Is that what it did, Bill? Did that boar come on me or what?"

Bill felt sorry for him now, frowned and became more serious. "Yeah, Jer. You just got in the way, though. Hell, the sons a bitches are just so horny they're a-humping each other, that's all. You best get 'em out there with the gilts quick, after they work their shots out. What's that take, a week? Just stay out of their way till then. All right?" Once again, Bill was trying hard to keep from laughing as he helped my dad out of the pen through the gate. Leroy handed him his hanky and backed up Bill. "That's right, Jerry. They're just raring and ready to go, that's all. You got you a horny pair, that's for sure. Looky here, now—we've gone and embarrassed the boys."

With the attention now on us, my father was able to finish cleaning his face under the spigot. Ronald and I walked inside the barn and pretended to be tidying up. The driver of the truck was pulling away, oblivious to the sex romp that had occurred behind his muddy axles. Ronald elbowed me in the ribs. He grimaced with the effort of holding in laughter. We ran farther back into the barn's recesses and flopped ourselves down on bales of straw, howling so intensely that it felt as if we were drunk. The laughter was a nervous kind we used around our friends when they'd tell an infamous "Jerry tale." It'd become a way for us to cope with the fact that our father was the county's court jester. When I got too loud, Ronald placed his hand over my mouth and said, while still trying to keep his own laughter quiet, "Shhhhh. Shut the crap up. Oh, piss—my side hurts."

We crept to the side of the barn. A glob of faint, gray light folded in on the concrete sleeping quarters of the boars. We peeked through the windowless frame to get another look. Bill and Leroy stood by our father as he continued to wash his entire head like an otter in a pond—both paws working in a circular, uniform motion. Bill and Leroy—and even Dad—were now chuckling as he stood up from the cleansing.

Ronald whispered, "He looks like he did when he got baptized out at Koon's Lake. Remember, he nearly drowned because he had two pairs of long underwear on? If it wasn't for Aunt Lee, he would've." We started laughing again at the story we'd overheard Aunt Lee tell our dad when she was mad at him, as if he had no recollection of the event, like he wasn't at the baptism at all.

We could hear my dad attempting to regain some composure. He said, "Well, I guess it was my fault. I should of put down some pea gravel or something. That ground in there is slick." He looked like a little boy, hair mussed and wet, his clothes hanging loose. We couldn't hear anything else they were saying as the rain began to pour down on the tin roof of the barn, making it sound as if we were inside a large kettledrum, hollow and thumping. The men all jumped up to flee the rain and scurried to the adjacent toolshed. On the way, my dad slipped in the marly slush again but was able to pick himself up. He looked back in dismay at the spot where he'd fallen, then stood in the rain alone, staring toward the pen that he'd spent so much time making. The raindrops lambasted the outbuildings; the old rusted farm equipment oozed small, ocher runnels of water into the gravel lane, flooding my father's feet. He tilted his head to the sky with eyes wide open and moved his palms slowly to his face, rubbing his hands up and down methodically, like a clown removing paint from around its features. For a good while he stared straight up into the sky, as if he saw something better up there, an object that was too high for him to reach. After a time, he dropped his arms to his sides and, with Bill and Leroy already in the shed, began to stroll toward them. Ronald and I watched until the rain poured so hard, all we could see were sheets of blustery spray. Ronald became serious. "I hope he just lets those boars be. You know how he is." In the mist of the rain, the two boars snuggled down in the straw, protecting each other from the weather.

CHAPTER TWO

For a week, the boars kept to themselves. It was hot, the sky reeling with black crows as the boars tried their best to fit in. I couldn't help but think of the circling birds as vultures, even though they only had eyes for grain. During feeding time the boars nibbled on the stray shelled corn lying on the ground at the outermost portion of the herd. If a gilt came by, they'd both frantically retreat to a knoll in the pasture, cowering and ducking their heads into the tall grass to hide, giving little grunts through their wet snouts until it was safe to come out after the female had passed them by. Then at the week's end, my dad came stomping into the house, mumbling under his breath. Aunt Lee frowned. "Good Lord, Gerald! What's wrong with you? You're dripping all over my floor."

"It's those damn boars! They're out there in a field chock-full of females and . . ." he hesitated and shot an uneasy look at his sister.

"Go ahead. I've heard a few breeding stories in my time."

His head nodded. "All right, then. They're out there screwing each other. Can you believe that? The pasture is swarming with bloody-tailed gilts in heat, and they're going at each other. This just beats everything, you know that!" Jerry Bancroft rubbed his red eyes like a baby and puffed out air, frustrated.

Aunt Lee tried to calm him down. "Why don't you just call Mr. Conner and ask him to swap you a pair that are fond of females?"

"Lee! Why don't you shut up and give me some time to think this thing through!" He looked at Aunt Lee, weary of what her reaction might be to his efforts to act rugged and firm.

"Now, Gerald, don't go biting off more than you can chew, which isn't ever very much. I was just saying."

"I know what you're saying, but Conner said the boars he sells are as is. No refunds, no exchanges." His eyes watered as he drew in a rough snort of breath.

Aunt Lee appeared frustrated, which was a shock to see. She was normally calm and not prone to overreaction, but now she had a look on her face that I didn't understand. She appeared sick of something, bored, or eager to get away.

Aunt Lee shot back: "Hey, Jer, you didn't leave your jacket behind, did you?" It was something she'd never used on him, a jest that had been reserved for Bill and Leroy and the others who gave him a hard time.

His eyes widened in disbelief that Aunt Lee had taunted him with the story. He looked hurt, the skin above his eyes pinched, his mouth open. Aunt Lee seemed to want to take it back, her lips in a whistle mode, as if she could suck the words back into her strong mouth. I stood by the sink, stuck in a moment they normally wouldn't let us see. When our dad was in high school, he'd tried to dodge a bill at the Waffle House near the city limits and left without paying. It'd been a dare, something a friend of his said would prove him cool, make up for his poorly coifed ducktail that stuck out lopsided at the back of his diminutive head. But he'd left his coat behind, with his paycheck from the meatpacking plant tucked into the interior pocket. The police had no trouble getting him to pay his bill, plus a tidy fine in criminal court. It was a notorious "Jerry story," one that Ronald and I'd endured since we were old enough to know that the fool in the story was our dad.

I wanted Aunt Lee to apologize and help him think through what to do. I closed my eyes and saw a perfectly etched horizon before me, the plane I was piloting humming along, with Aunt Lee, Ronald, and my dad behind me in the passenger seats, all of us normal and tanned bronze, back from an average family's vacation in Florida.

My dad tried to continue their argument but finally sat down at the table in defeat. He pulled out a bag of chewing tobacco from his yellow raincoat and stuffed a stringy wad into his mouth.

"You better not do that, Jerry. That's as foolish as can be. That allergy will get you sick." She trained her eyes on him, tried to stare him into his senses. He chomped and gagged some, his mouth stuffed to the brim. Aunt Lee tossed down her dish towel and stormed toward her bedroom.

I sat at the table with him now, munching a bowl of Cocoa Puffs. "Dad," I said, trying to stop him by pushing a saucer toward him so he could spit out the chew. But he had manly choices to make, something to prove yet again, even if that meant getting diarrhea in the process.

CHAPTER THREE

The next morning was Saturday, and I rose early to get a head start on the chores. When I got to the barn, I noticed that the boars had been brought in from the pasture but weren't in the pen. They'd been placed inside the old milking stalls that hadn't been used in years, where owl shit and the crunchy skeletons of mice littered a dirt floor. The boars were in separate areas, and both of them were groaning and biting the sides; their teeth left gnaw marks along the wooden rails. Their nervous behavior was accompanied by noisy breathing, watery and intense, like wet vacs. They paced rapidly along the partition that kept them apart. I heard a grating noise behind me. Ronald strutted through the door leading to the haymow, his denim shirt pressed and tucked in properly.

He winced. "What's he done now? There's no water in here! They could dehydrate. I swear, I think he's really lost it this time." Ronald seemed as though he'd taken on the same kind of attitude as Aunt Lee. His face was tense as he stomped toward the boars.

Ronald ripped open the jerry-rigged gates that my dad had fastened together with binder twine and made his way to the boars like an ambulance attendant at the scene of an accident. He let them into the same stall, and their breathing slowed as they rubbed their heads together. Ronald brought a trough into the area and filled it with water from a hose he'd stretched around the corner of the manger. They drank in the water as fast as it ran into the tank, the slurping sound so loud that Ronald yelled over them.

"Look at that! The son of a bitch just about killed them." Ronald's face turned pink, then red, and finally sank back into its usual olive color. Even from the time when we were little kids, I'd been one of his pets that he took such good care of. Now that both of us were older, he'd let up some—but not with the animals. Sometimes, when we were out in the hot fields together, he'd disappear and return with a fawn in his arms, its bony leg twisted but in a Fruit of the Loom sling. Or I'd come across my brother crouched down in a fallow ditch, stroking the head of a baby red fox.

Ronald let the boars drink for a while and then stopped them so they'd not get sick. He chaperoned the boars back to their pen, and I thought of the shepherds in the Bible. Before leaving to expertly perform other chores, he told me to keep an eye on them. "Don't let Dad separate them again. They need each other."

Over the next two days, Ronald and I found the boars tethered to posts, unfed and deprived of water, separated again, and, finally, on an afternoon when we were both home early, we discovered them together in the pen, listless and breathing shallowly. Ronald called Doc Stoops before even trying to determine what was wrong with them himself. We'd not seen our dad for a couple days, but his sickness from the chewing tobacco was splattered in the toilet bowl, accompanied by Aunt Lee's notes on the sink that read: "You're full grown. PLEASE clean up after yourself!"

When the vet arrived at the farm, Ronald filled him in on their condition. Doc Stoops washed his hands in an iodine solution, then pulled slip-on rubbers over his cowboy boots while he leaned against the bumper of his El Camino. Our dad was down at the feed store, making his first brave jaunt from the house since he'd chewed tobacco. It was the first time we'd ever called anyone to the farm ourselves. While Doc Stoops pulled on a sterile, light blue jumpsuit, Ronald touched my shoulder and said, "Lancey, let's promise to make this the last one, okay? I mean, he's going to keep on until the whole county thinks we're lunatics, too." Ronald was just as serious about finally putting an end to our dad's missteps as he was about protecting the animals, but it was scary to hear him say it aloud and, in a very palpable way, comforting, too. Things had to change, and it seemed Aunt Lee and Ronald were ready to charge ahead.

Doc Stoops examined the boars and found they'd been given oral sedatives, human ones, most likely, or perhaps they were old horse tranquilizers, but he couldn't be sure. He told us they'd be fine if we kept water in front of them and applied tepid washcloths to their heads every fifteen minutes.

Doc Stoops smelled like rubbing alcohol and spearmint gum. He chomped hard with his solid but yellow teeth. "You know, boys, your dad has quite a reputation for making matters worse. If I were you, I'd get a hold of the extension office up at Midland and see if they can send somebody down here to explain to him that these boars aren't gonna change. I mean, hell, Conner probably sold them to your dad knowing they were funny, and that isn't right, but they got a program where farmers can get trained in doing artificial insemination. So it won't matter if they're, well, you know, homosexual." Doc Stoops spit out his gum and plucked another stick from his shirt pocket, exasperation spreading across his stubbly face, as if he'd just felt an internal pain. "If you don't, there's no telling what your dad might come up with here."

Ronald walked Doc Stoops to his car and then came back to the pen. "I'll call tomorrow," he said, calmer, obviously intrigued that he might be able to get involved with Midland University, the Agri-Ed School of the World. "Come on. We have to get that old pile of tires started on fire. He left it on the list." Ronald pointed to a piece of paper he pulled from his hip pocket. Our dad made these lists out all the time, sometimes drawing complex arrows to the items on the list that he felt were most important. "You get the diesel fuel, and I'll meet you down there."

The tire mound was a monstrous collection of old radials, worn-out spares, and other odd pieces of rubber. Over the years, the pile had grown larger as my dad had invited anyone to make deposits on it whenever they wanted. It was one of the many offerings he'd make to other farmers in an attempt to gain their favor. Rubber was nothing but trouble, hard to burn and dirty, but he was always eager to please. Each spring we lit the mountain of rubber on fire, and it gave off a bituminous smoke.

In the strong sunlight, I poured the fuel around the entire base of the mound, while Ronald rounded up the stray tires that had rolled off the steep sides, throwing them back on the heap like an athlete in a track-and-field event. We'd performed the burning ceremony numerous times, and it had always felt sacred. It was something Ronald and I did alone, even though it wasn't safe. When we were smaller, we pretended that the smoke billowing off the top of the stack was a signal our mother could see. We would wait for hours, hoping she would notice the dark, rising vapors that spiraled up to the sky like a sluggish tornado, know it was us, and come running home to our rescue, her dark hair flouncing with each passionate stride toward her boys. But she never showed up, and we were left with soot on our skin and reddened eyes from the poisonous smoke.

I wet a burlap sack with the diesel while Ronald lit it from underneath with a handheld torch. I tossed the blazing cloth at the base of the mound as if it were a venomous snake, and fire spread around the bottom as we counted out loud the seconds it would take before the fire met its own end, flared up, and came full circle. When it did catch on fire, the heap of tires looked like a roasting topiary. We stood back as the blaze began to dance toward the sky. The mound spewed raven smoke out along the jagged edges of its flames. Ronald and I watched the air above the tires turn dark with acrid fumes and knew, even though neither of us had ever wanted to admit it, that what we once had pretended to be a signal for help was only a chore that would return again the next year. The intense heat made things at the edges of the fire appear like liquid.

Ronald scooped up crickets one by one from the mallow blooming defiantly around the fire and escorted them to safety. The fire was so hot that I spun around just in time to see my dad charging at us. His stride was bowlegged from the sickness. It was certain: Jerry was hurrying along with a chapped butt. Our dad was four feet and eleven and a half inches tall, and even to this day I can say I've not worked around a man so short or so thin. Now up close, he said, winded, "What was Doc Stoops doing here? I'm the one that's to do the calling! I heard he was out here from the fellas at the feed store. What's the deal?"

He wasn't angry, just intent on finding out what was happening so that he could exaggerate it down at the feed store, maybe even make the boar-purchase fiasco into something altogether different, like they were just too damn full of sex and spunk and superior lineage to do anything but fornicate. *And I'm talking all day long, boys,* as he'd wink knowingly at the other farmers actually at the feed store to get some work done.

Ronald hadn't looked up at our dad, even with the radio blaring, but now he placed a handful of crickets safely down inside a nest of fescue and stormed right up to him, towering over him by a foot. "What was he here for? I'll tell you what the fuck he was here for: you, dipshit! He came because I called him." Ronald poked a finger at his own chest. "He came because you just about killed the boars— that's what he was here for!"

My dad tried to understand what was happening. He hitched up his pants and looked around some. Ronald appeared as though blood might shoot from his eyes; he'd never challenged our dad but was clearly ready to make his point. I thought I could see a cloud of steam puff from both sides of his head. Hot flames of emotion streaked his face as my dad looked up at this older son and moved his lips before talking.

"Whoa there, Ronnie, now you keep in mind here that I'm your father and I won't have any of this malarkey here." He stepped closer to Ronald, peering up at him. Our dad asked in a weak, unsure voice, "You got that, mister?" He paused and thought harder. "Mister big pants?"

Ronald shook his head and turned in a half step toward the edge of the burning tires, but he swung around and punched Dad smack-dab in the nose. The sound it made was like a limb breaking. Dad clutched at his face and bent over. I went to him and tried to help as Ronald turned quickly away and stomped off toward the barn.

Dad looked up at me, his beady eyes between a swollen, bloody flange, and asked, stupefied, "What's up his butt or ass or whatever?" I shrugged my shoulders and sat him down away from the immense heat. The mound of tires was beginning to roar louder with the fine fuel of vulcanized rubber; the heat from the fire was still too intense, so we hobbled farther away as Dad dabbed at his nose with a sock he'd taken off his foot. I couldn't think of anything to say, so we sat listening to the crackling fire, faces red and sweaty.

I peered up near the barn lot and saw Ronald hosing down the boars, the sparkling water cascading off their strong backs, enshrining my brother in a silvery haze of heat, a partial rainbow arching over his dark hair. My dad had his head down, freeing his other sock from his petite foot. "Bill and Leroy asked if we wanted to go to a fish fry tonight," said Dad as he rolled up the sock in a neat ball and tucked it into his front pocket, tightened his mouth, and set his eyes across the field of dead grass. The fire behind us surged, belched black over our heads. "But I gotta get these boars acting right before I can have any fun."

"You should probably leave them alone, Dad," I said, not at all forcible like Aunt Lee or Ronald.

"Something's gotta be done about it," he said, trying to stand. He started to say something else but stopped. Dad glanced toward the barn and saw Ronald with the water and the boars. He stabilized himself on his bare feet and started to walk away, small boots in his hand. "Make sure he uses some of that water around the base of those tires when it's done. He's wasting his time on those boars, treating them like they're pets." Instead of walking toward Ronald, I watched as Dad took the long route behind the barn, up along the far end of the farm, where a little patch of blackberries grew and thrushes chirped, fiddling with tidy nests.

The briar patch had a secret opening on the backside, an arch Ronald and I made as kids. For a door we used an old sheet of plywood spray painted dark to blend in; it was our hiding place. Once, shortly after it became clear to us that our mother wasn't coming back, we held a ceremony inside. It was autumn, and the entire interior of the bushes smelled burnt and sad, fleeting. Ronald made a tombstone out of a piece of cardboard, and we pretended to be at the graveside services of our mom. We stood solemnly, Carhartt jackets draped over our shoulders like capes, John Deere caps held over our hearts, heads bowed. Ronald lit a candle, then blew it out and said something about ashes and dust and forever holding your peace.

As I watched our dad traverse the rutted ground on his pale bare feet, getting nearer and nearer the blackberry fort, I wondered how it all looked inside. It'd been a long time since Ronald and I had last hidden out there and that was to look at a *Sports Illustrated* Swimsuit Issue. When Dad approached the island of brambles, it seemed as if he'd read my mind. He stopped, stood stock-still, and waited, poised to take some action. As he took the turn, bypassing the blackberry patch, I could see that he was mumbling to himself.

CHAPTER FOUR

It was during a blizzard that Ronald and I first went looking for our mother. I was eight; Ronald was eleven. She'd been gone for almost four years by then. For one whole week, while the wind roared outside and the snow piled up, as fluffy as a commercial, we made our plans. We still slept together then, a mound of blankets piled on us; Aunt Lee punched holes through all of them at the corners and cinched them into one with jute rope. Once underneath, we could barely breathe, our pale, wintry dry skin sweaty, but that's when the idea of going after our mother came up.

"I bet she's down in Winston County," whispered Ronald, his hand holding mine as we flitted in and out of feverish sleep. I could smell the Vicks on his chest, under his thermal underwear. Downstairs Aunt Lee and Dad tried to keep their laughter low, holding back from busting out over a comedian on *The Tonight Show Starring Johnny Carson*.

"Why there?" I asked, not even knowing where it was. The television downstairs beeped with another Weather Service warning—precautions about windchill and frostbite, blowing and drifting snow. "Damn it," our dad said, bothered that the jokester on *Johnny* was drowned out. "Shush!" hissed Aunt Lee. "The boys will hear you."

Ronald stifled a cough. "Because, that's where that toolshed salesman lives. That's gotta be where she is. I think they're doing it without marriage. I bet they've already got a baby. It'd still be our brother or sister, just a half is all." I was mesmerized. The laughter commenced again on the TV. Aunt Lee and our dad went right back to trying to keep from laughing too loudly.

"You think we got a baby brother or sister over there in Winston County?" I asked, thrilled I might be a big brother like Ronald. School had been closed for over a week, and there wasn't an end in sight. The radio station man proclaimed kids might not see the inside of a classroom until planting time. We loved him.

"Not *over* there, Lancey, *down* there. Winston County is down south, almost to Kentucky. That guy sells those sheds all over, even in Illinois and Ohio, and some in Pennsylvania. He was their top seller the last three years in a row." I didn't know how Ronald was so up on the guy our mother had run off with but guessed it was from eavesdropping on Dad and Aunt Lee as they chatted, just like they were now doing downstairs. I didn't care how Ronald knew so much, though. I just wanted to see that little brother of mine. I saw him in my head then, as we lay sweltering under a foot of blankets, the snow falling outside, each flake a little gift. I wanted to sled with that baby boy, wrap him up good like Aunt Lee did for us, and tell him things he didn't know, just like Ronald did for me. I'd be the best big brother ever.

"We gotta go see that damn baby of ours." I'd started to cuss and loved it but usually got it wrong, thinking you added a curse word whenever you felt really happy about something or when you wanted to emphasize your feelings for anything. Ronald giggled.

"Lance, you can't say it that way! Besides, I was just talking. I don't know if Mom's had a baby with that man or not. Probably not." Ronald's words were an attempt to get me to calm down, knowing I'd fidget all night if he didn't at least try to take it back.

We fell asleep, the howling wind outside creating snowdrifts that covered tractors, hid fences, and made our mailbox at the end of the long lane vanish. In the morning, we got up and snuck out of the house, even before Aunt Lee was awake. She would've stopped us for sure.

Ronald wrapped a scarf around my face. "I can't breathe 'cause of this bastard thing," I said, pointing to my head as we stood on the porch outside, where the snow was up to our knees.

"Come on," Ronald managed to mumble through his own thick scarf. "We better get going."

We tromped through the yard and began the long trek down the lane toward the road. It was beautiful. White pristine snow clung to every inch of every tree. The silence was broken only by our own puffing of the hot air we expelled as we tried to hike through the snow. By the time we made it halfway down the lane, denim backpacks slung over our shoulders, chock-full of Saran-Wrapped sloppy joes and baggies of corn chips—we each carried a thermos full of black coffee, too—the drifts were as tall as our thighs. I followed behind Ronald, who removed his scarf from over his mouth when we reached the road. His face was sweaty, and his crow-colored hair steamed in the early morning cold. All I could think about was that baby brother I'd already assumed was named Daniel, little Danny. I prayed I wouldn't hug the little son of a bitch too hard when we finally got to see him.

"Man, that was something else," said Ronald, his face red. We both looked over our shoulders at the tracks we'd plowed, deep ruts in the otherwise undisturbed newly fallen snow. The wind picked up some more, blowing Ronald's scarf off. He bent to retrieve it, snot above his lip.

"Which way is it now?' I asked impatiently. The entire sky above us loomed gray, loaded with more snow; it looked as if the horizon might collapse into the high drifts, and the world would never again see sunshine. We'd be cold and stuck in the snow forever, and that baby would grow up before we could get into town and catch the bus.

"We go west on the county road, but if we don't hitch a ride, we'll never make it before they wake up and find we're gone."

"That damn Aunt Lee," I said, my scarf off now, too.

Ronald smiled. "You better stop that cussing before it becomes a habit." He had peach fuzz on his lip; crystals of water clung to the fine hairs like little silver beads. He wiped his face and came toward me. "You slip up in front of Aunt Lee and curse, and she'll spank your butt." He lifted the end of my loose scarf and started to wrap it around my face again.

"You mean my ass." Ronald ignored me as he expertly tightened the scarf until I could hear my hot breath in my own ears.

"Come on. Let's get going." We trudged over a large snowdrift and made our first cautious, wobbly steps onto the road, but it looked just like everything else—white and deep and difficult to walk on. There were tire tracks from a snowplow and another set from someone up early to brave it and go dig out their neighbor, but other than that, the road lay before us like the top of an icy summit, blustery and white, an expanse of treachery.

By midmorning we'd managed to lug our bodies down the first county road and onto another. Ronald figured we were about two miles out. The muscles in my thighs burned, and I felt my steps losing their power. To maneuver through the deep snow we had to resort to taking exaggerated high steps, and the extra energy it took to wade through the monstrous drifts left me sluggish. More wind picked up, and I toppled over the side of the road, slid down the embankment, arms flailing as I went, like a little penguin. It made me mad. Ronald purposely slid down the slickness to come to my aid. I pushed him away and yanked off my scarf. "That fucking snow. Son of a bitch!" I said. Ronald jerked me up and hauled me, kicking, to the top of the road. He pushed me down and told me to sit still.

"You're hungry, Lance. Let's eat a sandwich and drink some coffee." He reached over and flipped open my backpack, then did the same to his. I didn't want to stop. Danny was in his warm crib, and our beaming mother was watching over him; I had to get there to help out. Stubbornly I chewed loosely on a bite of sloppy joe. "Eat some corn chips, too," ordered Ronald, his mouth stuffed to the brim as his thermos steamed in the frigid air. Something had happened to the sky. It was getting dark out, though it wasn't even lunchtime yet. The slate horizon loomed before us like a concrete wall. My toes and fingers felt numb, and the food in my stomach seemed to rise and fall with each breath, as if unsure about whether it was inside the right organ.

Now Ronald had to talk louder because of the wind roaring. "Hurry up. We better get going before the snow starts again." I was all for that.

"Let's goddamn get moving, then," I said. We packed up our backpacks and fixed our scarves. We took three long strides through the deepest snow yet; it was near my waist, and I was stuck. Ronald was in front of me, but I didn't want him to see. I struggled to free myself, thinking of the movies I'd seen where some idiot got sucked into quicksand. The more I yanked and fought against the drift, the more my body sank farther in. The wind was so loud now that I couldn't hear my panting. I lurched forward and clawed at the snow as Ronald's figure grew fainter. The sky opened up, and flakes began to fall sideways, the wind whipping them like little pellets against my forehead. I gave up. I saw Danny finding another brother, maybe one our mother would make with that shitty toolshed salesman. It grew dark as my eyes closed, and the whole world went silent and warm.

I woke up in a state of dangling limbo, arms and legs flapping heavy and wet, the coveralls cold on the inside, the red lining like ice against my skin. Ronald's ear came into view. I opened my eyes fully and witnessed a total whiteout. I knew for certain we were heading back toward the house. Danny was getting farther and farther away, and I could feel it in my airy stomach. "Put me down," I mumbled, but Ronald couldn't hear me. His legs were growing weaker. The tracks from just a few hours before had filled up with more snow. He thrashed through drifts like a zombie, then slowly sank to his knees, still cradling me. Coldness touched the back of my neck as I lay motionless in his taut arms. Ronald seemed to be freezing, stuck in one position, and I was laid out like a sacrifice, half awake. All around us the vast whiteness wore on like the Arctic. Ronald finally dumped me from his arms, waking me up fully.

"Damn it," I yelled at him, his face barely visible. "I want to see our baby." Ronald flopped over into the snow as I tore into another foulmouthed rant about our little brother. Ronald was clearly in a state of exhaustion, having carried me for over two miles in a bodacious snowstorm, but I was pissed about not seeing Danny. I stood up and pointed at him like a brat. "You better get up and help me go to that goddamn baby, or I'll beat your ass!"

I felt a heavy hand on my shoulder. In the blinding blizzard, Aunt Lee turned me toward her with a strong and confident twist. "Lancey, once we get you boys back to the house and dry and warm, we're gonna have to have us a little talk." She wore snowshoes on her feet, and her thick hair was covered with a stocking cap. Behind her, I could barely make out a little figure wobbling and falling over, struggling to get up again.

"Help!" yelled our dad as he tried to make it across an enormous drift. He had on a papery-thin spring jacket and was wearing neither hat nor scarf. Aunt Lee helped Ronald to his feet and clutched us to her woolly sides. She pointed at our dad's gray, slanted figure, arms clawing the air, a stick man in trouble. "Now, let's get back to the house before your dad catches the pneumonia." We stumbled forward with her as our dad threw a tantrum like mine. "Help me!" he insisted. "I'm stuck, Lee. I'm stuck in the snow. Help!" Aunt Lee squeezed us and said, "Don't ever go out in a winter storm without a good coat on, boys. Especially if you're as scrawny as Gerald Bancroft." Over the wind she hollered, "Is it me or does it look like that little thing's sinking right into the middle of the earth?"

CHAPTER FIVE

After the fire died down, Ronald and I ran four hoses coupled together from the barn to spray at the base of the mound to cool the blistering rubber. When we were done, it was like the aftermath of a flood. Corroded wire from belted radials floated on top of six inches of oily water. Our dad had always been scared of fire, and out of years of habit we sauced those tires until the ground was a mess of scorched mud.

Ronald didn't bring up hitting our dad; he just pretty much stayed quiet. We headed back up toward the barn then, the skin on our arms and faces covered in soot, our boots caked heavily with gray sludge. Outside the boars' pen we sat on some old bales of straw in which small, green stalks of wheat had sprouted up from inside the sheaves. Ronald plucked one off and started sucking on it. It was nearing dusk. The katydids and crickets fought for each note in the humid air.

Ronald sniffed and hunched over, rested his elbows on his knees, and let out a forceful sigh. "What'd he say? You know, after down by the fire?" He looked away in the distance, over the tops of some poplar trees where a few quail hens trilled in the lowest branches.

"He didn't say anything about it." I didn't want to mention that Dad had talked about the boars, how he'd fix them, or else.

"That's good," said Ronald as he pulled the wheatgrass from his mouth and tossed it to the ground, a smile spreading over his face when the boars oinked in the background.

"I think he's in the house doing something now."

It was beginning to get dark. All around us bats and swallows dipped into splotches of cool air, snapping up circle flies and gnats. The smell of cremated rubber dominated the air; only a hint of manure and soggy muck was able to bleed through and make it to our noses where the cilia inside were gluey with particles of black sludge.

Ronald said, "Maybe he'll find something even more stupid to do with his time. I wish I hadn't hit him, though." Behind us, we heard rustling. The boars were coming out into the paddock, stretching and yawning. They walked side by side, rutting each other playfully. Overhead, a yard light clicked on. Ocher light spread across a portion of the lot. The boars came out of the shadows into the yellowness of the lamp. They dipped their heads in the water tank and slurped up what sounded like gallons. They were feeling better. Ronald and I watched as they finished drinking. With their wet snouts, they began nipping at each other's ears. The noise of more bats cutting through the swath of air above our heads sounded like a whirligig. One of the boars began sniffing the other's butt. Ronald and I tensed, unwilling to look away but uncomfortable watching, too. In one quick move, the boar behind reared up. He flopped on top of the other, his long, pink screw, jittery and moist, flailing around, trying to locate the object of his desire. It slapped to and fro until finally the tip sensed something and pushed all the way in, out of sight. We stood there in the dark night as the boars breathed hard. It was not a wild animal fuck, but rather a slow, measured transfer of something, as if one were trying to give the other energy.

The boar on top lingered, then eased down the back of the other and dismounted. Ronald and I looked at each other. He shrugged his shoulders. "I've been reading about it. Did you know the incidence of homosexuality in some animal species is even higher than humans?" Ronald seemed embarrassed all of a sudden. "It just makes you think, is all." He pulled his cap down and moved quickly to fill the tank with more water. "Doc Stoops gave me the number for the extension office. I'll call tomorrow. If we can keep numb-nuts away from them until we learn how to do artificial insemination, then maybe he'll leave them alone."

The boars meandered back into the barn. We heard the house door open; Aunt Lee stood in the harsh porch light. It was now as black as oil outside. "Boys," she yelled, "you out there? Come on in now for supper." I imagined flying at night, what the black fields of corn must look like from that high up, the contrast the city lights of Indianapolis or Cincinnati would make against all those quiet acres.

"Coming!" yelled Ronald, his voice hoarse. "I'm not looking forward to seeing him at dinner, I'll tell you that."

I tried to make it easier for him. "Well, his butt might still be sore from sitting on the toilet for three days. He shouldn't be able to move very quickly." Ronald laughed, but it was just out of kindness; he was too distracted for much more.

Inside the kitchen, Aunt Lee's pots of vegetables boiled, burping steam as the meat and gravy gave the air a sweet caramelized scent. We shucked off our dirty clothes, went to the table in T-shirts and underwear. Aunt Lee flitted around the table putting towels down for the hot pots to sit on. She yelled again, this time for our dad. "Gerald, get your skinny patootie in here if you want any of this cooking!" She winked at us, the loose skin under her arms jiggling ever so slightly. She whispered, "Probably still using baby powder in his shorts."

The door at the end of the stairwell eased open. Our dad stepped from around it, the hinges creaking. At first, he was too timid to step into the full light of the kitchen, but after a few moments, he crossed out of the shadows of the landing. He was decked out in camouflage and had black greasepaint on his face and a tight stocking cap pulled down to his ears. His small head looked like a turtle's in retreat. A wad of gauze stuck out of one nostril where Ronald had socked him.

"Oh, for God's sake, Gerald! What in the world are you doing?'" Aunt Lee shook her head but kept right on flipping lids and straining pans of grub. "You look like a fool in that mess! What are you up to?"

Dad walked stiffly to his chair at the head of the table, trying to look more erect than usual, as if the whole getup might melt right off if he moved too fast. Before he sat down, one of the gigantic black boots he was wearing—a pair he purposely bought way too big and stuffed tissue into the toes to make fit—got hung up on the other. He stumbled into his seat, making our glasses of milk spill over the sides. Ronald stopped shoveling food into his mouth and stared at our dad in complete wonderment. Aunt Lee didn't let up. "Gerald, what on God's green earth are you doing? If I wasn't right here, I wouldn't believe my eyes. You been watching those war movies again?"

His back was flat against the rungs of the chair. He asked in a regal tone, "Lee, could you please pass the gravy?" His face was serious; not a hint of self-consciousness played about his features. Without looking at anyone in particular he said proudly, "Me and the boys— that is, Bill and Leroy—are going over to Conner's place tonight. We decided to do some reconnaissance. See if Conner is purposely breeding *peculiar* boars. Bill's bringing his coon dog."

Aunt Lee piped up. "Now, Gerald, are you sure they're gonna be dolled up like this, too? What do you hope to find out—that he's got a whole herd dressed in tutus?" She motioned with her hand in his direction, walked closer to him, and made another large swipe in front of his face, as if she were trying to get him to blink. The movement must've given her a better look at his nose. "What have you gone and done now? Your schnozzle looks like a polecat got at it. You didn't try shaving the hairs off of it again and booger it up, did you?" My dad pretended to ignore her, but she knew how to get him to talk.

She wiped her hands on her apron, polishing each finger like it was a pistol barrel. Pointing at him, she raised her voice, becoming stern: "Gerald Bancroft, you stop with your nonsense and tell me what you did to your sniffer!"

He jumped, spilling a ladle of green beans on his camo shirt where they were well concealed. As he searched the cloth on his chest for the beans, he nervously tried to answer her. "Dang it, Lee, I'm trying to eat my supper here." He took a breath. Ronald busied himself with dolloping out more food onto his plate. He looked anxious about what Dad would say concerning his nose. Aunt Lee was good for goading our dad, but if it came to her getting wind of a fight between any of us, she'd smack us good in the face and make us shake hands, just like she did with Ronald and me when we were younger.

"Lee, I didn't cut it shaving," he paused, snatching the loose beans from his shirt and placing them on a napkin. "I was under the truck, and that torque wrench fell on my face, that's all."

"Gerald, the only thing you could do under a truck is sleep. Now, how on earth did that happen?" she demanded. My dad was getting irritated, was about to lose it and make a fool of himself. He picked up a remote from a side table near his chair and aimed it at a small TV on the counter across the room. It bleeped on and fuzzed into focus. Crop reports and the prices of hog bellies scrolled across the local access channel. It was called TV 23, and for the most part it ran stories on pesticide applications and fishing reports, cattle shows and the benefits of no-till farming, and, in the summer, there was always an entire night featuring the Fair Queen and Her Court of Runner-Ups. Aunt Lee stood with her hand on her hip as my dad flipped through the stations, coming back to TV 23 just as anchorman Roger Wolfrum, sporting a poor toupee that curled under like an ancient Roman senator's, was pinning a microphone to the lapel of a powder blue leisure suit. Aunt Lee started in again but was interrupted by my dad: "Shhh! Wolfrum is talking about the weather."

He turned up the TV, and we all eagerly watched. Dad had gone to high school with Roger Wolfrum and had once been interviewed by the anchorman for a segment on blister beetles, about which my father knew absolutely nothing. During the program, filmed at the Presbyterian Church in Peru, my dad couldn't answer a single question. By the end of the piece, Wolfrum was so sweaty from trying to improvise that his toupee had all but curved up into a beanie on top of his sweltering head. After that, whenever my dad would see the TV anchorman and old school chum, Wolfrum would look my dad dead in the eye and say, "Jerry, you're gonna get it one of these days, you know that?" A local saying, still in use today, "You know about as much as Jerry Bancroft does about blister beetles," is meant as a potent put-down.

Back on the TV, Roger Wolfrum caught a glimpse of himself in the teleprompter and realized he'd again missed the intro to active airtime. He flashed a quick smile and swiveled in his chair to align himself with the camera. Wolfrum delivered the weather report like it was one of the gospels, accenting certain syllables pertaining to precipitation.

Dad, now more confident, said, "Well, looks like we'll get to the bottom of this thing with Conner tonight." Ronald tensed, and only I saw him shake his head. It was difficult not to think of a child playing dress up. Our dad glanced down at his watch and stood up. Some of the camouflage paint on his little head had started to run. It was as if his face was oozing the same stuff the tires turned to in the fire.

Aunt Lee, now even more irritated with him, shook her head repeatedly. "Gerald, just let that mess with Conner alone. You're gonna get out there in that corn and get shot for sure. As God is my witness, that's what's gonna happen!" She cleared her voice for emphasis, and said, lower, "Just *let* it be, Jerry."

All at once, headlights from a vehicle slanted in through the kitchen's plate glass window, a noisy muffler backfiring as the engine shut down. My dad trotted quickly to the sink to rinse off his plate.

Aunt Lee was leaning there, and she coyly slapped at his shoulder and grabbed the plate away from him and shooed him off. After forty years of trying to keep him from making things worse, it seemed she was beginning to give up.

Bill and Leroy pounded on the door, making the pane of glass rattle. My dad skipped girlishly to answer it. As soon as they got inside the kitchen, wearing their normal attire, flannel shirts and faded Levis, they were laughing, their coon dog moving rapidly over the floor, sniffing for dropped food. The front door stood wide open, squeaking on its hinges. My dad said, "Hey, you guys, I thought we were going to wear dark clothes to go out there?"

Bill spoke for them. "Jer, thing is, we figgered we'd get you and Ole' Pecker here to go in them kern fields and stake out a spot for us to spy on Conner. See if he's got a whole mess of fairy hogs he's breeding." Bill and Leroy began tee-heeing. It was apparent to all of us except my dad that they were on the sauce, nearly falling down drunk to be more exact. Bill and Leroy hadn't noticed Aunt Lee at the sink until then, and they went all fidgety, taking off their hats and straightening their backs when she spoke up.

"I'd think three grown men would think a bit about the company they're in before opening their rotten yappers."

Bill and Leroy apologized as they declined her invitation to sit and eat. Aunt Lee had put more food on my plate, Ronald's, too. Now, as much as anything, she wanted these despicable men out of her house and away from her boys so we'd not be tainted by their idiotic behavior. Bill and Leroy sensed it, and they were turning to head out the backdoor when Ole' Pecker hiked his leg. Bill went after the dog, shoved his hand under the dog's collar and tried to pull him out the backdoor, but the smelly dog squirmed away from him and ran right up to Aunt Lee. Ole' Pecker, in one fell swoop, rushed his head up the skirt of Aunt Lee's flowered dress, his head lolling in between her slip and the dress itself. From where Ronald and I sat at the table, it looked like she was pregnant with some alien writhing in her abdomen. Bill hopped quickly to Aunt Lee as she threw wicked punches downward, hitting the hard head of the dog, her dish towel flailing. "Get out! You get out of there this instant, you dirty beast!"

Bill grabbed the kicking hind legs of Ole' Pecker, knowing better, even in his liquored stupor, than to approach Aunt Lee's personal areas. He dragged the dog backward; its claws screeched along the floorboards as he drug Ole' Pecker to the backdoor and tossed him out by the scruff of his neck. In seconds, my dad and Bill and Leroy were also gone, shooting out the backdoor, afraid of Aunt Lee.

Outside, the truck backfired as she tried to regain her composure. Ronald and I sat at the table, holding back deep laughter, trying to pretend to eat more so she could make herself presentable. Without another word, she washed her hands and went to the cutting board near the refrigerator to slice us both a juicy piece of apple pie. She watched with approval as we dug in, and then she said, "Your aunt Lee is gonna go take a bath. Just leave your dishes, and I'll clean up later." It was not her normal routine, but we didn't question it.

Before bedtime that night, Ronald came into my room with a catalog. He tossed it at me and said, "Got this at Doc Stoops's. He called Midland, and they're going to come train us in artificial insemination, AI."

I thumbed through the book as he sat down on the edge of my bed. He became serious, the smell of his freshly Ivory-soaped body filling the room. "Maybe this thing with Conner will keep him busy, keep him away from the boars, but if not, it's like Doc Stoops said: no telling what he'll do."

"But I don't think he's about to let us take over anything. I mean, he's not just going to step aside so we can whack off his prized pigs." Ronald looked at the side of my bed where I had airplane books stacked up. I thought he was going to mention something about them, but he didn't.

"Better look through that catalog good," he said, smiling. "Find you a real nice plastic smock you like so you won't get..." He grabbed the catalog away from me as he started to snicker and said, "What do they call it in here?" He searched the catalog, flipping from back to front. "Oh yeah, so you won't get any of the sire seed on you when you do the honors." He laughed and slugged me in the arm, then left the room quietly. He was in a good mood, readying himself to save the boars. I, on the other hand, felt the room tighten on me, and a low droning began in my ears. My stomach was tense, even as I started to drift off to sleep.

That night, I dreamed of my father, all made up in his hunter's gear, and the gay boars, who had corn tassels woven into their long tails. Dad and the fancied-up boars were inside an auction circle, and Ronald and I were the only bidders, sitting on bleachers, grunting out bids as my dad and the boars were showered in fluttering corn silk drifting down from some unknown location above them. A woman who was our mother—but didn't look a thing like her—walked into the ring and, with a wave of her long fingers, made our father disappear. I woke up confused and dazed, ready to fly away and make it all seem insignificant from a great height in the sky.

CHAPTER SIX

In the morning, Ronald woke me up earlier than usual. A gaggle of geese flew over the house honking. He threw my jeans at me and said, "Get up! They did something to the boars last night." He was somber. He walked out of the room with his head down, rubbing his right wrist slowly. I tugged my pants on and stuck my feet into my work boots, the laces loose and dragging on the floor as I ran through the house to the backdoor.

I jogged out across the hoary grass toward the paddock. The sun was emerging from a thicket of walnut trees down past the waterway; it looked as if half a pinwheel the color of Tang was stuck in the dark limbs, their tips clawing the belly of a cinder sky. I was groggy and tripped twice as I made my way to the edge of the enclosure. My dad's truck was gone, and there was no sign of him or Bill and Leroy anywhere. Another flock of geese floated overhead, so low that their honking sounded like a clown's gag horn just inches from my ear. They glided effortlessly up toward the house and disappeared over the cupola, swallowed up by the great ditch sloping away from the house. It got quiet. I couldn't see Ronald or the boars. The only thing out of order was a steaming pail of soapy water resting on top of one of the bales of straw near the pen.

From the darkness of the barn's sliding doors, Ronald appeared with a scrub brush in one hand and two empty cans of spray paint in the other; the paint cans rattled as he walked, the loose bearings inside banging decompressed air. He tossed the cans down like a DA presenting evidence and went back into the barn. His shoulders were sloped, and he seemed ready to either dry heave or go to battle— maybe both.

He reappeared, this time inside the confines of the boars' run, walking behind them, driving them forward. They looked as unawake as I felt. It was still gray outside, and from where I stood numb, I could see no cause for alarm, so I began to think that Ronald had tricked me just to get me up and at it. But then one of the boars' heads eased into a slash of light coming from a drop bulb Ronald had rigged up. Something about the boar's face appeared monsterlike, maybe burnt. His eyes were matted with black paint, and red globs were caked along the other's snout. As they became bathed in more light, I saw some letters sprayed along their muscular shanks. They'd been written on. "Faggot pig" and "gay bait" is what I could make out. As soon as I'd deciphered the writing, Ronald said quietly, "Lancey, hand me that bucket of water there."

I staggered toward the bucket and tried to imitate his dreary attitude. I lifted it over the fence to him, holding the handle as if it were a scalpel I was passing to a doctor. Ronald dipped the brush into the warm water. He withdrew it slowly and began to tenderly wipe at the painted words on one of the boars. The other, realizing he was going to have to wait, plopped down on his haunches. The lot was beginning to get brighter as the sun dawned over the farm. With more light, I could see that the eyes of the boar lying down were not just clogged with paint: he was blind. The daubed white washcloth in the back pocket of Ronald's jeans was testament that the boar's eyes had been the first thing he'd tried to soothe. The boar stared blankly at the space in front of him, every so often tilting his head almost imperceptibly to each side, trying to determine his predicament by sound rather than sight. The boar was in the early stages of learning to depend on one sense for survival after another had been sprayed away with a can of Forever Midnight with matte finish.

Ronald continued to work on the boars as if he were an apostle anointing a leper's feet in an open-air temple. He finished with the first boar, and really he was none the worse: the boar looked cleaner, free of the manure buildup on his hide, groomed. The other boar, the blind one, looked like he might bite Ronald as he approached. Ronald made cooing sounds to calm him and rubbed the boar's ears as he knelt down. With some patience, Ronald was able to get the boar's trust, but every time he tried to use the warm washcloth to swab at the crusty paint that clung in boogers to the long lashes and eyelids, the boar nipped at him. Ronald stood up and stretched his back. He said, low, "Lance, run over there to the field and get me a few ears of corn. Maybe he'll sit still if he's got something to eat on." I agreed with Ronald and did what I was told.

The cornfield was not ours. After our dad had flown out to California five years earlier with a supposed investment banker from Racine, Wisconsin, to meet about converting our measly two-hundred-acre corn-and-soybean farm into a state-of-the-art meatpacking facility, we'd done nothing but raise hogs. It turned out the banker from Racine took my dad's $20,000 brokerage fee (borrowed against the farm), which was supposed to put us in touch with bigwig pork men in The Golden State, and left him high and dry in a Ramada Inn somewhere outside San Diego. Aunt Lee wired him money for a bus ticket home and told him she'd never speak a word of the ordeal to another living soul if he turned over the bankbooks to her for safekeeping. In the end, the bank called the note on the tilled acres, and Aunt Lee had no other choice than to sell them cheap to avoid losing the farm, the house, and all the implements in a foreclosure sale. The man who ended up buying the ground, Fred Dickers, was sworn to secrecy by Aunt Lee to tell the story as she saw fit—which meant he was to let everyone around know how Ms.

Lee Bancroft could drive a bargain as hard as petrified oak stump. When Dickers slipped up once at the local bar after having one too many shots, Aunt Lee went to his house with a crowbar and shook it in his face, telling him she'd make sure he never again put that little nub he called a peter into old lady Struthers up Malloy way if he even as much as breathed another word, drunk on the devil's piss or not. Of course, she never told us the story—that would've violated her ideas of child rearing—but over the years, with both Ronald and me eavesdropping on her and my dad's late night squabbles, we picked it all up.

Ronald called lightly for me, so as not to spook the blind boar, wondering what was taking me so long with the corn. I'd been daydreaming about what Ronald might do when he saw our dad. As I hurried along to the field, in my distraction I fell once over my unlaced shoestrings. Getting up, I hoped I didn't look too much like my dad, and I scrambled to right myself so Ronald wouldn't see. I bent and tied my boots quickly and ran on to the edge of the field. Sunlight now lit up everything. The corn was the height of basketball backboards, the ears as big around as mason jars. The spring had been wet and warm, the early part of the summer humid and sunny, just the right combination to produce the kind of cornstalks that made a bounteous and dense forest where, the fall before, Ronald and I'd spread hog shit over what'd been a barren and cold plat of weeds.

I pulled my T-shirt off and made a tote out of it. I started twisting the swollen ears of corn this way and that, trying to loosen the strong tendons at the base. I decided to get plenty since I'd taken so long, thinking Ronald would see the gesture as me being as concerned about the boars as he was. I cradled about ten ears in my pouch and was just about to put one more in when I eyed a juicier ear two rows back. I stepped farther into the field, over the dirt ridge of the first row where a tier of roots clung like talons to the ground. I reached for the angelic ear of corn, careful not to let the razor edge of the leaves slice my bare rib cage. Just as my hand was about to grab it and turn the ear down to make the first break, I heard something farther back. I froze—didn't move a muscle—listened for what I assumed was probably a raccoon or possibly a brave young doe. I heard Ronald rasping out another plea for me to hurry up. I reached for the ear again. All at once something clamped onto my wrist like a vise. I didn't want to look but forced myself to, peeking sideways out the corner of one eye. The pressure on my wrist was firm, a pulsing heat that felt like it might stay there forever. I could see a family of daddy longlegs on the broad leaf in front of my face, but my head wouldn't turn. I was terrified, heart beating in my ear canals.

I unhitched the other eye, peeped through the slit. Floating amoeba shapes and light flickered around my lashes. The grip softened and released as I twisted my body in an attempt to get aligned with the force I thought was going to carry me off into the deep green, never to be seen again. I dropped the shirt full of ears and ran to the edge of the field. I peered back into the corn and saw an obscured image of a man dressed in church clothes—a short-sleeved shirt and a tie clip glimmering gold. He stood motionless just inside the second row, holding the robust ear of corn I'd reached for; it hung loosely at his side as if he were about to draw and shoot. His face was aged from the sun. On his feet he wore cowboy boots. He raised the ear of corn up and pointed it at me. "You're a Bancroft," he said, like it was an insult. He smiled a little hank of a grin; perfect dentures gleamed in the early rays of sun shooting sideways through the stalks. He tossed the corn at me, and I caught it. "God doesn't love homosexuals, even if they are pigs." He was off then, escaping into the corn as effortlessly and quietly as if he had been a deer crouched in the leafy shelter of the leaves. Something about the man's hair, the texture of it, and the way his face seemed to flatten, nearly flush with his neck—all of it reminded me of Wolfrum, the man we'd watched on the public access channel for years.

I stared out into the field, holding the ear of corn, shirtless and covered in goose bumps. Right then, Ronald came up behind me and turned me around with a mild but quick jerk. He had a puzzled look on his face as he caught a glimpse of my T-shirt lying on the ground inside the pile of corn. He pointed to it and asked, "What's your shirt in there for?"

I couldn't answer and didn't want to. I wanted this to be all mine. Besides, his mind was fully attached to the condition of the boars, and I wasn't sure I'd seen what I thought I had anyway. Telling Ronald would've made me sound too much like Jerry. Ronald wrenched the ear of corn from my hand and walked to the outside row, ripping three more ears loose before rushing past me again. Without looking back, he said, "I could use some help up here."

I slowly shook my head yes and watched the field a little longer. I walked toward the barn to help Ronald, half scared and half filled with the heady excitement of an accident victim.

Back at the boars' pen, Ronald had gotten the sightless boar to nibble on the corn as he continued to try to remove the hardening paint. After several failed attempts, Ronald tossed the washcloth over the fence and jumped it himself, his body filled with energy. "It's no use: that paint is all dried. I'm gonna go get the livestock truck and drive him in to Doc Stoops. He's blind for sure."

Ronald held back his tears; a thickness in his voice quavered as he told me to stay put while he pulled the truck around. I was still dazed. While I waited for Ronald, I thought about where my dad was and if he and Bill and Leroy had actually done the awful painting of the boars. Ronald and I hadn't talked about it, but it was obvious our dad had most likely gotten drunk with his friends and abused the boars.

A low groaning engine whined and strained; a clutch popped and reverberated off the sides of the cracked silos. Ronald steered the noisy panel truck from behind the barn, pulled it up beside me, and left it idling. He went to the pen and tried to get the boar up by waving a new ear of corn before his nostrils. The other boar, the one with sight, had gone to his lover's side while Ronald had been getting the truck and now used his snout to peck softly at the rear of the other. And it wasn't like before when that activity would've ended in some good lovin'. He was trying to tell the blind boar to get up and go with the man in the truck. Ronald smiled and looked back at me over his shoulder a couple times, impressed and touched by the unmaimed boar's intuitive assistance. With some more coaxing, Ronald was able to get the blind boar to his feet. He used a cane to drive him to a chute.

Ronald jumped in the truck and revved it. Black diesel fuel vapors puffed into the sky. He shoved the truck in park and slid across the seat, then rolled down the window. "If Dad comes back and asks, tell him the other boar got loose last night, and I'm out looking for him. He'll never notice the truck's gone. Okay?"

I agreed, and he was off. As he bounced over potholes, I could see the blind boar in the back through the slats; he was hangdog and staggering from side to side. I leaned against the fence and tried to calm myself. Instantly I felt something brush my hand and turned quickly; it was the other boar's cold nose. He pushed his twitching, wet nostrils onto my knuckles as I reached over with my free hand to rub his ears. I could still hear the faint snivel of Ronald's truck fading farther away as the boar grunted over and over in response to my petting.

It was now midmorning, and there'd not been a sign of my dad anywhere. For the first time since the boars had come to the farm, I was truly scared. It was becoming clear to me that Ronald was not going to back down from my dad. In fact, it appeared as though he were readying himself to take a real stand against him.

I looked back over in the direction of the cornfield. How far had the word traveled that we had gay boars on the farm? Was the man in the field kin to the Wolfrums? My thoughts raced as I jumped the fence and ran some water in the dry trough for the lone boar. As he sucked up the water, a spumous circle at the brim of his nose emerged. I focused on it and tried to picture how everything might end peacefully, but then a sound came from the hayloft.

I left the boar, went to the barn doors, and peered up through the rafters at the edge of the loft's thick planks. There, clad in only his flak jacket and oversized boots, stood my drunken father. He teetered on the edge of the hayloft, swaying back and forth, smiling dumbly at his luck, oblivious to his surroundings, the position of his feet. "Dad," I yelled up at him, shielding my eyes. "Just stay there. I'll be up in a second to help you." His head lolled from side to side, and he looked like he might vomit. Before I could scurry up the ladder, he lost his balance and went plummeting to the ground. The act made me want to run away. The boar, spooked by the crashing thud, ran to the farthest corner of the pen, while the little man who'd built it lay without a sound on the hard cement floor of the barn.

CHAPTER SEVEN

Barn swallows with beaks full of mud fortified with melted rubber from our fire crammed themselves under a roof beam fifteen feet above my dad. I walked closer to him, crouching down as I went, trying to determine if he was breathing or not. I thought he might be dead. For some reason, I got a metal rod, one that we used to pry the rusty cogs on the manure spreader, and used it to poke at my him. I nudged his elbow—nothing. I prodded his forehead, too, but he gave no signs of consciousness. Under his wee little nostrils two rivulets of blood were already drying. I tossed the rod to the side and went quickly to his body, which was curled in the fetal position. I rolled him over and stood above him, straddling his chest so I could get my arms up under his pits. When I jerked to get him up, I overestimated what it would take and nearly tossed him in the air like a rag doll. While I'd gotten stronger since the days he'd play-wrestled with Ronald and me, I was shocked at how negligible his weight was. He felt like the scarecrow Aunt Lee used to scare off jackrabbits, the ratty effigy she had my dad nail to the same cross she put out during Easter.

I pulled him to me and lifted him up, cradled him in my arms, and walked toward the house. He was breathing for sure, but his body felt cold. He stunk of liquor. It was as if I were carrying a drunken toddler.

I got him to the house and pushed the front door open with my foot. Aunt Lee was at the sink cracking eggs into a clear mixing bowl. She didn't look up when I stomped in, figuring it was either Ronald or me, late as always. I slammed the door behind me with a backward kick. My dad's eyes started to shimmy under the fluorescent lighting. His eyelids were like dainty hulls, translucent in the severe light. Aunt Lee spoke without looking up: "It's about time one of you boys got on in here. You know better than to leave this house without so much as waking me up." She was smiling down at an egg dripping from a brown shell onto a stick of margarine. She continued, "When you were babies—didn't matter what time it was—if you were up, you wanted Aunt Lee to . . ." She stopped when she looked up and saw me in the doorway, holding her limp brother in my arms like he was a dog that'd been hit on the road.

I held him out to her and said, "He fell from the loft." Aunt Lee dropped the eggs into the sink and wiped her hands on her apron with rapid-fire speed. She pulled two chairs out from the table and motioned for me to lay him down. When I didn't, she realized a better spot would be the floor. She moved the table back against the wall and yanked a throw rug from in front of the sink to where we were standing, then tossed two rolled-up kitchen towels down for his head; it was a perfect pallet. I placed him on the spot and backed off, spooked.

Aunt Lee knelt down next to her brother while I leaned against the counter. I watched as she got up and went to the sink to wet some towels under the faucet. I started feeling faint as she ran the cold tap at full blast, the water splashing out in all directions, splattering enough that it showered my forearms four feet away. She ducked back down to her brother and placed two of the towels to his forehead and two more behind his neck. She snatched up his arm and placed her big pink thumb on his wrist, checking his vital signs. His hands were stained with black and red paint. I stared at his nails as Aunt Lee timed his pulse with her slim silver watch. His nails were too long, as always, and were now full of the cakey remains of gummy paint.

For a moment, I wanted to just walk out the door and leave Aunt Lee and her pip-squeak of a nutty brother there alone on the floor while I crept silently into the cornfield. But instead I paused when Aunt Lee told me to run to the barn and get the livestock truck. She repeated herself calmly, slowly. "Lancey, didn't you hear Aunt Lee? I said go fetch the rigger, and let's get Jerry to the hospital. He's gonna need some doctoring."

I stood by the sink cracking my knuckles, trying to figure a way out of the situation that would allow me to keep Aunt Lee oblivious to Ronald and my dad's battle over the boars. Standing there against the sink, looking down at Aunt Lee without really seeing her, I thought of the English lit class from last year. I remembered the teacher, Ms. Wolfrum—yes, the TV anchor's daughter—and how she lectured us on the four points of literary conflict: *man versus nature, man versus man, man versus society, and man versus himself,* and how my father had managed to bag them all in one fell swoop from the hayloft. I cleared my throat and tried to speak. Aunt Lee insisted I get a move on and go get the truck, but I could do nothing more than point out the window toward the paddock, mumbling a little bit. I was about to tell her what was going on when I heard the familiar backfire on a piece-of-crap International livestock truck: Ronald! He was back.

I sprang from the counter and dashed out the backdoor. I ran in front of Ronald from the side of the weedy yard. He didn't see me coming as I jumped in front of his path, waving my arms in the air, just like I'd seen the tarmac workers on a runway do. He slammed on the brakes, and the truck hissed at me with its pneumatic brakes. Ronald blew the horn and shrugged his shoulders, held up his hands. He mouthed through the windshield, "What are you doing?"

I sprinted to the side of the truck and jumped up on the running board, hitting my left shoulder on the huge side mirror in the process. Ronald asked what the hell was wrong, and I told him all about our dad and the hayloft. He gunned the truck, telling me to hold on, and steered it in a broad half-circle up into the yard, mowing over the waist-high ragweed.

He yanked the emergency brake after we parked, and we both jumped from the truck. Ronald rushed through the backdoor, and I trailed behind him. I noticed there was a rolled-up newspaper in his back pocket. Inside the kitchen, Aunt Lee now held our dad in an upright position, trying to get him to sip water from a teacup. Ronald shot down next to her and scooped up my dad over his shoulder. Aunt Lee took the cup of water and tossed it in our dad's face as he hung upside down over Ronald's back. She said worriedly, "Little thing isn't coming to. Stubborn as all get-out, even when he's knocked to the moon." She shook her head and followed Ronald out the door.

I ran around them to the passenger's side door and pulled it open, forgetting that the bench seat on that side was unusable. It had caught fire once when our dad was trying to weld a new bracket to the floor. The hot flame had scared him, and he'd dropped the torch onto the vinyl seat. It was engulfed in seconds, but he somehow managed to put it out before the truck exploded.

Ronald yelled at me to open the rear gate of the truck. "Lance, you'll have to ride with him back there. Keep him from rolling around."

Aunt Lee went back to the house, reappearing shortly with the rug and a pillow from the couch in the living room. It was one of those overstuffed ones with tassels and fringe. Its mustard yellow velour matched perfectly the soiled straw in the back where the blind boar had crapped.

I crawled up the side of the wattled fence to the top of the truck and untied the rope that opened the hatch. I swung in and shook loose some clean straw from a half bale in the corner. Ronald righted my father on his shoulder and laid him into the straw softly, like he was a child going down for a nap. Aunt Lee tossed me the pillow and rug, which were more for looks than anything: she wouldn't have wanted the people at the hospital to think that the woman of the Bancroft house was mindless about the care of her men.

For a moment, we all just looked at him there, and I wondered if Ronald found the spectacle as ridiculous as I did: our father lying still and benign in the back of the same truck that his prized homosexual boar had just been transported in to visit a doctor, too. Overhead, a mile-high jet left white contrails in the sky like a fuzzy scar. Aunt Lee spoke up, "Well, get him to the doctor's. I think he's fine. Might have something broken, though. I can't ride in this truck, so you boys will have to take care of the bill." She shoved a red-and-white insurance card in my shirt pocket. Ronald pushed my dad's bony legs the rest of the way into the truck and battened down the hatch. Aunt Lee told Ronald to be careful, not to drive like a maniac. "Don't go forgetting your baby brother is in the back."

In a few minutes, we were out on the bumpy county roads heading east to the Malloy City Hospital. My dad was the same as before, but he was beginning to move a little; he'd twitch a bit whenever Ronald struck a pothole or took a sharp turn. Strong sunlight lasered between the slats on the side of the truck, crisscrossing each other at perfect angles. Some of the rays were distorted by the aluminum that lined the bottom foot of the truck's interior, and the refracted sunlight glittered over my father's face, making his skin look extremely white in some areas and dark brown from the contrasted shadows in others. I reached out to hold his hand when he moaned but withdrew it quickly, like it was a red-hot ring on a stove, as a smirk flashed on his lips. The smell of burped rotgut wafted up in my face as I bent in to take a closer look at my father; he'd thrown up in his mouth, and a frothy brown residue was lodged at the corners of his lips. I rolled him on his side as I'd seen Aunt Lee do when Ronald and I had the stomach flu.

He sputtered and spit, tried to sit up a little but fell back down, like a newborn foal. The truck bounced hard. I looked out the slats and saw that we'd just crossed a bridge. The truck railed against Ronald putting it into a lower gear, a prolonged, rumbling shudder that made my dad's bantam feet lazily wiper back and forth. The sight of his involuntary movements made me start to worry. I felt as if we might get snared inside the intricate metalwork of the old bridge and our dad would die a slow, hot death in the back of a shitty livestock truck. While I was certain that his condition, for the most part, was half hangover and half mild contusion, I wasn't about to take for granted my father's ability to make it through what most people would've seen as a slight mishap; he just seemed to have a way with taking the simple, everyday misfortunes and compounding them into life-or-death situations.

After we were off the bridge, Ronald revved the truck into a higher road gear, taking the last few miles to the hospital, which now consisted of finely paved side roads, at a clip that made me wonder if he had already figured a stay in the hospital for our father would keep the boars safe. As we got to the outskirts of town, we passed by a large billboard that proclaimed to travelers that they were now in Magnificent Malloy!

With the truck stopped at a light, I could hear Ronald open his door and jump out. As he passed by the side of the truck, he looked like he was whistling, but I couldn't hear it. He opened the hatch and looked in at me, trying to get his pupils accustomed to the darker confines. He blinked and held his hand up to shade his eyes from the sun. Our dad rolled in the straw from one side to the other, reacting to the traffic noise and overall melee; something was causing an unfathomable irritation that his small brain could not comprehend. Ronald spoke. "How's he doing?"

"Fine, I guess," I said. "But he puked once, and I think he's dreaming." We both looked at him for a while. Ronald stood in the intense sun watching it all. Our dad groped in the straw for something he couldn't find in his dream. He rolled over again. His little ass now reared up into the air. He coughed, and at the same time a runty fart made a delicate pop in his pants. He did it again, then again, and finally on the last one it sounded like he'd crapped himself. Ronald and I burst out laughing. There was some traffic, which was odd for Malloy. Two police cars were parked along the roadside, and an officer directed traffic.

In seconds, a brown sheriff's cruiser was at our side. The officer sprang out and clomped up to Ronald. I snuck up along the inside of the truck, trying to hear them, and peeked out of the chinking. The deputy nodded his head, and then Ronald did. Then they both did it in unison as if they were playing a game of mime. The cop jogged back to his car, and Ronald strode again to the rear of the truck.

"He's going to take Dad to the emergency room in the squad car. He told me to pull the truck off the road and onto the shoulder." I stood up straighter as the cop appeared at the back of the truck with an olive green stretcher and a matching blanket. Together, although the combined effort didn't take us both, we put our dad onto the makeshift gurney. I jumped down from the truck as the sheriff and Ronald toted him to the police car. We climbed in the back with our dad as the police officer put the collapsible stretcher in the wide trunk. We sat three across, our dad in a reclined position, leaning more on me than Ronald. The officer clicked his seat belt and took off his hat, putting it on the seat next to him. He adjusted the rearview mirror and flipped on the sirens. When he maneuvered around all the other stopped vehicles, Ronald looked pleased to be passing them by. The big cop turned down the squelch knob on his CB and asked us what had happened to our dad. Ronald poked me in the ribs, and I spoke up, telling the officer how our poor daddy had fallen from the hayloft while rushing through the morning chores. When I was through, the sheriff shook his head knowingly and gave me a reassuring wink to let me know that our pappy would be just fine now that we were in the custody of Malloy's finest.

We were near the hospital when we passed a long line of news vans. Ronald asked our cop, "What's all this about?"

The cop tilted the rearview mirror and looked at us, his dark shades making him appear buglike. "Not sure. Something's going on, though. We're just trying to make sure everyone who says he's supposed to be here really is." I felt my recently developed Adam's apple tighten; it was hard to swallow. As we pulled in under the breezeway of the emergency room, the cop said, "They say Wolfrum called them here. Must be some farm accident or something." The cop pulled up his sunglasses and added, "I dunno. Or maybe they got someone from Hollywood to keynote this year's Corn Festival. They been trying to get John Cougar Mellencamp for years."

Ronald and I looked at each other, wondering if we were both thinking the same thing.

CHAPTER EIGHT

The emergency rooms in this part of the Midwest have a way of smelling like an alloy of manure and rubbing alcohol. It's the rush to get so-and-so's finger reattached after the belt on a corn picker chewed it off or the scramble to get Grandpa's ticker jumped—he'd just happened to be feeding pigs at the time of his heart attack and then was nearly eaten alive in his unconsciousness by a hundred hungry snouts. In the hurry to get to the hospital, people forget to take off their boots and overalls that have hog shit packed in the fissures of the soles, splattered on the cuffs, and up the pant leg. So what you get is a waiting room that combines the stench of crap with the aroma of iodine-soaked gauze and sterile pads.

A gaunt-jawed man wheeled our dad down the hall to a room we were not allowed in. Ronald took the red-and-white insurance card to the front desk. After an hour of Ronald sitting in a cubbyhole with the paperwork, me standing behind him, leaning on his chair, the lady with hoot-owl glasses on the other side of the table told us that in most cases the deductible needed to be paid up-front but that just this once she'd let us mail it in. She winked at Ronald, snapping her gum, popping it with her rigid tongue.

A plump nurse told us that our dad was in observation. "It'll be a while, hons," she said, tiptoeing toward us with a chart in her hands.

"Just wait here." The nurse pranced past us toward another family, licking her lips. We sat down in a row of connected tweed chairs and idly flipped through the stacks of magazines on the veneered table in front of us. Ronald had a *National Geographic* with a picture on the front of a shark and a man. They were butting heads, face-to-face, the diver's bubbles trailing up along the spine of the magazine. The caption read, "Whose sea is it anyway?" He hissed at me: "Psst!" And again with more force and duration: "Pssssst!"

I looked over at him, and he flashed me a picture of an aboriginal woman wearing a brightly colored sarong but no top, her breasts upturned and slightly out of kilter as she leaped in a ceremonial dance. I smirked and looked around, trying to seem above it. He tossed the magazine onto the table and stood up, fished around in his pocket for some change, and said he was going to go call Aunt Lee and let her know we got there all right. I said okay and waited until he was out of sight to pick up the *National Geographic,* fumbling quickly through the pages to find the dancing, naked woman. I'd just found the page when, over the intercom, the family of Jerry Bancroft was called to the front desk. With the photo of the exotic, smiling beauty splayed on my thighs, I looked around for Ronald, thinking he would've heard the intercom, too, and would be taking the lead, sauntering up to the counter to get the details of my dad's condition. But he did not appear from anywhere, so I went up myself.

The charge nurse handed me a piece of paper that had the particulars of my dad's clinical status: blood pressure, heart rate, and other vital signs I could not decipher. At the top of the paper were his room and floor numbers. I went back to the waiting area half expecting Ronald to be again fully engrossed in the magazine, but he wasn't there, so I decided to take the elevators to the fourth floor myself.

As I stood waiting on the elevator, a man with the strong scent of calf scours approached me and stood a little closer than what seemed normal. He was old, with a shock of silver hair, and he wore thigh-high manure waders over a pair of fiber-teased tweed pants that were threadbare, the strands fluttering off his legs like tiny snakes underwater as the air conditioning vent above shot a strong breeze of cold down upon us. He stared straight ahead and cleared his throat.

"My wife is on the cancer wing. Yep, they found a tumor in her female part and said if they didn't get in there real good and all, we'd have a mess on our hands. Tumors would be breeding like rabbits if they didn't go in there and scrape her out real good."

The old man paused and pursed his lips, let his eyes cut my way. He continued, "Damnedest thing. 'Course you find that with an old cow, too: they go and get a vulva bit by flies, get pitted and all, and next time she calves, that little pit from some ole' fly bite last summer will commence to make a weak spot, and if she pushes too hard her . . . Well, you know. Then you got a mess on your hands. Sure enough do. Have to kill her when that happens. It's a sad damn thing." I liked how he cursed.

The old man never looked straight at me, and when the elevator came he didn't get on, just kept right on talking. I should've said something, helped him stagger onto the elevator, or told a nurse I thought he might be nutting out, but I felt too sorry for him to make a scene.

I got off the elevator, which smelled strongly of cheap lilac air freshener. An older nurse I'd seen behind the main desk was going around spraying it in stairwells and elevators, near the restrooms and along the waiting area seats. She sprayed the can at full tilt. I turned and went down the wrong way before figuring it out and heading back. I found my dad's room and slyly stepped inside the door.

A curtain was pulled around his bed, and I could hear a nurse telling him to read something. He was struggling with whatever it was and asked if he could try again, sort of laughing and sort of whimpering. It sounded like the baby groundhogs we'd accidentally mowed over in the clover field—the way they choked out dull clicks, lying on their backs with intestines exposed to the flat blue sky above them. It'd broken Ronald's heart. From then on, whenever we'd begin to cut the alfalfa, Ronald would first go through the field, stomping his feet and gently swinging a stick, but inevitably we'd chop into some concealed family of pests, and beheadings would ensue. The groundhogs always struck me as sadly absurd, their buckteeth bared, oblivious to why their heads were seeing their bodies from two feet away. It would sadden Ron so much that he'd spend more time giving them a proper burial than doing the mowing. So those were the thoughts I was having as the nurse, a young woman with extremely feathered hair and a profusion of green eye shadow, pulled the curtain open with a zing, smiled at me, and left the room. I was thinking of dead and dying groundhogs when I saw my father inclined in a hospital bed, several pillows behind his back to make it kind of like a crib. In all that crisp white sheeting, his head burgeoning forth from the deep fluff of all the pillows, he appeared as though he might truly be in a final stage of his last resting place, aglow with all that surrounded him: silver trash cans and similar bedpans, frosty tubing, snowy-colored extra blankets placed neatly in whiter shelving, and ghostly-toned window treatments. Everything was either white or mirrored.

When I saw him, it was clear that he was high on pain meds. He winked and said, "Got to be ferry, ferry quay-it. It's that rasc-qui wabbit." He pointed to the side table where a box of tissues did look as if a pair of rabbit ears were sticking from the slit. Later I found out he'd been given morphine for a set of severely broken ribs, but at that moment, I envisioned him being swiftly ushered onto the psych unit to be fitted for a doll-sized straitjacket, never to deny his gay boars again.

I asked him what was wrong, but he just kept talking like Elmer Fudd. The same young nurse came back into his room with a triad of capsules she told me were for any internal infections.

She handed him the pills, and he gulped them down with her coaxing him along. Then he fell fast asleep in the briefest of time.

As she left she asked, "You his son? I think he's the littlest man I've ever had. 'Cept midgets. I had me a midget once. She had a corn on her foot that got green in it. She was little, but, you know, they're supposed to be." She smiled and walked away.

The phone on the table rang, and a red light on it flashed. I picked it up. Aunt Lee was talking before I'd even gotten it to my ear. Her speech was racing as she told me that Ronald had already called her and told her of our dad's condition. She said, "Lancey, Aunt Lee is going to make a ride there to get you. I don't know what has gotten in to your big brother, but I'll come and get you in a jiffy, soon as I get that tractor started. Aunt Lee will surefire be there to get you."

Stellar fear weighed down my chest. The thought of Aunt Lee making the trek from the farm at willy-worm speed and the whole of Malloy seeing her come riding in to save her baby at the safest place in town was something I simply had to prevent. Otherwise I'd have to pack it in and join my dad in the land of idiocy. I finally got her to listen as I lied and told her that Bill and Leroy were there visiting and that I'd hitch a ride with them. She argued for a while, asking me for sure if they were acting sensible—were they drinking coffee? She believed that Ronald and I were unaware of things like sex and drinking and all the other foolish things grown men did to act like jackasses. And she would go to great lengths to pretend we were ignorant of all that was related to manhood and the general declining condition of the world. But in the end she agreed, telling me again that Ronald should not have left me there alone with my dad just to go get something from Doc Stoops. But I knew Ronald had only one thing on his mind—the boars and their protection.

Before we hung up she asked, "Well, how is that Gerald anyways?" I told her he was resting, and she tried to fool me again, thinking I'd not smelled the alcohol when I'd lugged him into her kitchen. "Don't worry about a thing, Lancey. Aunt Lee will set him straight on trying to do chores in the dark." I told her okay and hung up, already wondering about how to get a ride out of gridlocked Malloy.

It was now late afternoon as my father snored ever so gently in his cushy abundance of whiteness.

I went to the window and got underneath the curtains so I wouldn't wake him with any harsh sunlight. The air conditioner, a window unit that seemed wobbly in its installation, billowed the drapes off my back. I put my head against the glass pane and looked out over the rear portion of the hospital. There was a large newly paved parking lot and a series of tanks, drums, and cylinders located on the roof below. A barbed-wire fence quarantined off a backup generator and a miniature power plant, all coated in drab gray paint. Several yellow caution signs hung loosely from the chain-link fence. To the right of the parking lot were two loading docks and several brown Dumpsters. A pack of hospital workers unloaded refrigerated trucks. They hauled out crates of bananas and economy-sized canned goods, big plastic tubs of mayonnaise and other condiments. Seeing all the industrially packaged foodstuffs reminded me that I'd not eaten. Ronald had awakened me before dawn so we'd not had breakfast, and of course in the trip to get my dad seen by a doctor, we'd missed lunch, too. With my head still against the window, I burrowed in my pockets for some dough. I found three ones and decided to leave my dad and go to the cafeteria. I turned to get out from underneath the curtains and got caught up in the gauzy sheering. I thrashed around for a bit before freeing myself. When I was fully out of the curtains, I noticed that my father's eyes were open. He had a serene look on his face. He pointed at me and said meekly, "Are you an angel? Did I just see you born out of a cloud?" He was really getting the best of the drugs.

"No, Gerald, I am not an angel. Just sleep now." He stared at me in astonishment, not wanting to let go of what he thought he'd found. I decided to try a little bit of Aunt Lee on him, so I became firmer: "You go to sleep this instant, Gerald Hampton Bancroft!" He shifted backward in the bed some, still astonished but also confused by his angel's apparent curtness. He obeyed, though, closing his eyes promptly, worming his way farther down into the bed's comfort and mumbling sweet Jesus-es as he snuggled up to the fact of his divine revelation. At that moment, I thought about taking advantage of his drug-induced religion and ordering him, for Ron's sake, to back off the gay boars he had at home, but I was getting hungry, and, anyway, I was sure once he came to he'd not take the prophecy to heart. Our dad never took a warning—not for long anyway.

Downstairs in the cafeteria, lots of people were milling about on the Berber-carpeted floor, trampling over the square tables and loose three-rung chairs. They poured in from two exits facing the hallway. I'd ordered a cheap hamburger and a large orange fountain drink and had just thrown it all down in a flurry of consumption when the masses started to surge into the area that the hospital had dubbed Café Hospitality.

I got up and made my way through the crowd, filled my cup again with orange drink, and stood looking around the entire space. I'd not thought much more about what the cop had said— that there was a story brewing—and Ronald had disappeared too soon to talk about it with him. I tried to tell myself I was being silly, that word of the boars had only traveled to some Sunday school teacher I'd seen in the cornfield, but something about the way people were moving in the cafeteria gave me an unsettled feeling. The cafeteria seemed to be buzzing with people who were wearing brightly colored polo shirts and had tags hanging around their necks. I saw now that the laminated cards on silver-beaded necklaces read PRESS. I stayed put by the pop fountain and watched the scene. Then, just as I was about to fill my cup again, a man with a badge that read WTVR Fort Wayne walked right past me. He knelt at a table, his big sideburns like Velcro, and whispered to a woman feeding her toddler fries, "Ma'am, can you tell me where the Bancroft farm is?"

My stomach fizzed with pop, stunned by the notion that the press had an interest in our boars. I recalled what Aunt Lee had once told us about the nature of people's nosiness: "They'll believe anything that makes someone else seem worse than themselves."

CHAPTER NINE

I hitched a ride back to the farm with one of Wolfrum's kids. The public access cable newsman had sired about ten or twelve, and this one's name was Lucy, a voluptuous, round-faced girl who was four years older than me, closer to Ronald's age than my own.

After hearing the man ask where our farm was, I had buried my head and tried not to think about it. I went back up the elevator to visit my dad a final time before trying to figure out how to get home. Lucy was the CNA on duty, a title she said meant that she was fully certifiable in all areas of gross patient hygiene. She freely confessed some awful details of her job after I'd asked her if I could use the phone to try to call Ronald in the hope that Aunt Lee wouldn't answer. The phone rang and rang at the house. I knew Ronald was most likely with the blind boar, but still I let the phone ring until my ear itched. When I hung up at the deserted nurses' station, Lucy was creeping up the hall, pushing a bucket with a mop. She pulled the saturated mop from the rusted bucket and slapped it onto the gray linoleum, plowing the pool of soapy water across the floor, edging forward mindlessly. She swabbed around my feet as she passed me by, saying in a low, spectral voice, "Watch your feet." And then, as an afterthought, "If you want, I could take you home. You know we live out around you guys." She smiled at me a little, her strong forearms pulsing with each stroke of the mop. Lucy wasn't beautiful, but her face was round and her brown eyes were large and discriminating, and she seemed both irritated and smart—like she was on the brink of flipping someone off. I accepted her offer and helped her pour out the dirty water from the pail into a floor drain down the hall. Then I went to spend the last ten minutes or so of Lucy's shift with my father. Before she left me, Lucy said, "The last round is really just to see if someone needs diapering or if they were able to muster up the courage to ask me to slip a bedpan under their butt. I always tell them to crap now or hold your piece for the next shift. Try and make them laugh some." I tried to seem at ease with her forward approach to talking about bodily functions, but I am sure my face wore the expression of a recently post-puberized boy who had the county's most joked about pseudo-farmer as a daddy. I was always ill at ease in my skin, perpetually contemplating the possibility that the apple had not fallen far enough from the scrawny tree.

Killing time before Lucy could drive us home, I watched as my father slept more, enthroned in a bed half-lit by the flickering fluorescent tubes. I sat down in a vinyl chair and propped my feet up on the foot of his bed. The nurse had said they'd keep him a few days for observation to make sure his splintered ribs had not punctured anything he might need. They'd put another person in the room with him, an old man who seemed to be dying. A middle-aged couple prayed over him. I'd heard them from the hall before I came into the room, and now they were standing on both sides of the old coot, holding his hands as he, seemingly oblivious to their coddling and prayers, took deep, scratchy breaths under the foggy aid of an oxygen mask. As I sat there waiting for Lucy, whose dad wanted my dad *to really get it one of these days,* I found myself envying the sincerity of the couple's apparent desire for the old man to make it, to be healed so that they might spend even more time with him, maybe even enjoy it. Ronald and I had spent the majority of our time trying to find ways to contain our dad, make him somehow not so detrimental to our existence. And, just as when the boars first arrived, I felt a tinge of hope creep into my chest while witnessing the old man's family praying. I felt so good that I wanted to seal that feeling up, keep it freeze-dried so that it'd be ready when I needed it later. With my dad, there was always a need to have something stored up.

The couple standing over the old man chanted another prayer, but I was shocked to hear this added to the finale of their speech to God: *"And please, oh heavenly father, provide us the insight on how to combat the homosexuality that has crept into our homeland. Allow us the strength to contain all that is perverse, keeping all that is holy away from those who'd seek to taint your will. In your name, the Prince of Light, the Holy of Holiest, we pray these things and more. Amen."*

I was shocked, hoping still that the reference the man had made was just a coincidence, but the same feeling I'd had in the police cruiser earlier and then again in the cafeteria—the sense that things were buzzing, about to ignite—washed over me, and I was glad that Lucy walked into the room at the conclusion of the man's rhapsodic benediction. She'd already started to make her nurse's assistant uniform more comfortable. She had her hair down, which, when she had been in the hallway earlier mopping, had appeared to be an odd little dome of a thing, brown and compact in a net, but now it cascaded to the center of her back, and its length seemed to give her face some extra femininity. The top buttons of her starched dress were undone, revealing a milky white bosom, pearly and smooth. She walked past the old man's bed, offered a concerned, professional smile for his relatives, and stopped behind the chair I was sitting in. She leaned on the armrest with her plump hip grazing my shoulder. She said, without so much as one iota of quiet in her voice, "You ready? Let's get outta here. I'm sick of smelling shit today." I tensed and immediately thought of Aunt Lee and how she'd have told Lucy to her face that she needed a good and severe washing out of her mouth with Ivory soap.

I stood up and pushed the chair back in place. Lucy flipped opened her purse and removed a box of Virginia Slims 100s, fired up her Bic, and took a long drag. Burgundy lipstick was pressed onto the tip when she pulled it away and exhaled; it was the color of old blood. I went to my dad's bedside and stood there. I didn't know what to do, so I patted him on the head and put an extra blanket over his paltry body. Lucy sucked in some more smoke and let it out slowly. She said, pointing with the ashy tip of the cigarette at my dad, "He's a tiny little fucker, isn't he." I could hear the woman on the other side of the curtain gasp in shock. She whispered to her husband, "Is that child smoking? For heaven's sake, go over this minute and tell her to put that out. This is a hospital, Port. And you're a clergyman. Go tell her that it's a sin for a girl her age to smoke, let alone cuss like that."

Lucy snickered and frowned a sarcastic pout. We turned to walk out of the room, almost running directly into the man who was dispatched to straighten her out. Lucy sidestepped him like he was a runny cow pie she wanted to avoid getting on her shoes. He caught her by the arm and tried to speak, but before he could reprimand her, she'd yanked herself away from him so hard that I had to grab him to keep him from losing his balance and falling right on top of the old man in the bed. The woman cried out, "Oh, sweet Jesus, forgive these little heathens, for they know not how to behave in a hospital!"

I paused a moment and tried to give them a look that was supposed to let them know I was merely going along for the ride, literally, but with the man still struggling to keep himself upright, his frosted hair in a muss, and his wife's mouth agape with outrage, my gaze was interpreted by them as a taunt. As I ceded my attempt to make things right, I turned and ran down the hall after Lucy, who was well on her way to lighting up another smoke. I heard the man holler after me, "I do pray your daddy don't die tonight, son, although he'd be better off in God's world than the one you're shaming him in." If he only knew the man in the hospital bed next to his dying kin was the owner of gay boars.

I caught up with Lucy as she was stomping down the stairwell, dragging and puffing on the long cigarette as she took the flights at a considerable pace, her butt swaying nicely. Out in the parking lot, the sun was crouching down, trying to hide behind a mobile park of double-wide trailers across from a field of round hay bales, but there was still considerable heat and at least three more hours of sunlight to go before a sticky night would take its place. Lucy didn't speak to me until we got inside her red Chevy LUV. Thrusting a pack at me she said, "Wanna smoke?" I shook my head no. I'd never seen anything like her. She let her own cigarette dangle from her ample lips, something I'd only seen Leroy and Bill do. She fiddled with her colossal key ring, a chrome hoop as big around as a butter tub, and then cranked the motor, making it rev and squeal. She backed up without looking and never touched her cigarette, its long ash like a dying gray worm. We shot out on the main avenue, the truck tilting and the tires chirping.

The roads had cleared some, and the number of police cars lining the side ditches and grassy medians were no more than the usual squad car that was set up to patrol the speed traps. Aunt Lee had taught us to respect police, but even she often commented that our county sheriff's department reacted to everything—a funeral procession, a granary robbery, even the occasional banker's suicide—as if World War III were breaking out.

Unlike her TV father, Lucy seemed content with few words. Her dad used scads of words to depict everything from castration techniques to how to choose a perfectly ripe muskmelon. There were other differences, too, but on the ride home I started to forget about her polyester-clad daddy and focus more on how the hem of the CNA uniform rode up her thick thigh, baring a group of cellulite dents I wanted to touch.

We cruised along without talking, staring straight ahead at the scenes we passed: fenced-in tire shops and junkyards, so many used car dealerships with multicolored pennants that it looked as though a circus had decorated for blocks and blocks, and every twenty feet or so there was a sign promoting fast food.

Lucy talked for the first time since she'd asked me if I wanted a cigarette. "People are stupid. That guy in the hospital is probably a perv and his old lady doesn't even know it. I swear, living in this county is like being in exile."

She lit another cigarette and pulled the lever at her left side to ease the entire seat back about half a foot. Lucy threw a sharp right turn into a convenience store and said nothing as she whipped up next to the gas pumps and got out. She stood by the end of her truck, still smoking, as she stared at the pump. The cents per gallon clicked past in a blur of black and white. Lucy topped off the tank and flipped her cigarette out into the bright orange horizon. I watched her as she walked toward the store to pay. She looked to me then like she might either hold the place up or drop a five into a Lou Gehrig's donation bucket on the counter. She was strangely exotic to me, acting the way I felt about living in the middle of nowhere and saying it, too.

Lucy slammed the truck door shut and tossed me a brown bag that was ice-cold and beginning to wet through the paper. She drove us out of the lot and onto the streets of Malloy, then turned off the first back road to carry us out into the country, where decades before, our progenitors had decided to carve out a life in the stinking hog lots and lush cornfields of the Midwestern tundra.

We drove until we came to a dirt road that was called Wood's End. It stopped just short of a dense forest of craggy pines, an unfinished logging road that was left incomplete because the county had decided to issue permits for the sewage and wastewater plant to spread refined human feces on the three hundred barren acres that ran along the road on the east and west sides. Lucy pulled the truck up under an old tin-roof shed that covered several oil drums of a chemical used to keep the stink down. Supposedly, kids from the neighborhoods where there were no pigs or farming at all, in a remote part of the county that bordered an interstate, used the chemical to get high by heating it in Mountain Dew cans and sniffing the vapors.

But Lucy and I were going to drink beer, and when she asked me to pop a couple cans of it, my hands were shaking. I felt as far away from Aunt Lee's kitchen and my dad's hospital room and Ronald's gay boars as I thought I could. As I tipped the can back, the cold tangy hops trickling down my throat, I wondered what Lucy wanted from me. I'd barely finished the thought when she asked me to pass her another one. I tried my best to slug the rest of mine. Its suds foamed at the back of my throat, made me pray silently for a moment that I would not gag and upchuck the hospital café's orange drink all over Lucy's dashboard. She said bluntly, "What's the deal with your dad?"

"What do you mean?"

"You know, why is he such a weirdo and all? My old man says he lies like no one's shit. He hates him because of that beetle interview, you know. And didn't he poop all over himself once at the fair a long time ago?"

My feelings were hurt. It wasn't that she had it all wrong, but I'd started to think she was semi-interested in who I was, not my dad or even Ronald for that matter. She seemed mean as she waited for me to respond, both of her hands clutching the beer can like a baby bottle. She must've seen it in my eyes, the way I turned to look out the window toward a tanker spreading the good folk of Malloy's shit over their shit from last week. She must've noticed that what she'd said had sent me off in another direction because she reached over and patted my hand, became a softer presence.

"Hey, my dad's a weird shit, too. I just, you know, thought we had something in common that way. Just forget I said anything." She waved her hand in the air as if erasing her words from the interior of the truck. She slipped from behind the steering wheel and scooted over next to me. The sun had fallen behind the broken line of pine scrub. It glowed through the limbs, and the blaze looked as if it were

truly on fire. Out of nervousness, I reached into the soggy paper bag
and snagged another beer, popped it quickly and slurped loudly
on purpose. I could feel the heat from her torso warming my side.
She smelled like bleach and iodine and smoke, and something like
calamine was also there, sweet and medicinal. Lucy put her hand
on my thigh and snuggled under my chin. Her breath was hot. For
a moment, it was like she was a relative, maybe an older cousin or
young aunt needing some tenderness after having been dealt one
of life's simple little tragedies, perhaps a divorce or a DUI. But then,
in one passion-charged move, she untucked her head from my chin
and had her lips scrolling along my neck to my earlobe, back down
again to my chest, and then onto my mouth where she used the tip
of her tongue to pry my teeth apart.

We kissed and groped, spilled our beers onto the floorboard
of the truck. My feet slipped and slid in the mess as I tried to get
some traction to thrust my pelvis in her direction. Suddenly, my
mind did a flip-flop. I saw the boars screwing, my father dying,
and Ronald and Aunt Lee off in their own directions. I pulled
away from Lucy. We sat heaving and straightening our fronts. She
smiled and kissed me again, only this time it was one planted on
my cheek, meant to say she'd known all along I was trying too
hard. The sun was now completely down, and a sliver of moon
had taken hold over the trees. A blinking airplane droned past
a similarly blinking electrical tower. Lucy took her place once
more at my side, nuzzling next to me, soft and full of subsiding
fire. I smelled her hair and found the scent from earlier, maybe
chamomile shampoo. I felt love for her then. It'd all changed so
quickly, the way early lust does: one minute you're picking on
each other, making fun, and the next it's all heat and groping,
desperation. I felt close to her, wanted to give her something in
return for her generosity. I stared straight ahead, out onto the
fields of pine and human waste. I said, tentatively, "Lucy?"

"Yeah, what?"

"I saw this guy out in the cornfield. This morning. He knew my name. He looked sort of like your dad." I waited for her to respond, believing she'd see my confession as a sign of trust. She lifted her head from me and turned my chin toward her. She looked into my eyes; her features were negligible in the dark, and her hair looked raven in the shadows. She said, "It probably was my uncle. My shithead dad has been telling everyone about your gay boars." I felt sick. I stared at her.

"How did he hear?" I asked, sitting up straighter.

"I don't know, but he knows. He's the one who called the other news outlets. I heard him in his office." I wanted her to be more put out, to hate her father as much as I did at the moment.

"What a dickhead."

"Who? Your dad or mine?" We laughed some then.

I told Lucy all about the boars, how our dad was dead set on fixing them, how Ronald had punched my dad, and that Aunt Lee was in the dark. All the confessing got me some more kisses and led to us going at it again, this time ending with me awkwardly slipping my hand up her dress. She was mushy at her thighs, but the trip farther up was solid and full of wetness, as hot as a tailpipe. I didn't know what to do though. For several minutes Lucy had to keep putting my hand in the right spot; I was all over the place and had no idea how to please her. Finally, she provided the motion she needed, giving me hand-on-hand instruction. When she came, I was uncertain about what to do next. It held both the dreadful possibility of never happening again and the awful obligation of never going away.

As we drove the remainder of the miles to the farm, where I was convinced Aunt Lee sat at the kitchen table crying her eyes out for the boy she should've picked up in Malloy on a tractor, I felt my life was changing. I began to think I was not going to end up like my dad, that Ronald and I could save the boars, run the farm well enough to put us through college, and take care of Aunt Lee well into her golden years. A sense of confidence came over me as I watched the woman I'd just frisked into a heady state of pleasure glide the truck along the torn-up back roads with a faint but definite smile on her parted lips. We'd lost our mother, but it didn't mean I couldn't keep a girlfriend. I reached over and touched Lucy's knee. She smiled and winked. It was for sure: I was not Gerald Bancroft's son, not right then, no way, no how. I told myself over and over: *All I had to do was keep from getting on the news. All I had to do was keep from getting on the news.* It was a new kind of conflict, man versus the media. And I believed I could beat it as Lucy stroked my thigh and turned into the driveway that led to our farm.

Part TWO

CHAPTER TEN

It was almost a year after the blizzard incident when we tried again to find our mother. This time, though, the weather was mild, and while it was just after Thanksgiving, there was no snow. The temps had been unseasonably warm for over a week, which made us think now might be the perfect time to make another attempt. The sun was strong, bright yellow light everywhere, the sky like a big blue lick across the tops of the bare trees. We got hot and shucked off our Carhartt jackets and cinched them around our waists. A flitter of birds flashed over our heads and landed on the rusty fencerow, dead grass blasting from around the posts like brittle hair.

"I'm holding that damn baby first, Ronald." Even though Aunt Lee had made me write three hundred times, "I will not use foul language because I'm too much of a gentleman for that," I still cussed. But I made sure she was never in earshot.

"Okay, okay. Just let me say one thing, Lance." Ronald held his finger in the air and tested the wind, his mouth swollen with a wad of gum. "Yep, that's what I thought," he said, lowering his hand and patting his chest pocket for more Juicy Fruit.

"What?" I whined.

"The wind tells me we're going to make it this time. So if you want to hold that baby, you better really help out. We've got a long way to go, and this time if she catches us, we're probably going to get some whippings." Ronald let the idea sink in as I kicked stones with my feet. Our dad was off to Louisville for some farm show that he claimed had hired him to work for a week, and Aunt Lee had gone for her every other Saturday hairstyling appointment. If we didn't make it this time, it was our own fault. The weather was good, we were free, and our pockets had nearly forty bucks tucked in them from collecting pop bottles. Our backpacks were full of peanut butter sandwiches and Twizzlers, cans of pop, and a whole container of Pringles.

After the blizzard fiasco, Aunt Lee had sat us down and told us both, with honest love in her voice, that we had all we needed right where we were. While we'd not fessed up, Aunt Lee had figured it out herself that we'd tried finding our mother. When Christmas rolled around the next week and the snowdrifts climbed even higher— the worst blizzard our area had seen in decades—Ronald and I tore open our cards from our mother and found sketches of the newest addition to her family, a parrot that looked demonic, its beak a nasty hook. The two drawings were roughly the same. Each one had a full frontal view of Gizzard (that was his name) with intricately detailed feathers made realistic by our mother's deft hand and the use of colored pencils. Ronald's had the words "Eat, Sleep and Be Merry!!" at the bottom while mine read "Christmas is a Time for Sharing Loved Ones!" Ronald handed me his, knowing how much I liked staring at her handiwork. It would be a couple of years before he'd start simply tossing them in the trash can. Sometimes, after I'd fished them out, they'd have an eggshell stuck where a fine poplar tree's leaves shone in neon green, or there'd be coffee grounds over the face of an old man who was sitting on a park bench.

By late afternoon we were on the bus heading south toward Winston County. We'd made it onto the Greyhound and celebrated by drinking a warm Coke and scarfing down a whole tube of Pringles. The pop fizzed in my mouth, made my tongue itch. Before long, the bumpy ride lulled me to sleep, my head propped against the window. I woke up with a start, clutching my backpack, thinking it was being stolen. It was Ronald. "Come on," he said, still pulling me by the strap. "We're stopping for the restrooms." He smiled down at me, and suddenly I felt sad. Ronald had always been cautious of nearly everything; it was his curious mind, his love for biology and science. Now though, he seemed as positive as I was about seeing our mother. Handling your own disappointment is one thing; loading it onto a loved one is another thing altogether. Getting off the bus, we met a man calling himself Captain Electro-Man who was operating a booth to promote his business. There were food vendors on either side. He told us he was opening an electrical company in Winston, but all I cared about was the pens he gave us and the two-dollar bill he pulled from his wallet. Ronald tried to tell him we had our own money, but Captain Electro-Man told us it was always good to have a bill in your wallet that you didn't really want to spend, so Ronald put the two-dollar bill in his John Deere billfold, and we shook the Captain's hand.

The gas station smelled like grease, urine, and popcorn. Several of our fellow bus riders waited in line to buy a bag of buttery Orville Redenbacher (our state's claim to fame) after they'd just waited in line to use the foul restrooms. Ronald and I passed the group, weaving in between aisles of fan belts and tuna cans to make our way outside.

We sat on the edge of the curb and shared a Milky Way that Ronald had bought. Chewing a big bite, he passed it to me. "You better button up your coat. It's getting colder."

"I'm not fucking cold. Thanks for the candy bar." I was a cranky kid or at least pretended to be that way so I could cuss. I passed the Milky Way back to my brother.

Ronald took the last bite, broke it in two, and handed me a chunk.

"It won't be long now. We've got to go through four more counties, and then we'll be in Winston. I think the address is right off the town square." Ronald pulled an empty envelope from his coat pocket and read it again. "Yep, it's 106 Williams Street." I swallowed my candy bar bite and opened my backpack for another can of warm pop. "You're gonna have to pee real bad before we stop again," said Ronald, grinning.

I was still groggy from sleeping. "I'm not gonna have to piss. Besides, my tallywhacker is so long, I can whip it out the window and just let it go." Ronald was laughing before I even got the whole one-liner out. I'd heard men boast about how long theirs were, and if I got the chance to use the stupid jokes myself, I never hesitated—at least around Ronald.

"That little wee wee of yours wouldn't even come close. You might want to name it Wormy," said Ronald, trying to rile me. We played this type of game all the time, insulting each other just for fun.

"Shoot," I said grabbing my crotch, "this thing here's so big, its name should be Boa."

Ronald slugged me in the arm as the bus driver sounded the horn and yelled, "Five minutes and we're taking off!"

Passengers started filing toward the open doors of the Greyhound, but we remained on the hard concrete curb, tailbones tender. Ronald said, "I guess they'd know we're gone by now—if they found the note. I tried to make it easy to find but also hard enough to give us time." He spit on the pavement and turned toward me. I slugged back some more pop and burped. He hesitated, then scooted closer.

"You know, there's every chance in the world she won't be home, or they might be on vacation somewhere, too." He was trying to convince himself as much as me.

The bus driver blew the horn and called out, "Last reminder: all aboard."

"She'll be there," I said. Ronald raised his eyebrows as we stood. "They better fucking be there," I added. An old lady walking toward her car overheard and shook her head in disgust. "What the hell is she looking at?" I said. Ronald rushed to put his hand over my mouth. I had the taste of his salty skin on my tongue as we climbed onto the bus, the doors shutting behind us with a hiss.

We were the first ones off at the Winston stop. It was dark now, and while we hadn't planned on arriving at night, it was nice, secretive, but did nothing to quell the jitters in my stomach. Our backpacks were light, all the food eaten and pops sucked down. As we plodded along, it was clear our bodies were coming off the sugar high. Ronald held the address before him like a map, referencing it as we took syncopated steps around the square, trying to read the signs of the streets that shot off in multiple directions. We made a complete trip on Main Street and ended up right back where the bus had left us off. I tagged along beside Ronald. "Where the hell is it?" I asked, picking my nose.

Ronald was looking up, then back down again at the envelope. "I don't know. Shut up a second and let me think."

I wanted to respond with a vile tirade, but Ronald might've given up, so I kept my mouth shut. I took a step away from him so he had room to work it out. The entire square was just like the one in Malloy—antique stores and sandwich shops galore, a whole block dedicated to insurance agents, realtors, lawyers, and the farm bureau. We were two hundred miles from home, but it looked exactly the same. Even the sounds and smells were similar: the empty intersection that hummed, the roasted scent of burning leaves. Everything here made it seem like we were feeling our way through a strange but familiar schematic.

"It's gotta be that way," pleaded Ronald, pointing in the direction of where we'd just come. A white clapboard fence enclosed the town square, and in the dark a tomcat prowled around the base, its yellow eyes glinting like caution lights. We took mechanical strides forward, then backward again, as Ronald inspected the envelope like a tourist getting his bearings. He stopped and looked around as a car passed by slowly. The man driving, who was staring at us, looked like George Washington. He gunned the motor, and the car roared out of sight.

Ronald pointed to the center of the square, where the tomcat had been. "Over there. I think it's one of those maps like in the mall." He squinted and took me by the hand, let go of it as I tensed. We looked both ways before crossing the street, then jogged to the fence, hopped it, and approached the map. It was cloaked in a dark shadow.

I pointed up and nudged Ronald. "Why they still got their leaves on?"

"Because," said Ronald as he tried to see the map in the dark, "we're farther south." He tilted his head and tried to turn the sign toward the little light coming off the street, but it was no use. "Damn," he said, shoving the envelope into his front pocket. "I wish I'd brought my compass. If I had a good map, I could figure it out." Ronald sucked his bottom lip and twisted his mouth. A row of benches lined a simple stage to our right. In the dark it was hard to tell what the town used the area for, but if it was like Malloy, they hosted country groups that performed covers of Oak Ridge Boys' songs.

We were about to turn and take another stab at it—walk around the square again—when someone spoke out of the darkness. "What are you boys looking for?" The voice was tired and strained, as if the man behind it had been using his deep baritone for too long on the nearby stage. I scooted as close to Ronald as I could and had no problem this time when he clutched my hand in his.

A figure sat up on one of the benches and coughed. "Don't worry, kids. I sleep here, homeless after a drought stole my future a couple summers ago. I can help. Where you trying to get to?" His outline was slender, and as he stood up, a long coat made him appear like the shadow of a poltergeist. I tightened my grip on Ronald's sweaty hand. The leaves rustled above us, and it grew colder.

The man stepped out of the shadows and came toward us. I could feel Ronald's body ready itself for flight. In the faint light, the man's face opened up. He was pale but strong-jawed. A few lines etched his brow and trailed under his sleepy eyes.

"We're trying to find Williams Street, sir," said Ronald, as if addressing a teacher. The man shook our hands, first Ronald's, then mine, bowing slightly to each of us. His fingers were cold and rough. "Well, good news is you're close; the bad news is there's not much on Williams that'd be open now."

"What about houses?" asked Ronald.

"There are several, but Williams runs all the way out of town to the country, dead-ends into State Road 129. What's the address?" Ronald gave him the envelope, his hand shaking. The man pulled a penlight from his shirt pocket, and the beam made him look like an alien. I was scared. He switched off the flashlight as if he were a doctor and handed the envelope back to Ronald. Something in him changed. It was as if his body temperature rose.

"What you want with those people?" he asked, sounding more irritated, groggy, and impatient. Ronald shrugged his shoulders and nudged me secretly to keep quiet. The man lit a cigarette and puffed smoke out the side of his mouth. The smoking calmed him, and he changed the subject, sighing.

"Before I lost it all, I had a goat that could speak French." The tip of the cigarette glowed in the dark like a tiny sun. Since his comment had to do with animal behavior, Ronald let his guard down.

"What do you mean?" he asked, more than a trace of disbelief in his voice. The homeless farmer sniffled as the tomcat caterwauled from some hidden spot in a nearby tree trunk. The man chortled to himself as he blew more smoke, the plumes fogging his head.

"He could speak French. I'm serious. People thought I was crazy, but I taught that old billy goat to neigh in French. He could say, 'il fait froid.'" The man sucked in as much of the cigarette as his sunken cheeks would allow, then silently expelled a large cloud of smoke. He rubbed the butt into the wet grass, picked it up, and tucked it into his shirt pocket.

"No way," said Ronald, smiling. "Animals can't speak human languages."

I asked, "What does that mean?"

"Sure they can. There's a Malamute that can howl 'I love you.' And in St. Louis once I saw a cow moo the word 'bullshit.'" The man tilted his shoulders toward me. "It means 'it's cold' in French."

"No way," said Ronald, shaking his head, his voice like a little boy's.

The man turned toward the benches. He was exhausted now. "Either you believe or you don't, men, and that's that." He crawled onto the bench and rolled over, turning his back to us. He took a deep breath. "Don't go out to that house. I think you'll be disappointed." He sounded like he was drifting off. "Besides, it's five miles. Bed down here on the benches if you want. It's as safe as anything." His words trailed off, and he was dead asleep, snoring slightly.

Ronald looked at me, his eyes shiny, silvery wet. "You sleep, Lance. I'll keep watch."

"For what?" I asked. With the homeless farmer whistling from a stuffed-up nostril, I'd lost my fear.

Ronald unhitched the backpack from my shoulder and placed it over his. "Nothing really. But you get some sleep, and I'll sit up and make sure no cops come by." He took his coat off and made a pillow out of it for me. He sat down and patted a spot. I stretched out on the bench and put my feet across Ron's legs. The stars in the sky were twinkling, a few so big I thought they were white planets. My eyes grew heavy.

"Ronald?"

"What?" he asked, his voice dreary.

"You think that fucking goat could speak goddamn French?"

It was so quiet that I could hear his lips smack with a smile. "I don't think so, but you never know." He had his head tilted back, peering up at the stars, too. His hair was longer than mine, and in the light some of the strands glittered like chrome. I could tell he was falling asleep.

I dozed and woke up over and over again. "You think they got a baby or not, Ronald? Tell the truth."

"I don't know, Lance. He'd be a half if they do." His voice quavered.

The man on the creaky bench farted and talked in his sleep, rolled over, and began snoring again. The entire square became darker as every other streetlight flicked off. I was glad to have a solid connection with Ronald, his legs under mine so I could trust sleep.

The last thing I remember was Ronald's answer to my question about Dad and Aunt Lee.

"I'm sure they're worried. I be they're looking for us right now, Lancey."

The morning came so quickly, it felt as if we'd only been asleep for a few minutes. The homeless man was gone, not a trace of him left. Ronald had curled up in the night and was still soundly asleep. Overhead the leaves were yellow, gold, and orange, wet with dew, and the sky stretched out pale blue, as close as a ceiling.

"Ronald," I whispered. He didn't move. "Hey, Ronald. Get up. It's morning time."

He sat up straight and stretched. It was very early, just after sunrise. The town square was empty and lonely, desolate.

In silence we arranged our backpacks and buttoned up our coats. It was cold. I shivered and watched Ronald as he did the same. "Where's that fucking goat when you need him?"

Ronald tousled my hair. "Come on. Let's see if we can get a ride out there."

"I'm hungry."

"Then we'll just stay here and get some breakfast first," taunted Ronald, knowing I wanted to see if there was indeed a baby Daniel.

I rushed to catch up with him. "That's okay. I can eat later."

We walked for twenty minutes until an old man in a grain truck pulled over when Ronald waved him down. He was smoking a smelly cigar, and his windows were open. "What's the problem, boys?"

"Nothing," said Ronald. "Can you drive us out to where Williams and 129 meet?"

The old codger nodded and revved the engine, fiddled with the clutch. "Well, get in then. You're about five minutes away from it." We yanked the rusty passenger door open and scrambled inside. As the truck gained speed, the smell of stale cigar and dried manure whipped around our heads. Snickers bar wrappers and Styrofoam cups swirled at our feet. Damp cold wind lashed our faces as the old man floored the truck, hunched over the steering wheel like a monkey. Up ahead a blinking red light indicated a three-way stop. "What address you boys looking for?"

Ronald craned his neck, pointing out the back window. "That one," he said as we overshot our mother's house. "Sorry, I should've told you sooner. I must've missed the numbers on the other mailboxes."

The old man tossed his withered arm across the back of the seat, peered over his sloped shoulder, and began backing up with considerable speed, his cigar like the stack on a tugboat. "Hell, ain't no problem. That's what they make reverse for."

He shot into the driveway and nodded. "Life ain't nothing but a steaming pile of shit on a plate, but, hell, you still gotta eat," he said, his grimy teeth clenched and bared. We squirmed out of the truck and watched as he backfired onto the road, smoke trailing the bumper. After a few seconds, he was gone, and the front yard of the house was quiet.

Ronald looked at his watch. "It's just after six. You think they're up?" I couldn't think clearly; I wanted to hold my baby brother. The house was small but well cared for, and it had a really big toolshed off to the side where a nice field lay plowed and fenced.

"Just go knock."

Ronald rubbed his head and then his chin. He pointed toward the toolshed. "Looks like they've got company." Half a dozen cars sat parked in thick fescue, their windows covered in frost.

We took two steps on the cement sidewalk before laughter rang out inside the house, a high-pitched trill that seemed to be all kinds of fun. The house rumbled, as if kids were chasing one another inside. "Oh shit," I whispered. "They must've had a whole goddamn bunch of kids."

Ronald cut his eyes at me. "Shhh." He stood very still and listened, motioned for us to take a few more steps toward the house. Another delighted scream was followed by a giggle. The house rattled. A loud song started, then skipped, the needle on the turntable scratching several times before it could get going right. Music thumped against the windows. I couldn't take it anymore, knowing for certain our mom had married the kind of man who fathered kids that liked to have a boatload of fun during sunrise. I saw the rambunctious family in my head—four, five, maybe even six kids, all of them looking somewhat like Ronald and me, their faces beaming as we burst in. "Your half brothers are here! Let's eat Lucky Charms and listen to some more music!"

I took three long strides toward the house. Ronald caught me by the jacket sleeve, trying to pull me back. I lurched from his grasp as he tried to stop me. "Lance, wait!" he rasped. I approached the door and knocked, but the music was too loud. Those fun-loving little bastards couldn't hear me. I pounded again. Ronald crept up the steps and grabbed me around the waist. He said hotly into my ear, "Let's wait a little bit and figure out what we're going to say." Ronald dragged me, kicking, down the steps as someone whistled a catcall and turned up the music some more. The windows didn't have any curtains or blinds. I wrestled free from Ronald and jumped back onto the porch. He followed me but not as close as before. Trying the door seemed a waste, and the way those brothers and sisters of ours were acting, I knew they wouldn't mind me going to the window to wave them outside. Ronald was by my side, and he tried one last time to stop me but gave up and cupped his hands, too, as we peered into the house. In a circle stood several ladies and men, naked and pale, their private parts as hairy as bears.

"What in the hell are they up to?" The music was so loud, they had to yell over it, but we couldn't make out what they were saying. A woman I instantly recognized as our mother appeared from a side room with a man in tow, holding his hand, both of them naked. Another naked man—who I assumed must have been the toolshed salesman since a big picture of him and our mother hung on the wall—greeted them and kissed our mother on her neck where her dark hair fell around her shoulders. Ronald yanked me away from the window. He looked dejected, as sad as a hound. "Come on," he said, turning to go back down the steps.

"Wait," I said. He turned and looked at me as if I were a bird with a broken wing. I struggled to come up with something, shoved my hands in my pockets. I said, real low, "They still might have some kids. Maybe they're staying over at someone's house." Ronald let out a little sob, then sucked in a deep breath. I hoped Danny was safe somewhere, away from the adult party. I tried to seem tough and not be a baby, but that damn mother of ours didn't seem like she was missing us at all. The light was coming up across the flat plains in a blast of orange and pink. I felt my bottom lip quiver as we walked together toward the road, the music from the house growing fainter, sparrows flittering on the ground before us, an owl hooting a sad refrain.

Once out on the road, Ronald said, "We've just got to forget her. Let's tear down that blackberry hideout." I didn't want to agree. I loved that space, the way it was just ours, musty and covert; it was the place where a part of our vanished mother lived.

A couple of livestock trucks blasted past us on the road, blowing our jackets and mussing our hair. After we walked all the way back to the square to catch the bus, we sat down on the same benches we'd slept on, exhausted. Ronald bought us sausage-and-cheese biscuits from a restaurant that served breakfast, and we ate them in big bites. I could've eaten three more, but we had to save the money for the ride home. We tried hard to leave behind what we'd seen, make it just another part of our laughable parents. The bus wouldn't be in town for another two hours, so we thumb-wrestled and told jokes, and I got to ask Ronald questions about sex.

"Your mother's a whore."

Ronald held back a full smile. "She's your mother, too," he said, and the two of us bent over with laughter, eyes watering, but it was painful. Something like homesickness lodged in my throat. We cackled some more, but I could feel a well of tears about to break free, too.

We looked like we were drunk when a cop car pulled up and Aunt Lee and our dad crawled out. It was good to see them, even if our dad was dressed in a pair of Ronald's jeans and wore my Fonzie T-shirt. "Come on now, Gerald," Aunt Lee instructed him as she rushed toward us with him in tow.

CHAPTER ELEVEN

I awoke to the sound of what seemed like a hundred coon dogs barking and braying, coursing in a zigzag over the spoor of something. They were just outside my bedroom window. I got up and took a peek through the blinds. My head felt a bit groggy from Lucy's beer, and my underwear was scratchy at the fly. The bedroom was stuffy, my skin clammy and hair damp. The dogs swarmed past, and I could see there were only about ten of them. One of the hounds, a tan-and-black skinny boy with sad eyes, stopped briefly to sniff at the window seal. The coon dog licked the base of the window as I continued to steal a look, but then one of the men yelled, "Come on, Knight!" and the dog took off toward the rest. I jerked away from the blinds, and they slapped the wall.

Lucy had dropped me off at the end of the lane after we'd arranged to meet again when she was through with work and I had visited with my father. Secretly I wasn't sure how I would handle seeing her again, particularly if it occurred while I was with Aunt Lee to see my dad, which I assumed would most likely be the case. But that was a concern for the afternoon. Now I hurried around my small paneled bedroom searching for my pants, sweat already beading like mercury droplets along my forearms.

Finally I located my jeans and pulled them on, hopping all over the place in an attempt to get the jump on Ronald, who might charge into my room and order me to get up, saying madly: "The posse is here!" I was sure he'd sense something in me, that he would be able to figure out what had happened with Lucy just by looking at me. I had my pants on and a clean T-shirt tucked in sloppily, and even my work boots were laced, but there was no Ronald, or Aunt Lee, for that matter. The dogs had stealthily slipped away from the side of my bedroom and sounded as if they were now down around the paddock. Howling and yapping in unison, they blasted like rapid fire on a distant test range, all hyper and intense, sending out signals that all was not well.

I weaved out of the bedroom and into the kitchen. There were no plates on the table or any evidence that a breakfast had been made: a skillet with coagulating bacon grease, the cutoff crusts of toast on Ronald's plate, Aunt Lee's soiled apron on a nail by the sink—none of it was there, only the muffled racket of the dogs outside. I pushed the backdoor open and almost knocked Ronald and Aunt Lee right off the porch. They were both standing quietly with their arms folded, watching what I could now see were over twenty men and twice as many coon dogs disappearing around the barn, working their way toward the precipice, aiming for the steep road that spiraled down toward the fertile river bottom. Aunt Lee turned and surprised me by saying only, "Well, good morning, sleepyhead." She didn't quiz me about why I'd taken so long in getting home, and I didn't get the feeling from her that she'd talked with Bill or Leroy to find out if they indeed were the ones who'd brought me back from the hospital. She was asleep when I got home, and I'd not bothered to see if Ronald was still awake then. I wanted only to get to my room and play over in my head the way Lucy felt between her legs, the smell of her hair and the contours of her mouth.

"Good morning. What's going on?" I pointed to the vague line of dogs and men slipping over the brow of the hill. The barking was now almost inaudible.

Ronald spoke up, "Nothing. They just wanted to run the dogs out here along the river. They needed access is all." He held a steaming coffee mug in his hands and took a sip of it when he was through talking. Usually Aunt Lee would complain if she saw us drinking coffee, saying it would stunt our growth, but this morning she turned toward Ronald and said, "How's the cup-a-coffee? You boys hungry? I'm gonna cook you up some omelets and bacon before I get in to see your daddy." She eased past me and went through the backdoor, leaving Ronald and me alone on the porch.

He sipped some more from the mug, tapped the rail he was leaning on with the fingertips of his other hand. He asked, "Got home okay last night?" I didn't get to answer. He said, "Sorry about leaving you at the hospital, but I just had to see about our boar. Doc Stoops was trying to clean the boar's eyes out with a new kind of laser, and when I stopped by his office he invited me to help him. Besides, I found out at the desk that Dad was all right. You know, before I left and all." I listened, surprised by Ronald's need to do some explaining, particularly when I thought I'd be the one put on the spot. But I didn't want to jinx the reprieve, so I changed the subject from our dad back to the boar.

"How is he—the boar, that is?"

Ronald shifted his weight from one hip to another, contemplated how he was going to answer the question. "He's not going to see. The paint stunned the retinas in his eyes. The laser helped some, but for the most part he's blind. I'm going to pick him up tomorrow." Ronald looked down inside the coffee cup. His big lashes batted away the moisture collecting at his lids. I tried to think of something to say, but nothing would come. We were at a crossroads really. It wasn't that I didn't care about the boars—I did, and I hated our dad and Bill and Leroy for what we'd alleged they'd done—but I also knew the boars represented a fight my dad would take to any extreme. At the same time, I knew my big brother well enough to understand that animals, or for that matter any creature, symbolized to him the purest of acts: to take care of and nurture that which nature had charged us with. To Ronald, that meant mending broken wings, giving extra shots of painkiller during pig birth, holding a family pet after it'd been mangled by a car, and so on. It was indeed a part of him I envied, the portion of his person I most wanted to be like. I assumed he got it from our clandestine mother, and I had given up trying to imitate him after I hit puberty. Some things you just can't fake; it's either part of your biology or not, a simple truth that's not always easy to accept.

So standing there on the porch with him, I not only felt inept at offering him some support for the blinded boar, but I also felt guilty for not being able to get to the same level of hurt concerning the treatment of the boars. As I started to move away from him, to go back inside and wait for Aunt Lee to finish breakfast, I wondered if I'd ever be as good a person as he was. Ronald spoke again, "Lancey?" I stopped and looked at him.

He asked, "You going to help me with the boars? I mean, the thing is, Doc Stoops is sending the guys out tomorrow morning to train me in the AI stuff. It's just that, well, I was hoping, since I never really asked you, that you'd help me. I don't want to do it by myself."

Ronald had never asked me to do anything. It was either an order or somehow understood, through his benign bullying, that I was to do what he said. So when he asked me to help with the gay boars, which meant help whack them off so they wouldn't die, so that my dad would see them as useful since they could still sire baby pigs, I felt like I had the night before with Lucy, all manly and full of pride. I told Ronald I would, and he seemed as if a burden had been lifted from his shoulders. He threw back the rest of his coffee and told me he'd catch up with me in the evening to go over what we needed to have ready for the men from Midland University Animal Sciences Pathology Division. Ronald was going to go back to the vet's to pick up the blind boar and then swing by the hospital to see our dad. Aunt Lee had been up early as usual and had phoned the hospital.

She'd told Ronald how he was doing. He said, before going inside with me to eat, "She said the nurse told her he was doing fine and that as soon as his ribs healed good they'd let him come home. You know one of his ribs tore his lung a little, right?"

I didn't let Ronald know that the most I could've told him about the hospital and the staff was that one of them, doe-eyed and plump, let me touch her and kiss her. "Anyway," he said, "I'm not going to tell him about the boars and all. When he gets home, we'll try to show him. That's all. Period. And remember: don't tell Aunt Lee anything, or she'll just get worked up and get in the way. Just keep quiet about it, okay?"

"That might be a problem." Ronald's eyes widened. "When I was at the hospital, there were some reporters there. I overheard a guy ask where the Bancroft farm was. I think Wolfrum has gotten wind of the boars, Ronald." I couldn't confess seeing the man in the field or what he'd said. Ronald looked sick, and for the first time in our lives, it seemed he wanted me to make things better. "But I'm sure it's nothing," I added, trying to smile. "They would've made it out here by now, right? If they were coming, I mean."

Ronald gave a weak grin, his face still etched with concern. We walked into the house. In the kitchen, Aunt Lee seemed more refreshed than usual. She was light on her feet, turning quickly from one hot pan to the other, seemingly joyful with the food preparation, her face stippled with rosy blotches from the grease heat. She trotted to the pantry and brought out some lemon meringue Pop-Tarts. "Have to hide these blasted things from your daddy or he'll eat every last one before we even get so much as a snip," she said and smiled a devilish grin. She set the box on the table for us while she served everything else onto our plates.

We ate until we were so stuffed that we couldn't move. For a while we just sat and stared and rubbed our guts. But once we did get up, it was supposed to go like this: Aunt Lee was going to clean the table and then ride into town with Ronald (for all she knew he was going to drop off some blood samples to Doc Stoops) while I was to take care of the morning chores and tidy up the barn lot for the Midland men (Aunt Lee was led to believe they were coming down to examine the boars, nothing else), and then, and this surprised me, Aunt Lee said, "Lancey, your friend Lucy called, and she's coming by before she goes to work to pick you up so you can see your daddy."

Aunt Lee began to act as she thought a mother would. "Now, Lance, I ain't got a darn problem with you boys having crushes and all, but the devil lives in too much time alone, and I'm gonna make an exception this time, with your daddy being in the hospital and she works there and such, but don't go to thinking Aunt Lee is gonna let you ride all over this godforsaken county with just anybody."

I felt my face redden and tried to change the subject before Ronald could tease me. I said, half holding back a grin, Ronald raising his eyebrows, "Let's turn on the TV and see if the weather's gonna hold out today." Aunt Lee and Ronald chuckled, and my face felt hotter than ever.

The small television set on Aunt Lee's kitchen counter flickered, then buzzed, came into focus. All three of us immediately recognized a sketch of two boars that was intended to represent ours. The agriculture reporter who sometimes sat in for Mr. Wolfrum and looked a great deal like Wilford Brimley narrated as the drawing shook slightly on the screen. "This was drawn by the high school art teacher at Malloy County Schools, a fine lady named Corine Somerset." The words "Bancroft Farm" were penciled below the charcoaled boars. "We're hearing that boars, which resemble these, a Hampshire crossbreed, are purported to be acting very *peculiarly* on the Bancroft farm," said the anchorman, his face scrunched up, appearing disgusted. He went on to report that church groups, ag teachers, and the general public are curious to know just what was happening on our farm, that they had a right to know what was happening under their noses in Malloy County, Indiana.

CHAPTER TWELVE

That night the little television in the kitchen couldn't meet our needs. All three of us were now captivated by the news. I turned up the TV set in the living room. Aunt Lee heard the racket and trotted in, wiping her hands on a towel. I did a double take when I saw that she was wearing culottes—new, nonetheless. They had the Malloy City Hospital logo at the bottom of each pleat, and I could hardly fathom the fact that she would've had to have bought them in the gift shop of the hospital.

Ronald said louder, "Turn it up, Lance!" Aunt Lee stared at the television with intensity. The TV screen went to a test pattern, a fixed picture of bars of various colors, while dubbed over the tape you could hear the guy that Lucy's father was interviewing, an expert on animal behavior. "It's not uncommon, no. But we don't often see this kind of thing in domesticated animals. To be quite frank, these types of individuals are usually culled in adolescence or are selected out in breeding programs. Still, it does happen from time to time."

The test pattern flickered and bounced on the screen. Finally they got it right, and the video started. The live cameras zoomed back in on the Mr. Wolfrum and one of his sons, Lucy's brother, as they sat opposite the animal behaviorist on the same rickety set our dad had embarrassed Wolfrum on years ago. Lucy's brother tried to look downtrodden, even stuck out his bottom lip some, and as I sat there with Aunt Culottes and General Boar Jerker, I was reminded of Lucy's lips. My whole body was tense. My toes curled into the work boots on my feet. The media was onto us, and I couldn't help thinking how our father had managed to take his penchant for muddling up everything to a larger audience.

"So," said Mr. Wolfrum, "these boars on the Bancroft farm are in essence a kind of crime against nature, then. They aren't supposed to be here is what I'm hearing." Aunt Lee and Ronald both swallowed loudly. The animal behaviorist stammered and shook his head, "No, not at all. You've misunderstood. What I was stating was ..." Wolfrum talked loudly over the man until some music started playing. The segment ended, and the coverage switched to a garden expert named Sally Greenfield.

I shut the TV off. When I turned to say something to them, Aunt Lee and Ronald were already in the kitchen area, talking about the possible upsides to the farm being named on the news. Listening to them carry on in there, with Aunt Lee's Eddie Rabbitt tape keeping a ludicrously simple beat and Ronald's more buoyant and cheerful demeanor coming out in the way in which he asked Aunt Lee if he could give her a hand, I wanted to run in and yell at them good, let them know just how stupid they both sounded, even as Ronald enthusiastically quizzed her about her opinion on erecting a sign at the end of the lane that would display the moniker Bancroft Farms. I thought of letting them have it, telling them both that Jerry Bancroft would not stay in the hospital forever, that the AI process would not keep the boars from certain death, and that the last thing any of us needed was more attention from the same people in the county who had mocked Dad—and us, in the process—since his ill-fated plane trip back in high school.

But I did none of these things. Instead I went to the table and joined them in eating fried chicken, baked beans, stuffing, marmalade succotash, and, of course, corn on the cob. At the table, I held back my anger and kept my head down, pretending to be so famished that all I could do was eat and eat, but it was an act. Aunt Lee was nibbling and singing at the same time. With a mouthful of white Wonder Bread stuffing like a chaw of tabbacci, she sang along with her Eddie Rabbitt tape about loving a rainy night.

Aunt Lee's rheumy eyes seemed to be less bleary. Something about her was more feminine, as if the energy she didn't have to expend on keeping our dad in check had gone to where it was most needed. More than anything, she seemed happy. Ronald sucked down Aunt Lee's toothsome chow and only looked up every so often to gulp some milk; when he drank, he smiled at us and then went back to eating. The Eddie Rabbitt tape clicked off, and we were left with the sounds of three people digesting. Aunt Lee's stomach growled as she ate, made little internal gassy noises as she continued to sing without the aid of Eddie's voice to drown her out. I used my irritation as willpower to wolf down the rest of my food. I got up and excused myself, went to the sink and rinsed off my plate. As the rush of clear water poured over the blue stoneware, an idea came to me that completely soothed my rancor with Ronald and Aunt Lee. I'd felt so alive and purposeful with Lucy when I'd brushed her nipples with my clumsy fingertips, stroked her thighs, kissed her rosy neck. Standing there at the sink, I realized I was angry with Aunt Lee and Ronald for what they held in their heads, even if it was to be brief, as their purpose: Aunt Lee to celebrate while her goony brother was away, and Ronald to save, with my enlisted help, the boars via masturbation.

I stood there, cold water cascading over the plate like a miniature white rapid, and thought of how Lucy had made me feel alive and bigger than myself. As I toweled off the plate and flipped over the cassette tape at Aunt Lee's request, I decided I'd make a break for it. Even though I masqueraded as being tired and ready for bed, I was making plans in my head on how to escape the house later and not be detected. How I'd sneak off to Lucy's house and climb her trellis, if she had one, and make her leave with me into the dark copse of the endless cornfields. My woman and me would make love in the narrow, silty rows during a sticky hot night and then scamper off deeper into the corn, as I told her that one day I could fly her above it all, give her a view of the heartland below as if she were a goddess looking down from the heavens on our former homes.

CHAPTER THIRTEEN

I got out of the window with not much clatter, but when I tried to get my bike from the portico I made such a rumpus that I could hear the boars, almost a hundred feet away, grunt and stir due to what they probably determined was someone out again to spray paint their eyes shut or do them some other type of ignorant harm. The smell of Aunt Lee's softener sheets swirling inside the dryer were puffed out into the sticky air via a vent at the side of the house. It was the same vent Ronald and I often warmed our hands under during a winter snowball fight, and the scent always made me feel happier and somehow less Bancroft-ish.

I gave up on wrestling the bike free and turned to begin my walk down the long lane and then onto County Road 24, where a slight right turn off to the east would bring me to Lucy's house. I was scared and chock-full of adrenaline. I also felt like I was striking a blow against her father for ratting us out on television, but then again part of me understood why he'd want to get back at Jerry Bancroft.

When I stepped on some potsherds from an old drainage tile, I nearly let out a scream of terror, but somehow I managed to keep my mouth shut and continue the pilgrimage that would bring me the completeness I'd craved earlier when I left the house. Aunt Lee had been snoring under her macramé blanket, falling asleep on the couch after watching so much of the news, and Ronald was dutifully to bed early in anticipation of the arrival in the morning of the men from Midland U. As I walked, I imagined him dreaming of all the semen he'd collect and how the AI process would make him a shoo-in for the veterinarian school in Lafayette. I thought of Aunt Lee's dreaming, too, how she might be in the throes of envisioning a life without her zany brother. I wondered what she'd do or become without him pestering her to death with his risible antics. Would she settle down with a seed corn salesman? Or could she live alone, not be tied to making our meals, washing our manure-caked laundry? Would it be too much for her to think of life without her brother's boys? I didn't know and, really, at that moment, didn't understand so much. These were just passing thoughts I used to keep my fear down. It wasn't that I didn't care at all about their dreams; it was more like I was ready to take that first step into making my own desires more than just the foolish urges of a boy.

As I trudged down the lane, a hoot owl called its eerie sound, and bats fluttered about overhead. On either side of the lane, the cornfields of Mr. Dickers cropped up full and ripe, tassels tickling the dark air above. The slight breeze rustled the leaves of the corn; they looked like broad knife blades under the shadows. I smelled the pungent scent of a skunk buoying over the air, refusing to drown in the stifling heat. Sweat began to issue from the pores behind my kneecaps. It drained along my forehead and made my underpants, a pair of Ronald's colored Jockeys I'd snuck out of the laundry room, damp. I thought they'd make me sexier for Lucy, but they were now as wet as if I'd been in Koon's Lake for a baptism, just like my dad. I tightened at the thought of our similarities, what my face would look like on television and if my eyes and nose, like some people had said, resembled my father's.

I looked up at the sky to clear my head. Viscous clouds pushed along in the midnight blue. They seemed to be confused, stuck in a gluey pattern that wouldn't allow them to naturally move on. And then, as if my gaze had given them the thrust they needed to forge ahead, a gap appeared and the full moon was exposed, the clouds visibly gaining speed, moving out of the airspace of Malloy, just like the planes I'd never get to fly, the planes I'd started to try to forget about and replace with thoughts of Lucy's full body.

Something swished in the ditch, and I jumped back. With the light of the moon, I'd gotten the pounding in my chest to subside some, but now with even more sounds coming from the ditch, I felt as if my heart would pop from all the pulsing. The sound escalated to that unmistakable level in which you know for sure death is but moments away. I began to run in the opposite direction, back toward the house, back to my big brother and kind, gentle, all-protecting Aunt Lee. I stumbled some as I sprinted. The huffing and puffing and the blood coursing through my veins all echoed between my ears like I was standing alone deep inside a dry, wide gulch. I felt the gravel beneath my feet spit backward as I picked up the pace, ran as hard as I knew I could to the place I'd just minutes ago escaped.

I tripped and fell, rolled onto my side instinctively to shield my vital organs from what I thought was either a rabid dog or the Sunday school man from the cornfield, ready to kill a Bancroft and strike a godly blow for clean living.

A sheet of loose plastic overtook my face as it consummated its attack on me with the help of a stronger gust of hot air from the wind shift. Even there alone, lying curled up in the center of the lane under the film of dirty Visqueen, arms flailing to get air, trying to come to terms with being a wuss, I felt a blood rush heat up my face and chest in utter embarrassment. The splotches of red could've shown up on a radar system, would've provided enough infrared light to illuminate the darkness around me.

I kicked and swatted at the plastic until finally I was able to get to my feet and catch my breath. The awful reality that I was making up for my dad's absence from the farm hit me full force. I was talking myself out of it when again something stirred at the edge of the corn. I wasn't about to be taken twice in one evening, so I refused to look in the direction of the sound, until, that is, I heard someone cough, hawk up a loogie, and spit it out, their lips blubbering.

While my mind was unsure that I should begin running again, my body made the required moves anyway. Before I knew it, I was crouched down in a timothy field on the other side of the lane, near the brim of a gorge that held discarded appliances and rolls of rusty fence bales. The main road was close, so I assumed the person hacking up mucilage was a hired hand of one of our neighbors, drunk on aqua vitae from one of the illegal barn bars that hawked the stuff to anyone from five to ninety-five. My knees shook, and a stale taste filled my mouth.

I could barely make out the figure as I parted a fold of the hay grass and kept low to the ground. The moon was hidden again by some more clouds, making it difficult to determine if the person was just stopping off to piss or had become disoriented and was heading down our lane toward Ronald and Aunt Lee. I started to feel better about the misadventure earlier, rationalizing that it was entirely possible that I was merely being tested by the countryside, prepared for what was happening now.

The thought soothed me, and I was ready to go on to Lucy's place. I eased up on my haunches to let the numbness building up in the backs of my thighs loosen. I was preparing to stand when I heard not just one voice (one would've indicated that the drunk was simply talking to himself) but two or three voices all murmuring, shushing one another if they got too loud. They tittered and scraped around in the gravel as if they were dancing a jig. I could tell they were moving closer to me, so I belly crawled through the timothy to a tree only yards away, where I was able to stand up and hide behind the fat trunk. The earlier fear prior to the plastic attack had built me up some; I was not nearly as afraid as I should've been.

I now began to make out the voices more clearly. The loudest, low-pitched and raspy, was the most familiar. Out of nowhere, headlights flashed. A van pulled into our lane from off the main road, casting its rays of light onto the grassy field, almost illuminating the tree I was hiding behind. I promenaded around the trunk to avoid the light. The driver backed up the vehicle and rearranged it across the lane entrance, blocking anyone else from going in or leaving.

The familiar voice refrained again; it was clearer as the wind had died down and the van was shut off. It said, "Oh yeah, ya see, we go by what we call a corn-to-hog-ratio. That's the current market price per hunnard pounds to the cost of one bushel of corn. Ya see, that gives us the profit margin on raising pigs. That way we'll know if we can buy the missus a new kitchen set or not." Whoever it was chuckled, proud of the quip. It registered in my brain, and something caught, made the connection. The voice on our television, the one I'd been listening to for years.

Behind the tree, I felt like I might just give up and go back toward the house. Lucy's dad talked on and on about how the Wolfrums first settled the area back when the Miami Indians still fished the rivers near Huntington. He started to tell those who were with him some more farming principles but was cut off by a voice I'd heard that day at the hospital when Dad was first admitted. And now, as the voice spoke, I could tell he was one of the newspeople who'd been in the hospital cafeteria. He said, "Hey, mister, are you sure this is the place? I mean, to me this whole county looks like one big corn fuck, but you better be certain this is not some wild-goose chase you got me on here. I mean, if you think you can bring me out here and go snipe hunting or something, you better think again. I'll slap a lawsuit on you so fast that toupee of yours will be covering your ass."

Lucy's dad went to blubbering about he'd never think of doing that to a fellow newsman and how he knew for sure this was the farm, that this was the place where the gay boars were housed. "I know for sure, Mr. Rhodes, that this Bancroft farm is the place. You see, my daughter Lucy—you didn't meet her when we were at the square there tonight in Malloy, she was at work, anyhow—she told her sister that the Bancroft boy told her that he was afraid their old man was going to do anything to get these boars right." He took a breath and started in again, "Fact is, Mr. Rhodes, this corn here doesn't even belong to Jerry Bancroft. They say he sold it, but I think . . ."

"Look, I could care less what yahoo owns this field, okay? I just want to try to get some footage of it so we can have a fucking visual shot for the early morning piece, all right? I don't care if those swine are homos or not, but with the protests starting at the churches in town, I think this will make a good story, might even make the national headlines."

I had to admit, I liked how he could fling his curse words. The man threw down a cigarette, and I could hear him grind it into the gravel with some force, the same pressure I bet he wanted to use on Lucy's dad's throat. Lucy was right: her dad was nearly as needy as my father when it came to feeling like he was a big shot.

As I heard the door on the van being quietly forced shut with a slight metallic click, I wondered if the reason Lucy had been interested in me was somehow connected to her father's desire to spread the story about the boars, but that seemed too illogical to think about for long.

The other man from the parked van approached, also smoking a cigarette. When he reached the others, he flicked the butt out into the cornfield, unaware that even green corn could burn, start a blaze from its high fructose gases and flame out of control for days, like an exposed pipeline that has to burn out before it will stop. Lucy's dad, aware of that detail, skipped over to where the orange butt glowed like a tiny devil in the dark base of the first row of corn. He said, "Oh no, fellers, that there is a no-no out here around Malloy. Ya see, forests aren't the only things that can conjure up one heck of a fire. No sirree. One time out around Urbana, a kid—I guess he was about twelve or something, I can't recall right yet, anyhow—he was smoking some of that wacky weed, hiding out in the corn from his pappy, about this time of year and he . . ." The newsman interrupted. "Mister, if you don't shut that fucking trap of yours, I'm going to shut it for you real good. You got that?"

Lucy's dad tried to explain, "Oh no, Mr. Rhodes, ya got me all wrong, I was just saying, you know, I thought with us being in the same business and all . . ."

He was interrupted again. The irritated newsman mockingly laughed and said, "You think we're in the same business, huh? Is that it?"

Lucy's dad tried to laugh, too, to show he was seeing whatever inside joke there was. He said, "Well, yeah, Mr. Rhodes, I do. We're both news chaps, men trying to get the good word out about the world and all. Know what I mean?"

In the light of the moon I could see the guy look at his coworker, and they laughed together. A killdeer, probably hovering over a ground nest of chicks, bleated its call from somewhere out in the timothy behind me. I twisted around the tree, thinking they'd be distracted by the bird's cry and look in my direction, but they didn't. Lucy's dad looked uneasy in the full moonlight that shone down once more through the migrating clouds. Mr. Wolfrum stood in front of the guys, glancing back and forth at them both, looking as if his lodged smile were glued onto a dummy's head. The news guy looked once at his friend, both of them still laughing.

The moon was brighter than ever, and it shone like a spotlight on the three men as if they were on a stage. The other two men stopped laughing and walked away from the scene, lighting up new cigarettes and talking about how they were going to shoot the cornfield and— if time permitted and no one showed up to shoo them off the land— they'd take a hydraulic lift a few feet out into the corn and shoot a panoramic view of the field. "Great idea," one said to the other. "We'll use a tag like, 'The Heartland's morals are adrift in a sea of maize.' What do ya think about them apples?" They were excited by the possibilities the corn offered up in the way of media hype. They ignored Lucy's dad. It was as if he were just another stalk of corn. Rage swarmed up into my gullet, bit me multiple times as I began looking around the bottom of the tree until I found a rock about the size of a baseball. Someone had to protect our inept dads. I strike a blow for the little daddies everywhere. I moved out from behind the tree slowly so as not to stir their peripheral vision, took my time aiming. I wound up, pulled back, and let the rock fly, chucking it with all the strength I could muster. I heard a dull smack. At the same time, a moan like that of a horse's neigh echoed in all directions of the field, over the tops of the corn, through the scant blades of timothy, and up and down the hilly lane.

I ran as quick as a cat back to the tree, ducked behind the trunk again, and peeked out from around the enormous curve of bark, proud of hitting my target with so much precision and effect. At first, I couldn't see what was happening; the bodies out in the lane scurried around, trying to get a handle on the disturbance. When they quieted down and began grilling one another about what had happened—when they finally convinced themselves that what had been thrown had come from the fields—I clenched my teeth and shut my eyes tightly, pressing my forehead hard into the bark of the tree for a quick, eclipsed moment of utter regret. "Shit," I whispered.

Holding his ear, Mr. Wolfrum rasped, "We best get outta here then, 'cause if I'm right about what I'm thinking about here, then some of those church protesters are out in those fields just waiting for anything to move. We belong to the Quaker Church—pacifists, you know. The first congregations to protest the Vietnam . . ." He was cut off again, overruled. The media duo decided they'd get a rifle from the van and take turns watching out. The newsman who'd mocked Lucy's dad said in a low hiss, "Now's the time to see if you're a real *news chap*. Stay out here with us till the light comes up, and we'll make you part of our coverage team for this thing. If we can get footage of those gay boars, this whole fucking county will be crawling with even more press rats."

Lucy's dad said, "Ohhh yes," in hushed delight, as if he were being given a tasty treat or a sexual favor. It was the sound I am sure my own dad would've made if the men down at the grain elevator had asked him to run for the county's livestock magistrate. It was an utterance that contained all the heat and covetousness of a crime of passion. They sidled toward the van, deciding Mr. Wolfrum would take the first shift, maybe the second, too.

I felt sorry for Lucy's dad as he agreed to something that would end up with him guarding the other two until dawn, so just to make them jumpy enough not to trust a public access mouthpiece with a shoddy hair weave to do all the guarding, I picked up another rock and heaved it at the van. Mr. Wolfrum screamed. One of the newsmen grabbed the rifle out of the van. He said in an annoyed tone, "I'll take the gun. You stand over there," pointing to where they thought the rocks were coming from, "and if you see anything, let me know. Last thing I'm up for is a gunshot wound, not out here."

I worked my way farther up the fence line. It was past 2:00 a.m., and the sun would be making things less scary for them in just a few hours. As I veered off into the grassy hummocks, looking over my shoulder to make sure I wasn't being tracked and inadvertently shot, I felt better than I thought I would. I hadn't gotten to Lucy's, but I'd acted. I'd somehow altered the way people and things bumped into one another. I couldn't have known how true the statement the newsman had made about the media would be in a matter of just a few hours.

As I crept back into the house—Aunt Lee still sprawled out on the couch in her new hospital clothing and Ronald dead to the world in his room, his khaki pants and blue denim shirt already laid out on the kitchen table for his debut with the Midland men—I could not have possibly known how significant the stones I'd thrown would become. As they say, it's the ripple effect of our actions that can bring down the king or the house or, for that matter, an entire way of life.

CHAPTER FOURTEEN

The newsman at the end of the lane was dead-on right. After the story Wolfrum had aired on his public access channel was picked up by first the local affiliates and then by stations in Ohio, Illinois, Pennsylvania, and Nebraska, the outrage was on. It spurred even more protesters to come out, carrying signs that read: "God doesn't love fags even if they're pigs." The town square in Malloy became a parking lot of coaxial cable and satellite dishes, with news reporters from Chicago and Pittsburgh being mocked behind their backs by the farmers as they tried their best to speak above the taunting accents of grown men. Business in Malloy's cafés and Wal-Mart peaked to an all-time high that has never since been remotely challenged.

While I slept, a late night newsman, who later we'd find out hadn't even visited our county, reported, "I can tell you by being here now for a month that this place can have an intoxicating effect on a person, with its plethora of summer smells: the rotten gunnysacks on fire in the earthy ditches, the fescued pastures alive with syrupy blooms, the slightly heated aroma of milkweed pistils twitching with the touch of fat bees, the sweet stench of tepid hog manure seething in low-rise waterways, the wind soured with the leaking vapors of anhydrous tanks, the night air pungent with run-over skunks. It's these aromas, these Midwestern colognes of the Heartland, if you will, that make this place the perfect location for a story about nature versus nurture."

All of that was just getting revved up, however, when Ronald woke me. At the time, I was unaware, as was he, that the sideshow was about to begin. He shook me awake, and I tried to roll into my clumps of covers to keep him from doing any more damage to my fatigued teenage body. After all, it had yearned for Lucy, been nearly frightened into a coma several times, and walked the mile lane round-trip, all of it on less than three hours of sleep. But, of course, Ronald had no way of knowing this and now stood above me in his pressed, dapper clothes, looking down at me with mild, agitated disgust, trying hard to make it look the other way and seem like he was giving me some encouragement to rise and shine.

"Get up, Lance!" he pleaded. "The men from Midland University are supposed to be here at seven. It's already six thirty. Come on, get up. You said you'd help me. Now, get up!"

I struggled to gain a sense of balance. My mind whirled in every direction, trying to determine if the activities of the night before were real or part of the dream I was having. I'd dreamed I was inside the belly of a boar, then climbed his trachea to watch the world out of his earhole. Everything was knee-high, and the sounds were muted. But as I flopped around under the covers, still feeling Ronald at the side of my head, wobbling the headboard to get me up (his way of making sure I was not comfortable), I reached down and felt the scrapes on my knees, then ran my hands over my elbows to feel the knotty dried blood that was there, too—all indications to my tired head that I had been out of my bed and had seen what I thought I did, that I'd fallen and gotten back up.

Ronald made another plea, and, mostly out of wanting him to stop his mulish whining, I jumped out of bed and did an exaggerated dog-out-of-water shake to make Ronald think he'd really gotten to me, but it was just so I could get dressed in peace and not have to look at his schoolboy clothes any longer. While my mood had improved after the stoning, I was still craving seeing Lucy and for sure was not looking forward to listening to total strangers teach my big brother and me how to pleasure a boar real fine like.

As I searched my floor for a pair of semi-clean socks, a feeling of alarm came over me. It occurred to me that Lucy's dad and the guys in the news van might still be at the end of the road. They could possibly be talking to the Midland men at the very moment I was picking up socks and sniffing them like a coon dog might. The revelation made me stop and think for a moment. I stood frozen, holding a pair of mismatched socks in my hands. I came to the conclusion, after I'd cleared my head some more, that I was being silly. It was impossible for anyone to know that it was me who'd thrown the rocks, that it was Lance Bancroft who'd hit Lucy's dad with a heavy hunk of limestone. I talked myself through the worst that could happen: the Midland U. men would think the people on the farm that Doc Stoops had called them about, the family with the gay boars, were zealous hosts who'd come to the end of the lane to welcome them to their homestead. That was it, period. Still, I could sense that the day was going to be one that I would recall years later, that it would mark some specific era in the Bancroft family's history.

Ronald came back into my room a second time to make sure I was up and at it. He poked his head through the door crack and, seeing me completely clothed, said, "Oh good. You're ready. I made some pancakes for those guys. Do you want some? 'Cause I'll have to drum up some more batter if you do. I'm not eating."

"Why don't you get Aunt Lee to cook for them?" I asked, still muzzy, half paying attention.

"Because," Ronald licked his lips nervously, "she left real early this morning. Old Man Dickers took her to the bus station. She's going to take some time off while Dad is in the hospital. You know she hasn't been away from this farm since she took you to Terre Haute that time for the Weebolos Cub Scout thing? She was telling me last night how she thought she would go see her sister up in South Bend, maybe stay a couple days and visit. When she calls—she said she would—don't tell her I said anything, though. She didn't want you to know about her taking a vacation. You know how she is. She's going to tell you she's there to take care of Aunt Willy, so act like you don't know. Anyway, hurry up. They'll be here any minute."

I pulled on my work boots with the disorienting knowledge that I was not the only person in the house secretly trying to redeem some part of their life. While I was happy that Aunt Lee saw the whole situation as an opportunity to get away and do a few things for herself, I was also hurt that she and Ronald were developing a more mature relationship. It made me feel like I had the night before: the lone descendant of a buffoonish klutz, the sole heir to the jester's throne.

Ronald had decided that we'd wait for the Midland U. men at the end of the lane. His mentioning it, after we'd checked on the boars real quick and made sure they had plenty of water, caused me to stutter a little in response. "Well, what d-d-do you w-w-want to do that for?"

Ronald looked at me queerly and asked, "You okay, man? Sounds like you were trying to get a motor started there."

"I'm f-f-fine, just c-c-cold is all."

"Okay, whatever. It's seventy-five degrees already, but, sure, you're cold. Anyway, I just thought it would be a nice gesture if we were down there, you know, so they know they're in the right place. I mean, that lane is really long. They might think they're on another road or something. Come on. We can drive the tractor down there."

He looked at his watch and tapped it. "Looks like we got about ten minutes. Let's get going. Come on."

I couldn't think of an excuse not to go and was pretty certain Lucy's dad and the news guys had more than likely gotten their cornfield shot and were on their way, but I knew there was an outside chance they were still there. My face would flush with guilt if I happened to see Mr. Wolfrum with a knot on his head.

Ronald and I walked to the John Deere and climbed aboard. I sat on the wheel well to his left, just as we always had while spreading manure or whacking down weeds with the pull-behind mower. The morning was crisp and clear, the full moon from the night before still visible in the bright blue sky. It got me thinking, even though I tried not to, about flying, about taking off and piloting a gorgeous silvery bird into the horizon. While Ronald steered us toward the end of the lane, bouncing roughly over the hilly places and ruts, I allowed myself to see the ascension of the plane I was navigating, my older, sturdier hands on the controls, climbing higher and higher into the sky with a woman at my side, half Lucy and half someone I'd meet at the aviation school in Chicago. The tractor puttered idly along on the gravel, some of the rocks popping up and pinging the underbelly of the engine while Ronald, with his serious face and jaw set at an upward angle, steered the tractor toward what I determined was his dream. Like me, he wanted out of the county, away from our dad. Maybe not a mile up in the sky, but perhaps several counties up the map to the university, where he could demonstrate his passion for animal husbandry.

Without warning, we hit a large hole in the lane, and the tractor bounced unevenly on its duallies. I grabbed at the side of the slick wheel well but couldn't find any help there. I tilted back and lost my balance, started to fall off the tractor. Ronald popped the clutch, shoved the tractor into neutral, and let go of the steering wheel. He grabbed my thighs with both hands and pulled me back onto the wheel well with some effort. I could see the veins in his forearms and temple bulge with blood. The tractor sputtered and died. We were on an upward slope, the last climb before coming to the end of the lane. It was quiet except for a covey of crows chattering in the treetops. Ronald looked at me sourly, then changed his expression to one of concern. He said, "Lancey, come on now. Pay attention. This is important to me. Besides, if we're ever going to do something, it's gotta be now. Okay?"

I was embarrassed about nearly falling off the tractor and was going to apologize for not hanging on like we'd been taught when the clamor of a pack of vehicles made us both look in the direction of the hill. Several news vans, all with different insignias appliquéd in bright colors to the hoods, doors, and side panels, zoomed past us without slowing down. I thought I saw the van from the night before. Was Lucy's dad looking out of the back window like a ghost? An urgent roiling began in my stomach. I was afraid they might be after me, that they'd somehow figured out that I was the one who'd thrown the first stone.

In the very back of the line, like a caboose, was a plain red Ford F-150 with a small magnet on the passenger's side door that read Midland University Animal Sciences. The truck moved slowly, in complete contrast to the vans spitting gravel. Ronald was out of sorts with the entourage of media vehicles converging upon us but managed to gain his senses enough to flag down the truck. The three men inside, packed in tight and close, had what I assumed were the same dumbfounded expressions Ronald and I wore stupidly on our faces.

The trio pulled over. A glint of morning light flickered on the windshield of the truck. The driver had a perplexed look on his brow. He rolled down his window and spoke. "This the Bancroft place?" He asked it as if he knew the answer could be nothing but no.

Ronald introduced himself and apologized for all the commotion, saying, "Well, you've probably heard on the news about this, but it's okay, though. Everything will be just fine." He made a scooping motion with his arm, like he was about to do a cartwheel, to let them know to follow us to the circus. He said, trying to sound a bit like Bill and Leroy, "Come on. We got some pancakes and coffee for you boys if you got a hankering for it."

The men didn't respond, their expressions blank. Ronald's face fell some. He knew he'd overdone it with the "howdy, boys" malarkey. Ronald took me by the arm, and we sheepishly climbed back on the John Deere. He fired up the tractor, which blew plumes of oily smoke into the air, idled soupy, flooded. The men in the truck waited patiently as Ronald did a U-turn into the ditch. His hands were so tight on the wheel, I could have sworn his knuckles were lumps of the white limestone from the lane. He gunned the tractor to its max, pumping the hydraulics handle to release the buildup in the hoses, not that it did anything to speed up the tractor, but I assumed he was merely trying to look competent in front of the Midland men who followed us in their truck behind a pristine shield of glass. They looked like serious surgeons in an observation booth.

When we got to the house and barn lot, several of the crews were out of their vans hoping to be the first to knock on our door. Ronald looked at me and tried to talk out of the side of his mouth, as if the Midland U. men might actually hear him from their quarantined truck pulling up next to us in the grassy lane. He asked, "What the hell are they doing?"

I was tense, still unsure of what part I was to play in the whole mess. I knew I didn't want cameras in my face. We climbed down from the tractor. Ronald signaled for the men to stay put in their truck as we went to investigate. The driver gave a slight nod and then started charting something on a clipboard with a pen he'd pulled from a pocket protector. Ronald marched with authority up to the newsmen swarming on the porch. He hopped up onto the bottom step. They hadn't noticed us drive in and were now also unaware that we were behind them as they continued to jockey for the chance to meet whoever came to the door. Ronald cleared his throat, but they did not turn around.

He said loudly, "Excuse me," but they did not respond. Finally, he shouted, "Can we help you!" The throng of men with cameras on their shoulders and booms at their hips all came at Ronald blurting out pleas about getting our permission to set up and film. At the back of the pack, which had been the front when it was aimed at the house door, I saw the wiry flap of Mr. Wolfrum's toupee. He was holding a stack of cords and poles and trying to keep his balance.

The two newsmen he'd been with at the end of the lane heaped more equipment on him so they could get down the steps and through the masses to talk with Ronald directly.

When the burliest of the two approached Ronald bellowing out something over the din of the rest about getting first dibs, I was sure he was one of the guys at the end of the lane the night before. He said, "All right. All right, everyone, quiet down." And they did. He sounded like he could sing bass in a barbershop quartet. He walked up to Ronald and poked him in the chest with his finger. He said, "Listen, I was here first, last night even—almost got killed by some crazies—and I'll be damned if I'm not gonna get to stay here and try to get some film. You got it?"

Ronald looked scared. He glanced back at me, and I shrugged my shoulders. I wanted to tell him no way, but the group seemed in a slow boiling frenzy, so I decided to just blend in. Ronald started to protest but thought twice about it and told them they could set up their equipment but that it had to be out of the way of the barn lot and the driveway. The guy sneered and said, "Fair enough, boys." Then he motioned for Lucy's dad to haul his stuff down the steps and across the lane to the edge of the cornfield. The rest of the news carnies set up their gear along the field, too, some of them already removing hibachis and gas grills, battery-operated mini-fridges and Igloo water jugs that held a red drink they called Hairy Buffalo. In a matter of ten minutes they'd taken over the outer lip of the farm.

Ronald and I remained at the end of the steps. He said, "This doesn't look good."

We both watched as four more vans full of TV personnel pulled in behind the others. The doors flew open, and people with headsets on and ID tags around their necks spilled out. Someone with a headset yelled that two churches in Malloy were holding vigils, praying that our homo boars would be turned around by their Savior.

More men climbed out of the vans, gave high fives to the ones who were already barbecuing and checking sound levels with handheld gadgets that beeped like metal detectors. Ronald was in a slight trance, almost as if he'd forgotten he had his prized Midland U. messiahs in the truck, waiting for us to retrieve them and get to whacking. I nudged him in the side with my elbow. He looked at me vacantly as I motioned toward the truck with my eyebrows. Ronald continued to stare at the vans, then he said, as I hit him in the ribs again, motioned with my head again, too, "Oh yeah. The boars." He didn't take his eyes off the fracas as we walked together in the direction of the ag men who sat obediently in the truck, seemingly never lifting their heads from their clipboards to even take a peek at what was going on behind them.

Ronald tried to shake things off. He smoothed his shirt and hiked up his pleated pants. He opened the door of the truck as the driver continued to write something in his chart. The driver did not get out right away but instead held his hand up and said, "Just a moment." Finally, he slapped shut his notebook and stepped from the truck.

Ronald introduced himself, gestured toward me, and said, "This is Lance, my brother. He'll be assisting us today."

The driver likewise introduced his coworkers, stopping briefly before each introduction to allow for firm handshakes and the repeating of names. The main man was Randall Feirst. The other two were referred to as Mr. Simon and Mr. Steart. All three men wore crisp white jumpsuits with disposable blue rubber boots designed to stop the spread of disease to other swine herds on other farms. The men were all of similar height, and had it not been for the straight-lined mustache of the driver, Mr. Feirst, I would've bet they were triplets. Their hair was of the same auburn tint, they all had light green eyes, and they even took the same type of small steps when they walked. These three men who were about to show us the fine art of masturbating pigs looked like the health officials and poster boys for some gene-cloning company: clean, purposeful, and erect.

Mr. Feirst asked Ronald where the sires were kept. Ronald pointed toward the paddock and said, "Right over here." I was glad to hear he'd relaxed some with the fake talk, and for the most part he seemed to have been able to forget about the news invasion and focus on the task at hand. I, however, was doing a bit of my own daydreaming, wondering again if anyone would be able to detect that I was the one who'd thrown the stone. Could they find fingerprints on a shard of limestone? I purposely tried to make myself seem small, unnoticeable. Surely I could duck if the cameras were trained on us. I could steal away behind a towering round bale of straw or belly crawl from the barn to the river bottom like a military man.

While the Midland U. staff surveyed the boars for the first time, I glanced back toward the bevy of news vans. Mr. Wolfrum was standing by the only female reporter or perhaps techie—it was difficult to tell what her role was from that distance. He had his wallet out while still trying to balance all the crap the news guys had made him carry. He was showing the woman pictures of his kids in the long plastic accordion-like sleeve that hung down to his knees. She seemed authentically interested, saying things like, "Oh, aren't they precious" and "Well, he's certainly a handsome young man."

Mr. Wolfrum flipped the dangling plastic over and showed her the others. I heard him faintly say, "And this here is Lucy." I hadn't been with Lucy since she'd driven me to the hospital to see my dad, and now with her name being uttered in this strange new world of media frenzy and hog fondling, it made me want to take off right then and sneak over to her place and have sex with her in the apiary she'd told me was located behind their house, bees buzzing a sticky song as the sweet flow of amber honey dripped from the sieves, from the edges of the white boxes and onto the ground where we'd lie writhing.

Ronald brought me back from my dreamland when he called me over to talk while the AI men went to the truck to get their equipment. He said, trying to be covert, cupping his hand around my ear, "Lance, look: they think the one boar is going to get spooked—you know, with him being blind and all—but they've got a solution that usually works." He looked intense as if he were about to ask me to kill myself in the name of artificial insemination. He continued, "You see, they have this dummy sow, or, I guess, dummy boar in this case, that they use to, well, you know, collect the semen. The boar mounts it, and the collector, well, you know what the collector does. Anyway, they're telling me that the blind boar will need something with blood in it. It will need to smell blood to know it's in the right place since it can't see now."

I interrupted him, partly because his hot breath in my ear while we were talking about boar sex was starting to give me the creeps and also because I was having a hard time hearing very well. "Ronald, what the hell are you trying to say?"

He looked at me as if he'd just been goosed, nervous but determined. He blurted out, "Okay! They want to know if you'll let the blind boar mount you while I collect his seed." For a moment, I believed I was some poor sap being crucified in a candid camera hoax, but Ronald nixed that comforting mirage. He said, "Oh, come on. Please? All of them have done it. Sometimes it just makes it easier. They said they thought you would be the perfect height—on your hands and knees, that is." I saw, in my peripheral vision, a barn swallow swoop past. Inside my ears I heard the swirling sound of blood racing through major arteries. I hadn't touched him, but in my hands I felt Ronald's throat under my tight grip, his corporeal neck in such a tight squeeze that the skin oozed out between my clenched fingers like melting plastic. He knew what he was asking was the kind of thing my dad would fall for. And it was that dastardly fact that made me haul off and punch my brother right in the kisser as hard as I could—hitting him just like he had our father.

CHAPTER FIFTEEN

The Midland men looked uncomfortable when they saw that Ronald was bleeding from his nose, the trail of thick blood easing onto his top lip like maroon glue. My aim had been off, but the punch was strong. They'd come back from their truck with an armload of instruments and devices that would've been more appropriately displayed in a sex toy catalog than in their sterile and poised arms.

For Ronald's part, when I hit him he acted as if he'd expected it to happen. He didn't flinch and afterward said despondently, "Okay." The AI triplets didn't mention their indecent proposal to me but rather started immediately talking about how they could do the training on the boar with vision, and, if all went well, they could try using pheromones on the blind boar in order to get him to screw the metal dummy hog. My earlier anger subsided in a few deep breaths, but I tried to be more alert about the cameramen near the cornfield.

Ronald blotted his nose with a piece of burlap from the barn floor, and I realized at that moment how much of the event was not going well for him. He had the news media rooting around in the corn, only a hundred feet away, encroaching minute by minute; his brother had just socked him but good; and one of the boars he was hoping to utilize for semen production was so blind that it needed a boy's blood-scented butt to get the honors done. I told him, "Sorry about that," pointing to his face.

"It's okay, Lance. I'm just glad you're out here." We smiled at each other.

The Midland men did not mention anything about the boars' sexual orientation until they had arranged all their AI instruments on the straw floor just inside the overhang of the barn, placing the vulgar items in rows on swatches of blue cloth. They asked if we'd please sit down on the bales of straw they'd arranged for our comfort, creating a little stage area. It was as if they were performers in a traveling minstrel show and we'd paid a penny to see them dance and sing. Ronald and I took our seats, both of us sucked in by their method. As I sat next to him, he dabbed at his nose, looking at the snotty blood on the gunnysack as if he'd never seen such a thing before. I began feeling worse about the punch. I kept an eye on the news vans and the men filming the house, barn, and fields. It was like I knew what was about to happen.

The leader, Mr. Feirst, said, "Let us first discuss the need for this type of reproduction method." The minstrel show had turned into a Sunday school lesson. "According to Dr. Stoops, DVM, your purported sire swine are homosexual; that is, as in many cases we see, they are only interested in mating with each other. Is that correct?"

I glanced at Ronald, who was sitting nearly on top of me. He responded to Mr. Feirst's question as if in a daze, like he was a patron at a dusty roadside stand about to buy the brown bottle of placebo at any cost. Ronald said, "Yes, they seem to only want to be together, even when we put them in with gilts in heat."

Mr. Feirst chimed in. "I see, I see. And have you noticed any sexual activity between the two; that is, have you noticed, when they are mating with each other, if ejaculation is achieved?"

Ronald turned and looked at me to confirm. He didn't want to be the only one to confess. We both shook our heads yes, and underneath the burlap he still held to his nose I saw the slightest of grins appear. I shouldn't have hit him.

Mr. Feirst said, "Okay, it is just as I expected. Based on their age, health—other than the blindness in the one—and the fact that they do indeed produce semen, I would say you have qualified candidates for artificial insemination."

Mr. Feirst closed his notebook, stuffed his pen into his pocket, walked over to one of his cohorts, and gave him a quick nod to indicate that he was to take over. The next of the three look-alikes walked stiffly into the area before us, knelt down on one knee in the straw, and looked Ronald right in the eye. He said, "Son, do you think of yourself as an open, broad-minded type of person?"

Ronald didn't speak, only nodded his head. The man scrambled quickly to his feet, straw flying in all directions. "That's a good thing, son, because AI takes a person who isn't afraid of what his fellow farmers might think. This AI business is relatively new out here." He threw out his arms to indicate our county. He continued, "And we only train those who we know are going to be able to hack it, to rise above the flak they might get from any uncouth peers."

He got back onto his knee as if he were about to ask us if we had God in our hearts. He looked me in the eye now and asked the same question. I was unsure of what was going on. I could hear the news crews up by the field in their own little world yelling and shouting about tape length and intros. I pictured Lucy's face and wondered what she'd think of my volunteering in the hog masturbation cult. My mind was swarming with visions of Aunt Lee and our hospitalized father. I hadn't answered, so the man took hold of my forearm, squeezing tightly. He repeated himself through clenched teeth, "Son, I said are you an open-minded individual?"

I wanted to push him away and then give him a good kick, but instead I nodded slowly, contemplating whether or not my refusal to be mounted by the blind boar had anything to do with his intense cross-examination of my resolve. Once again he stood up. An audible pop in his knee made him blush as he, too, went offstage to cue the last of the three to take his place before us.

The last man smiled at us as we sat on the bale of straw like two pollywogs. He was cockier than the other two and had an air of disbelief about him. I'm not sure what it was, but something about the way he carried himself suggested he'd done time. He said, "You two punks want to play with some pig dicks, huh? Wanna get right down there and git ya a snoot full of that nasty shit, huh? What are ya, a couple faggots yourselves? That it? Hoping ya might get a little dick yourselves this way? Huh?"

He turned his back and spit at his feet, swung around with crazy eyes and leaped at us, stopping just inches before our faces, glancing back and forth, breathing like he was about to have a coronary.

Then he said, in a more restrained tone, almost like a counselor, "You know that's what all the others are going to say, don't you? Can you handle that kind of disdain?" He combed the wild head hairs off his brow, smoothed them back, and slurped the excess saliva from his bottom lip as he stared us down, walking toward the others like he'd just played a part in the Scared Straight program.

Ronald and I didn't budge from the bale. We were both waiting for the men to perform some grand conclusion to the show, but all they did was begin shining the instruments on the cloth, like the pieces were a row of brogues in a storefront. We got up from the bale shyly and eased quietly to the edge of the barn, leaving the three clones behind as they knelt on the blue cloth and closely examined the AI items as if they were checking sights on guns. When we were out of earshot, Ronald said, "What do you think?"

"What do you mean?"

Ronald seemed concerned but ready to partake. "Well, you know, about all this?"

"I guess it's okay, but what choice do we have? Dad will be home from the hospital in a few days, and if we don't do this now . . . well, you know." Ronald agreed with me. A loud electrical pop accompanied by a buzzing surge echoed across the farm. We both looked up at the same time toward the vans near the cornfield. Two men stood holding a coaxial cable as big around as an arm. It was on fire, the blue flames snaking over the shiny black insulation, dissipating in dying swirls. One of the men was laughing while the other had a sour expression on his face. They stamped on it while a man appeared out of nowhere with a bucket of sand and emptied it over the fire. The cornfield rustled as the sun shone bright and the farm droned with electricity.

Ronald said, "That can't be a good thing. How are we going to get rid of those people?"

I didn't have an answer, but it didn't matter. Mr. Feirst called us to come back in so we could get started with the hands-on portion of the training. At that moment, I suspected Ronald and I were having the same emotions: we felt stuck, over our heads, and bewildered. But we went back into the barn anyway.

I felt air slink from my body when the two other men said they'd go into town and make sure their hotel room was booked while Mr. Feirst finished up with the terminology and equipment explanations. The tough one said, "No use getting going on the collection process today. They need to get familiar with it all before that."

Mr. Feirst agreed and waved to them as they left in the truck, neither of the two even looking in the direction of the teeming newsmen. Mr. Feirst seemed relieved to be on his own. He showed us the metal dummy hog the university would allow us to keep, told us how we'd be wise to cover it in foam rubber and then strap some canvas over it to make it feel as mushy as a sow's, or, in this case, boar's, rear end. He let us touch the beakers, inspect the slides, and hold the test tubes we'd use. He told us about how the boar's semen consistency is classified in three ways: creamy, milk, or skim milk. He preached to us that the collected semen should be maintained at 64°F to insure maximum fertility and that we should always be in the right mood when jerking off the boars. He said, "Never work with a boar when you are short on time or in a bad mood. They'll sense it, and that will be all she wrote."

It was now after lunchtime, and Mr. Feirst asked us about what kind of sandwich places Malloy had to offer, as he appeared to be getting bored with talking about AI. He told us that he and the other two men would be back the next morning to actually show us how to "collect" the boars. He said, "Oh, I wouldn't worry about it much. Once you get used to it, the whole thing seems as natural as cleaning up their defecation. It's as simple as that."

He went over to the blue cloth on the ground and packed all the AI equipment back into a velvet-lined carrying case. He got up and started to walk away without saying anything else. Ronald called after him. "Hey, Mr. Feirst! How are you going to get into town?"

Mr. Feirst looked over his shoulder and said, "Easy. I'm going to ask one of these people up here to take me. Maybe I'll make a good story for them." He laughed as he strode up to one of the guys and talked considerably with his hands. In a flash, he was inside a van and barreling out of the lane in a cloud of limestone scurf. Ronald and I stood together at the edge of the pen. The boars were asleep next to each other, completely unaware that the next day we'd be stroking their corkscrew penises into pink-tinted beakers. Up near the vans, the scent of meat sizzling in a tangy sauce drifted our way. The boars, eyes shut and by all apparent indications asleep, sniffed the air, their snouts wiggling to catch the rich bouquet. As I stood there with Ronald at my side, watching the boars' noses twitching, the meaty aroma hanging in the farm's swale like a curtain, I remembered what we'd been taught in 4-H—that pigs are omnivores, just like humans. They can, and *will*, eat anything. Just then, one of the cameramen started toward us toting a video recorder on his shoulder. I ducked behind Ronald, then ran like crazy into the barn, out a backdoor, and toward the river.

CHAPTER SIXTEEN

It was getting dark outside. Summer evenings in Indiana are magical. The lightning bugs cling to the hinterland between day and night as if the purple shade of evening were their lifeblood.

Ronald sat at the kitchen table, fumbling with a two-yard fold of muslin he'd fished out of Aunt Lee's trunk at the end of her bed, something she would've normally scolded him for taking without asking. But she was not there. When she called, she'd told us she was settling in for a few days with her sister and that she'd made a long-distance phone call to the hospital to check on our dad. She told me on the phone, "Now, Lance, sweetie, I want you to see if you can get a ride into Malloy. He's all fussy about you boys not coming in to see him for a day. He's fine, but you get in there to see him for Aunt Lee, okay?"

I told her I would, and she acted like she was just as proud of me as she would've been if I'd brought home straight A's or solved the world's energy crisis. So I sat waiting for Lucy to pick me up, trying hard to not act as if she were anything more than a friend when Ronald teased me. He said, sounding more like himself than before, "Ooh, little Lance's gonna get him some older poontang." I ignored him as he sewed the muslin and then cut the string with his white teeth.

The cloth Ronald fussed over was to be used on the hog dummy. He cut the muslin with a pair of pinking shears along black felt-tip marker lines that I'd helped him trace earlier. The outline he worked on looked like the profile of a bullfrog. Outside, fires crackled, and when one of the embers burst so loudly that it sounded like a popgun, Ronald jumped, even though he was deeply engrossed in cutting the fabric. He didn't look up when he said, "Those guys are gonna burn down the farm with those fires. I asked them if they could make sure to put water on them before they went to sleep, but I don't think they listened to me."

The newsmen had hoped to get some footage of the church protesters, but so far no one had shown up at the farm. On the television, the sketches of the boars were compared to the shot of the real ones. Ronald sort of glanced at me when the video from earlier in the day, when I'd run toward the river, played. Ronald's profile was just barely visible at the edge of the screen. He was pointing at the boars and saying something, but the reporter's voice was dubbed over, talking about how clear it was that young Ronald Bancroft cared about the creatures. As it turned out, several camera crews had filmed the boars, but most were unimpressed. "I thought they were homo pigs," one had said. "They don't look no different than other pigs I've seen before." Now the crews were waiting for something to happen. From the kitchen window, I saw them sitting in the dark next to pit fires, watching portable TVs.

When Ronald and I had slunk into the house after the late chores, one of the nicer guys, an older man with pink skin, ran up to us at the steps to the house and said, "You guys better watch the news tonight. All the networks will have your cornfields on." He was a helicopter pilot, he told us, and Ronald wasted no time introducing me as his brother who wanted to fly. "Well, good," said the pilot. "Call me at this number when this is all over, and we can talk about a career in aviation."

Then he ran back to the masses of boisterous men standing around blazing fires, drinking longnecks, and smoking cigars and cigarettes. The guy didn't know the cornfield was not ours, and it occurred to me that Mr. Dickers might get mad at us for giving permission to film it without his knowledge, not to mention they seemed to be using the field as their own personal campground now. But Ronald told me not to worry about it. "Dickers is Aunt Lee's puppet. He's not going to give us any trouble. Besides, Aunt Lee told me that he was going out of town for a few days, too. After she brought it up, he just got to thinking he might take a few days of vacation. She told me he said it'd be his last chance before the fall harvest. So that old fart isn't even around to complain. I wish he were, though. Those guys make me nervous."

When a horn blew, I thought it was just one of the newsmen getting rowdy after a shot or two of schnapps, but when I heard some catcalls and whistling, I realized it must be Lucy. I became tense. I was unsure if she knew her father had signed over his soul for the chance to be one of the network's piddly-assed gophers, all with the promise of fame and recognition. Or could it be that Mr. Wolfrum had already called home to spill the beans to the entire family about how he was now going to be the next Dan Rather?

I told Ronald bye and hurried out the door. Lucy was standing next to her truck wearing a jean miniskirt and a low-cut halter top. She was not scheduled to work and so was taking me to see my dad out of something other than it being no bother. "Hi," I said, and I was suddenly aware of how stupidly I walked. My arms seemed to puff out too much, and my stride seemed like I was trying to prove something.

Lucy smiled at me as I scuffed around to the passenger's side door. As I got into the truck, I saw Mr. Wolfrum fetching beers from an ice chest tied to one of the van's bumpers for the two guys who now owned him. One of the scraggly-looking cameramen at the rear of the fire yelled, "Hey, kid, fuck her real good for me, too."

The crowd around the fire roared with laughter. Mr. Wolfrum looked up to laugh himself, trying to go along with the group for the sake of his career. His face went blank when he recognized the truck and the girl driving it. Inside the cab Lucy tried to act like she hadn't heard the harassment. "Man, it's just like in town—fucking media is everywhere." She was backing up as she talked, nearly ramming right into the news vans. Before I could answer or try to explain the things from the night before, including how I'd tried to sneak over to her place, she caught a glimpse of her father as she slammed the truck into first. Mr. Wolfrum was standing dumbly by the blazing fire, an armload of beers tucked under his chin for delivery. Lucy looked at him for a moment while he blankly stared in at her through the rolled-up window. She flipped him off, then peeled the tires with considerable gusto. The white road dust shooting out behind us was visible in the firelight. It hung in the air like a grimy ghost.

As we sped down the lane in her truck, Lucy did not speak. I'd not seen her look hurt before, but now with the fact that her father had been part of the awful thing the cameraman had said, she held back tears. Her lip trembled when we traveled under a light. I reached out to touch her hand, but she withdrew it, like my fingers held the same poison her father had used earlier. She sat straighter behind the wheel, taking a deep breath to make herself tough it out. She changed the subject. With a slight thickness in her voice she said, "So what are all those fuckheads doing back there? Are they waiting for your boars to immaculately conceive?" She didn't look at me when she talked, her eyes fixed on the curvy road before her.

"No," I said, trying to think of something that would make her feel better. "But last night at the end of our lane I hit your dad in the head with a rock."

Lucy smiled a little and giggled some when she said in dismay, "What happened?"

I told her everything as she drove, taking time in between sentences to inhale the air laced with the Gloria Vanderbilt perfume she told me she'd bought at Hook's Drug Store. I spilled my guts about her dad and the rock I hit him with.

At that part of the story she said with enthusiasm, "Good. I'm glad.

I wish you would've hit him with ten. No! I mean a hundred rocks!"

I confessed everything about the scene at the end of the lane. I even got into the boars and my dad and how Ronald would never let him or anyone else hurt them, not again at least.

Interrupting my tirade, she said, "You know he gets released tomorrow, right?"

"Who?" I said, thinking more about how to move Lucy into a hot lather than what she was saying.

"Your dad. He's supposed to be released tomorrow."

Aunt Lee had not told us—if she knew, that is—but it made no difference. Or maybe she'd decided to stay away a little while longer, unable to accept more days of his tiring antics. The fact that he was going to be back, undetained from the hospital and able to wreak havoc again in our lives, made me feel nauseous. I was glad he was okay, but, truthfully, the freedom we'd had was intoxicating. Lucy tried to comfort me regarding my father. "It's going to be okay. He's got orders for bed rest for two weeks." I stopped myself short of envisioning what two weeks of him holed up in the house with Aunt Lee taking care of him would turn into.

"Thanks," I said halfheartedly.

We were near the hospital, just two blocks outside of Malloy. Lucy pulled the truck off the main road and onto a dead-end drive where an uncompleted housing subdivision was cobbled together. She turned off the motor and scooted closer to me on the seat. She smelled wonderful, and her skin was cool even though I was sweaty and hot. I resisted looking at her body. She said casually, "The square in town is full of protesters. Church nutjobs." She let out a long breath, as if she were about to fall asleep.

I didn't say anything but took her face in my hands. We kissed for a long time, and her mouth tasted like Big Red gum, sweet and burning. She pulled my hand to her legs, spread her knees so I could put my hand on her warm, damp panties. Outside the truck, the headlights from cars passing by lit up the dashboard, made Lucy's hair gleam with arcs of chrome light. She stopped me, panted hoarsely. "Let's go to the woods."

Other than it going lightning fast—and that I had some difficulty not thinking of the boars and artificial insemination—my first time went off without a hitch, even if it did happen too quickly. Lucy and I had found a spot under a huge tree and groped and pushed ourselves against each other on a mossy bed of black dirt until seconds later I felt my toes curl and my midsection buckle.

If the act had been a disappointment for her, she didn't let on that way. We took turns brushing the leaves and smudged spots off the backs of each other's clothes, kissing more after it was over than before it had started. It was getting late, and visiting hours would be ending soon, so we decided to hurry back to the truck and get over to see my dad, knowing the last couple of blocks would be jammed with more news vans and the feral camera crews. We were just about to the truck, tromping through some brambly weeds, which gave off the scent of stale mint, when a blaring knelled over Malloy's town emergency alert system. It was the same one used when a tornado had been spotted. The piercing siren made our heads hurt. We both held our hands over our ears. It went on screaming for a while, then stopped abruptly.

Mayor Danter spoke over the crackling PA system from his office in the courthouse less than a hundred feet away. "This is a mayoral directive. Any and all protests on the town square are hereby restricted. I repeat: anyone gathered in groups is ordered to cease and desist. The town of Malloy has nothing to do with the recent developments surrounding a certain hog farm in the county. Anyone, including the media present on the town square a half an hour from now, will be arrested. Thank you."

Lucy looked at me like she'd been shot as cars and trucks blasted past on the road. She said, "We better get back there. Your brother is going to need some help." We got into her truck and sped away from Malloy without seeing my dad. As Lucy dodged other cars and charged down back roads I'd never been on, I thought of my father in his bed at the hospital and how his farm was finally getting the recognition he'd always wanted. Halfway back to the house, I wondered if he'd ever felt as manly and big as me when Lucy pulled the truck over for two more minutes of my quick and eager love.

CHAPTER SEVENTEEN

The three of us sat at the kitchen table with bottles of ice-cold pop before us, the TV bright and loud sitting on the countertop. When Lucy and I'd finally gotten through all the roadblocks and traffic detours, we had still beaten the masses of sightseers and additional news crews to the farm. They simply didn't know where they were going, and we did. Ronald had not heard the news, and when I interrogated him, he seemed lost. "They're quieting down for the night," he said, trying to hide the dummy boar from Lucy's view by stepping in front of it. "A few of them ventured off into the cornfield with spotlights. They must've seen something."

"What's that thing?" asked Lucy, pointing to the dummy. Ronald was still at work on the covering. We told Lucy the boars were going to mount it as a prop while we got the great honor of whacking them off. "Yuck," she said, sipping her pop. "Sometimes guys get boners when you put the bedpan under them." It was silent in the kitchen, so Ronald left and made sure the doors were all locked.

Outside, the roar of cars and high-strung commotion made us go to the windows. More vans and trucks were pulling into the barn lot and front yard. There were police cruisers and some groups of protesters with signs. The entire area was becoming lit up with floodlights that clicked on as soon as the men erecting them like beams at a barn raising got them stable on their bases. The news came on and mentioned something about Malloy, so the three of us pulled ourselves away from the windows and went back to the table to watch. A newsman with gray hair and bushy sideburns showed a picture of the town square with the words "Malloy, Ind." pasted over a cornucopia horn, which overflowed with vegetables, fruit, and flowers. The man said, "Malloy, Indiana, is usually a place of serene beauty and homespun, traditional values, but ever since local churches and other nonsectarian groups got wind of a pair of homosexual boars, the town, and the county for that matter, has been gaining attention in neighboring states. There's even a national petition being circulated by an organization called Americans for Wholesome Virtues that is asking that the animals be euthanized and studied for their abnormalities. We now go live with Peter Losey at the farm for the details."

Our faces fell. It was surreal to see part of the farm right outside our door on the nightly news. It gave me a sense of disorientation. My head filled with vertigo as the edge of the well-lit cornfield came into focus. Mayor Danter and two policemen stood posed before the backdrop of shadowy corn. The news anchor said, "Peter, what can you tell us there?"

The on-location reporter said, "Well, Frank, I am here live with a Mr. Hank Speicher, who as you can see is not happy about what he considers an abomination." The reporter shoved the microphone in the man's face. "Tell us why you and your church group are out here."

The man spoke directly into the microphone. "We have come out here to this farm to make a plea to the owners. If they'll give us the boars freely, let us take them to a Christian vet, we can promise they'll not be harmed." After the newscast had finished, the studio anchor moved on to a story about the influence of heavy metal music on teenage sexual behavior.

"Shit," said Ronald as he rubbed his head and paced the kitchen, thinking. Lucy looked at me and sort of widened her eyes. I could hear footsteps on the porch and a knock at the door, quick and hard. Ronald got up and answered it. From the kitchen table, I could see a bluish light cast over him, and he stared directly into it while a man asked him questions. He froze, unable to answer.

"Hey, kid. Kid?" said the man. "Did you hear me? You gonna answer the question?" After a few moments, the bluish light went black, and Ronald shut the door. He walked back to the table with a blank look on his face.

We agreed then to avoid the press, sneak around and steer clear. We were about to talk about his news debut, the way he looked as if an alien had greeted him at the front door, but Ronald opened, then closed his mouth, just as the phone rang in the kitchen. Ronald rushed to answer it while I talked with Lucy about how she should call her mom, could even stay at the farm for the night since the place was most likely surrounded and she couldn't get out of the lane if she had to.

Ronald looked scared on the phone. He came back to the table and sat down, took a big gulp out of the wrong bottle of pop. After guzzling down the dregs of the Mountain Dew he said, "That was the hospital. They said Dad checked himself out against their orders. The charge nurse said he seemed pretty wound up when he saw our farm on the news."

Ronald appeared dazed, like he was seeing a flower for the first time or trying to understand a foreign language. Before we could even take in the stinging reality of our dad's return, the phone rang again. It was Aunt Lee. Lucy rubbed my back as Ronald solemnly talked on the phone, leaning against the doorjamb, winding the long coil of phone cord around his wrist and then letting it unfurl in a blur. He hung up and came back to the table. He said, "Aunt Lee told me to tell you hello. She's trying to get back here. She knew Dad left the hospital."

"What else did she say?" I asked. Ronald seemed to look through me, his eyes fixed on the backdoor, which was behind my head. When a pounding at the door made Lucy and me jump, I believed then that Ronald was working on another level of perception; it was like he was becoming tuned into things before they happened.

Ronald didn't get up, just kept staring at the door, and it was true that we all felt certain our dad couldn't possibly have gotten to the farm so quickly, but no one wanted to be the one who opened the portal to that possibility. We both figured, too, that maybe we'd have another camera shoved in our faces. Lucy watched us both and then got up and slowly went to the door. She let a man in who looked familiar, but I couldn't place him. I knew him, but the face seemed out of kilter, like a favorite actor you struggle to detect in a movie when they wear a different hair color or put on extra weight.

The man wore a pair of ultra-blue dungarees and a yellow short-sleeved button-down shirt with perfect creases at the shoulders. As he stepped farther into the kitchen, he tipped a nonexistent hat to Lucy and said, "Ma'am."

Ronald stood up and went to him. "Mr. Feirst?"

"That's right, son. I thought I'd come out here tonight. By the looks of it, your whole farm might be roped off before the sun rises. You know they've got that cornfield half mashed down already? Those newspeople are a rowdy bunch."

Ronald offered Mr. Feirst a seat while Lucy boiled some coffee on the stove. Mr. Feirst began to explain why he'd decided to come out to the farm during the media carnival. "Thing is, when I got a ride into town with one of those fellas, he started telling me about this whole mess out here, and I thought I'd better see—you know, for purposes of saving time and headaches—if I could stay out here with you and get a fresh start on the AI work tomorrow."

Ronald eagerly spoke up. "Well, of course you're welcome to stay here with us. You can have Aunt Lee's room. She's up visiting her sister." Mr. Feirst was quiet then, and for a period of time we all just sat and listened to the ruckus outside. With horns honking and people yapping away at one another, it sounded like what I imagined living in Chicago might be like. My mind drifted away from the farm to a small two-hangar air hut on the outskirts of a generic metropolis. I was landing a fine private jet with plush seating and a state-of-the-art instrument panel. Lucy was by my side this time, wearing a full-length sequin dress, presumably due to our just having returned from some special evening where I'd flown us in to eat at a fine restaurant.

"Lance. Hey, Lance?" Lucy was pushing against my shoulder with her hip, a steaming coffeepot in one hand and a cup in the other. She said, "Hey, do you want some, too, or not?" She had a smirk on her face.

"Uh, no. No thanks."

Lucy put the pot on the stove and walked to the table with her own cup of coffee. Ronald and Mr. Feirst had gotten well into their cups as I'd daydreamed. They were talking about how to best get the boars to respond with all the racket from the news vans. Mr. Feirst said, "Listen, kids, I got to be honest with you here about something. When we were at the motel earlier, in Malloy, there were just as many idiots there talking about all this hubbub. There in the lobby were a couple fellas talking to a couple others, and I happened to overhear them when I was waiting in line. Anyway, these two guys were saying how they loved watching this other guy named Jerry get all bent out of shape and all over some gay boars. And then one of them said something I latched onto right away. He said, 'Yeah, he sprayed those boars mighty good with paint. One of 'em is blinded.' They kept on about how this Jerry was in the hospital, and they were going to help him break out or something. And they said how he was going to shit when he saw the media was on his farm without his consent. Anyway, I didn't think there were two farms out this way with a gay, blind boar."

Mr. Feirst leaned back in his chair and sipped some more coffee. Ronald looked like he was about to puke. He'd taken the goal of getting into Midland U. for vet training very seriously, and now an ag man from there was seeing how screwed up his family and farm were. When yet another knock at the door came, Mr. Feirst told us to sit still, that he'd get it.

CHAPTER EIGHTEEN

The newsman with the greasy mustache sat at the table looking like Pat Harrington, the man who played Schneider on *One Day at a Time*. He had on tight blue jeans and a turquoise belt buckle that squeezed him at the waist like a boa constrictor. After Mr. Feirst had let the guy in, Lucy insisted he have a cup of coffee. Having him in the house made me nervous. He'd told Mr. Feirst that he had a proposal to make, to which Mr. Feirst announced, "Well, don't talk with me. These kids here are the ones in charge." I could see Ronald puff up. The comment from his mentor made null, even if temporarily, everything that had gone wrong.

The newsman combed his 'stache with bony white fingers. His nails were long, with gray arcs over fingertips that I could've sworn were printless. The newsman said, "See, we in the TV biz have always got to be thinking of what the viewer is into, you dig?" He surveyed us all.

"Why don't you get to the point, mister," said Mr. Feirst.

"Okay, dig this. All these other crews are goin' in to town interviewing church officials and shit like that, so what I wanna do is feature you babies as sorta the 'Forgotten Teenage Farmers' in all this hoopla. What do you babies think about them sweet-ass apples?" He pointed to Ronald and added, "You'd look great on video, brother. Them eyes of yours would light up like jewels, my man."

Ronald didn't say anything. None of us said anything. It was as if, by the newsman's presence, we'd finally come to grips with the absurdity of the situation. Mr. Feirst pushed his chair back, the legs vibrating along the floor, rumbling like thunder. He stood up and said, "Mister, I think you ought to leave. These kids here are trying to keep this farm running, and that's quite a chore, and unless I'm wrong," he paused and looked at each of us separately, "they're not interested in your proposal."

The newsman stood up, too. He sauntered over and got in Mr. Feirst's face, stared him in the eye. He looked like he was going to say something else but left out the backdoor as if he were sneaking out of church. I went to the window to watch him strut away. I could see his upright figure trailing across the yard, heading for the tribe of news roadies by the dying fire. It was getting late, and they were simmering down, some even cocooned in sleeping bags by the flames. I turned away from the window. Lucy looked tired around her eyes as she smoked the last cigarette in a crumpled pack lying on the table. Ronald asked me if I'd put new sheets on Aunt Lee's bed for Mr. Feirst, but before I could, Lucy was saying she'd do it.

She hopped up and went instinctively to the linen closet. I could hear her closing the thin door on its creaky hinges and then her muffled footsteps on the floor. Thinking of Lucy making up the room made me wonder how she'd be in a real bed, not the woods. As Ronald and Mr. Feirst went back to talking about the boars, I determined that she would be like the women I'd seen at tractor pulls: fierce with their love but vulnerable, too, like they might slap you and then cry about it, pulling you close for a hug, the scent of fabric softener their only perfume.

Lucy glided back into the kitchen. Ronald whispered something to Mr. Feirst and then stood up and cleared his throat, like he was about to get a crowd's attention to make a toast. It was a formal moment that reminded me too much of something our dad might have overblown. Ronald said, "Mr. Feirst and I have been talking," (now he really sounded like our dad) "and he thinks—that is, he and I think—we should divvy up the night and go in watches." He addressed himself to Lucy, "Of course, Lucy, we don't expect you to take a shift." Lucy rolled her eyes. Ronald continued, "Now, we all know that Dad and Bill and Leroy are going to try to get here tonight, and we also know that they're going to try to do something to the boars. So as long as we keep our eyes peeled and guard the boars, everything should be all right. I'd thought about calling the sheriff about this—you know, to see if he could pick Dad up and convince him to get back to the hospital—but for now we'll try to get a handle on this ourselves."

Ronald looked at me. He said, "Lance, you kosher with all this?"

The moment struck me as humorous—I don't know what it was, maybe Ronald saying "kosher" did it, or maybe it was the fact that it seemed so silly and melodramatic to be talking about guarding what amounted to ham and bacon still on the hoof—but I let out a burst of laughter that rattled the table. In seconds Lucy was cracking up, too. When Mr. Feirst got bitten by the bug, the strong giggle that Ronald had been holding back for his mentor's sake busted through, making his eyes water as he tried to get it under control. The four of us leaned on the table and counters laughing until Lucy's laughter began to lessen, the smile draining from around her features. She started shushing us. She said, "The phone. The phone is ringing."

Ronald wiped his eyes and used his sleeve on his nose. He answered the phone, and no more had he gotten it to his ear than a look of utter relief spread across his face, as if he'd just taken a long piss by the side of a road. He hung up and let out a hot sigh.

"That was the hospital again. Some farmer just brought Dad in. The guy told the nurse he heard a commotion out by his shoat lot, and when he went out there, two guys ran off into the weeds. He found Dad covered with manure and brought him in."

Ronald smiled a little bit and then realized it might look like he was happy about his own father's misfortune, so he quickly switched back to a more concerned expression. He said, "Anyway, the nurse says they're worried that infection from the manure could set up in his cuts. They're going to clean him with some type of antibacterial wash and apply topical antibiotics. She's gonna call us in the morning."

"What about those other two yahoos? You think they'll stay put?" asked Mr. Feirst.

Ronald lost some of his lightheartedness. He answered, "That's a good point. They might still try to get out here, just to egg things on. We should still guard the boars. But listen, I'll just stay out there tonight. There's no reason all of us should have to miss sleep."

Mr. Feirst tried to talk Ronald out of it, but after some time he said, "Well, son, it's your farm. You do what you think is best." With that, Mr. Feirst went into Aunt Lee's bedroom to go to bed. The Listerine he'd used at her small basin in her pink bathroom made the whole living room smell like it had been sanitized.

Ronald packed a backpack and got the shotgun down from the shelf on the back porch. He seemed like a little boy playing war. The nape of his neck looked like the sweet, perfect skin of a newborn as he turned and left the house out the backdoor. He stepped back in and whispered, "Make sure Mr. Feirst is comfortable, okay?" I didn't know what that comment was supposed to mean, but I shook my head yes anyway. When he walked down the steps toward the barn, there were a few stragglers left around the newsmen's campfire, and the groups of protesters had put up tents of their own. It was as if the media and the do-gooders were resting up, getting ready for a big day tomorrow. The air was thick with the scent of the corn's pollinating tassels, and a whip-poor-will sang alone somewhere over the house, confused by the late evening racket.

That night Lucy and I slept on the couch together, too afraid that if we were in my bedroom, Mr. Feirst might think less than decently of Lucy. Before we drifted off to sleep, clutching each other in sweaty, stale clothes, we watched the news. One of the networks was doing an in-depth interview with a woman named Florence Graves. When the old woman's purplish hair flashed onto the muted screen, Lucy said, "Hey, turn that up, Lance. Isn't that Mrs. Graves, the old kindergarten teacher?" I turned up the TV slightly, but I didn't want to wake Mr. Feirst, so I pulled Lucy by the hand to sit closer. She willingly let me lead her across the floor where we plopped down in front of the TV, legs crossed as if about to do yoga.

Mrs. Graves had an overbite—well, at least now she did—but Lucy and I decided it hadn't always been that way. It had to be her dentures that she was trying to hold in. The reporter kept pulling the microphone away from her mouth because her choppers kept hitting it, making it sound as if a pair of castanets were being clacked as accompanying music for the segment. Whenever the reporter pulled the mic away though, Mrs. Graves just kept yanking it back to her noisy mouth. Lucy and I had to smother each other's laughs. When she put her hand over my mouth, I could taste the coffee and salt on her palm. I tickled her away so that we could listen to the woman who'd had everyone from my dad to Mr. Wolfrum and myself in her kindergarten class. Once the reporter had gotten used to the rhythm it took to keep Mrs. Graves's false teeth at bay, he was able to get down to the essence of what she was supposed to be exposing. She was describing how she had a nephew who was gay. "He's nothing but a good, well-mannered boy, and I think people should keep their noses out of other people's bedrooms." She paused, then held up a crooked, wrinkly finger. "Or in this case, the barnyard." I loved Mrs. Graves at that moment, even if all I could do was laugh.

Her teeth slipped again, this time so violently that the banging on the microphone even made her jump. She jerked her head back and said to the reporter, "I think that instrument of yours just shocked me. I hope you have it grounded." The reporter brushed her hand away as she tried in vain to inspect the microphone for a malfunction. He bent over and whispered sternly in her ear. She straightened up and started talking at a faster clip, saying, "Anyway, if God wants them boars out there at the Bancroft place—if he wants them dead like the folks at the First United Savior's Way congregation on Walnut Street in Malloy say he does—well then, I'm not about to tithe them anymore."

Mrs. Graves shot her hands in the air and shook them into the darkness toward the heavens. She was louder when she talked into the microphone again, the feedback distorting her voice, "Praise the Lord Almighty. Life's too short to worry about who or what is putting their privates where!" When her teeth finally fell out from all the skyward head movements she was using to exalt God's holiness, she ducked down to get them and then was out of the picture as the cameraman on the live remote did the best thing he could, taking a zoom-in of one of the many churches in Malloy. The on-site reporter sent the broadcast back to the studio in New York, where a panel of sexual behavior experts, including a woman who had just published a book about her platonic but long-lasting relationship with a gay wolf, discussed our boars. It was strange, like watching an old videotape of some event in your past. I guess it felt as if something of this magnitude had always been on its way to us. When Lucy began rubbing my leg, I switched the TV off, its slow dying buzz and fading glow like an alien life-form in the darkness of the living room.

We kissed and kissed until, apparently, we passed out into a deep sleep in each other's arms on the floor, because the next thing I knew, Mr. Feirst was shaking me, saying, "Come on, son. It's time."

CHAPTER NINETEEN

After I'd eased my arm out from beneath Lucy's head, I didn't bother to change clothes. Not because I was in too much of a hurry, but because when he woke me up, standing over me in his official AI attire like a spotless column, Mr. Feirst already held in his other hand a white jumpsuit from the university that he tossed at me. "Scrub your hands good in the kitchen sink. I've filled it with a bleach-and-iodine solution. You can't be touching a boar's penis with bacteria or the like." With that he left me to my woman so I could produce the kind of tenderness he thought a man should display after a night had been spent and a gift had been given, but, of course, he was wrong. Like I said, we kissed ourselves into slumber that night, and that was it.

In the kitchen sink, the nicks and cuts on my knuckles burnt as I scrubbed them in the frothy hot water. From the window, I could see Ronald and Mr. Feirst already prepping the boars like he'd instructed us during our training the day before: a light meal, a warm water brush bath, and lots and lots of petting, which I could see the two of them doing as I finished drying my red hands on Aunt Lee's noel towel. It was clear that Ronald had stood watch over the boars, his sleeping bag now rolled up next to his pillow on a bale of straw. I saw that Ronald was keeping pace with Mr. Feirst, who was scratching the blind boar behind his ears, by imitating everything he saw him do. Now he was at the head of his own boar, scratching at his floppier ears.

Outside the fence, I could see yet another pail of steaming water and realized my current hand scrubbing was more to set the tone than to provide antibacterial protection to the boars' dicks. I'd need to wash them again when I got out there. I felt a tugging at my insides as I prepared to leave the house and go out across the paddock in front of the swarm of news goons, who I figured, after last night's news with chattering Mrs. Graves, were whipped up into a feeding frenzy. It was a feeling of premonition, one that told me we were only going to make matters worse with the AI thing. But out of loyalty to my big brother, I forced myself to stumble out the backdoor, pulling the hood of my sweatshirt up over my head and trying to take on the quiet, unassuming nature of a praying mantis.

The news crews had retreated some. Only a handful remained, and I started to think that most of them had gone back into Malloy after having seen the national coverage of Mrs. Graves the night before, thinking they'd better get to where the action was. Since she'd come out that strongly, it was likely only a matter of time before a confrontation took place, maybe right inside one of the churches, where a congregation might accost the county's most beloved kindergarten teacher for spewing her soulless message.

As I snuck by, careful not to catch their attention, I inspected the news vans, the paraphernalia strapped to the sides, leaning in tangles against open doors. Two cameramen were passed out, mouths open. The story-hungry reporters were not about to leave now as more and more news coverage focused on our farm. The television stations looped Mrs. Graves's bold views, and her simple but heartwarming words made the protesters ratchet up their activity—a fact I was unaware of as I snuck toward the barn and saw only a few crews setting up cameras, checking lighting levels, and performing the general duties of creating B-roll tape they could use for their continuous coverage. Still, I crept past as if they were bears, able to kill with just one blow.

Anyway, I was happy to see less of them around. It soothed me some, made me think that my gut feeling in the house was not based on anything tangible. Maybe the crews would begin to lose interest. I even had a thought that my own dad might be healing well in the hospital, that maybe his new infection from leaving the nurses' care too early had brought him to his senses somewhat. I felt hopeful that the incident might have led him to consider not listening to Bill and Leroy anymore, at least until he was officially released from the hospital and back at the farm, and by that time Aunt Lee would most likely be home to keep him under her thumb. This was the nonsense that filled my head as I approached the boar pen.

Ronald and Mr. Feirst were in good moods, ready to engage in some real intimate animal science. The dummy hog was farther inside the barn, now tightly strapped with the white muslin that Ronald had worked on so diligently. He saw me eyeing it and said, "What do you think, Lance? I was able to get it just right last night out here. I didn't get much sleep, but it gave me a lot of time to work on the dummy."

Mr. Feirst gave Ronald what I am sure the older man detected was some much needed praise on the job. "Yep, Lance, your brother here is gonna make a good vet. That's about the best homemade dummy I've ever seen." Mr. Feirst wanted to make sure he thought of a younger boy's needs, too. He asked, for my benefit, as he continued to scrub up, bending over the pail, "What is it you got your mind set on for the future? In the way of work, that is?" I wasn't going to answer, but even so it made me a little miffed when Ronald spoke up for me.

"Lance is going to be a pilot. He's got all kinds of books on planes."

"Well yes, sir, you Bancroft boys as far as I can tell are gonna make your daddy real proud." He realized, even though he'd only been around us for a little while, that by bringing our dad into the picture he'd made both of us quietly unsure of what our lives really would be like, and so he changed the subject to the boars. "Here's what we're going to do today, boys, and it's only gonna take you a little while to get this down. By the end of the day you will be able to collect the semen from these two, or at least the one that can see, and that'll pretty much be it. I can come back if you have any troubles, but this whole thing could be done by a chimp if need be." He paused and dried his hands on a rag tucked in at his hip. "Anyway, what we're going to do today is get you boys used to the collection process. It's just like anything else on a farm: once you got it, you got it, like driving a grainer."

Ronald let the boar that could see out of the pen. He lovingly steered it to another enclosure that he and Mr. Feirst had fashioned out of some bales of straw and loose tires. Ronald had pulled the tractor into the space, too, and its chassis blocked the boar off from the rest of the barn. The boar went into the new area and began sniffing around. The blind boar whimpered for his partner to return, running into the fence boards that separated them like a sparrow flying into a window. Mr. Feirst looked concerned, not scared or irritated, but more like how a doctor might look if a critical patient lying on an emergency table had a nervous and out-of-control loved one going nuts. The blind boar kept at it, almost wailing now, guttural and excited.

The pandemonium of the blind boar got the attention of a couple of the cameramen standing aimlessly by the vans near the cornfield. They snatched up their cameras and came running, long hair flowing in the breeze. My stomach flip-flopped, and I chanted silently my mantra: "Just stay off the news." Even though Ronald had frozen up for the cameras the day before, and we'd successfully turned down that gross newsman for a feature interview, it seemed as though we couldn't avoid their all-seeing eyes any longer.

I tried to say something to Ronald and Mr. Feirst about the news guys charging us, but they were both so involved in trying to calm the blind boar that they just waved me off. Mr. Feirst called out to me, "Lance! There's no time for talk right now. Can you take the other boar somewhere? Maybe let him out into some grass to graze?"

The cameramen dropped down on their knees just outside the barn doors and began taping us. I did what I was told and let out the blind boar. I couldn't stop it once it was loose. It sniffed the air, its eyes milky and fixed. It charged the bales of straw like a train. It nearly knocked Mr. Feirst down. Ronald fell over into a stack of the tires he and Mr. Feirst had arranged earlier. He sat in them looking stuck, as much a son of Jerry Bancroft as he could be. The blind boar was antsy and went to the other one quickly, using his upturned snout to find it. They grunted at each other until the time in between the grunts lessened and the blind boar calmed down.

I hurried and pulled Ronald out of the tires as Mr. Feirst took off his cap and ran his hands through his hair. He said, "Let's just try to get one of them up on that dummy to collect. I don't care if it can see or not. Let's just try and get this thing done today." He got a tub of what looked like Vicks VapoRub from his carrying case. I thought he would've seen the cameramen then, but he didn't. Either that or he just didn't care that they were rolling tape, recording his every move. I yanked my hood back over my head and slunk into the barn's shadow.

When Mr. Feirst opened the container of jelly, the feeble breeze carried the scent outward. It smelled gamey and reminded me of a seafood counter. Both the boars began sniffing the air. Mr. Feirst walked over to the dummy, dipped his hand in the tub, and scooped out a big dollop of the goo. He rubbed it all over the tail end of the dummy, where Ronald's upholstered muslin puckered into a ruffled bunch. He said, "This is what I normally use to get old sows to come into heat. It's petroleum with sheath fluid mixed in from an old boar we have in the lab at Midland. The sows go crazy for this stuff. I figure these boys here might like it, too, you know."

Mr. Feirst finished smearing the dummy with the pheromones and glided across the barn floor. He pulled down a shovel from a peg on the wall. He spread the excess jelly he had on his hand up and down the length of the handle. He held the coated handle in front of the sighted boar's snout. It sniffed it and nibbled at the slime along the wood. The blind boar was standing close by, its eyes like a doll's, vacant and fixed. Mr. Feirst moved the handle nearer the gluey rear of the dummy, hoping the boar would mount the contraption so we could collect semen from it, but the boar turned to his partner and began grunting lowly, pushing his nose into the soft brisket of his mate. Slowly the boar's penis spiraled out of its sheath, pink and stiff, as if it were a device used to bore the cork of a humongous bottle of wine. When the boar mounted the blind one, his penis began to search for familiar territory. Mr. Feirst looked happy. The expression on his face shone with insight and assurance. It was the look of a man with a dawning idea. He quickly grabbed a pair of surgical gloves from his splayed case and snapped them on, then tossed Ronald some and told him to do the same. He picked up one of the big glass beakers and said to Ronald, "Come on over here. Quick now, before he gets it in."

Ronald's gloves went on awkwardly. They were twisted about his knuckles, making his hands look slightly deformed, like a burn victim's. I tried again to get Ronald's attention, to alert him about the cameramen quietly capturing our gay boars on tape, but it was no use. He was all too eager to please Mr. Feirst, and I didn't want to risk detection myself. I stood very still and just watched.

Mr. Feirst made Ronald stand next to him. While looking under the belly of the boar on top, he said, "Good. He hasn't got it in yet." He handed Ronald the beaker. "When I get down there, you hold the beaker good and low. I think I can get the semen that way." Mr. Feirst moved with the brave intuition of an emergency room doctor. He knelt down by the boars and grabbed ahold of the penis. Ronald dropped down beside him, offering the beaker like it was

a housewarming gift. Mr. Feirst pulled Ronald closer with his free
arm. With a couple of purposeful strokes, his cheek lying flat against
the boar's side, Mr. Feirst moved quickly and said in a determined,
calculated voice, "Now! Here it comes." The boars didn't move, and
when Mr. Feirst stood up, he yanked Ronald up with him. In a daze
from the rapid pace of the procedure, Ronald didn't look down at
the beaker that now held a creamy dose of semen.

Mr. Feirst, pleased, took the beaker from Ronald's hands and held
it up to the light. A few stray pieces of straw stuck to the glass, but,
other than that, the material inside gleamed like liquidized pearls.
It was then, as Ronald began to look proud, too, that Mr. Feirst saw
the two men with cameras silently securing the whole scene on tape.
But before he could say anything, the beaker in his hands burst, the
glass and sperm exploding like shrapnel in all directions—a liquid
and a solid now in plasmatic blur. The single gunshot rang in our ears
as Mr. Feirst jumped behind the tractor. Ronald and I ran there, too.
The cameramen kept rolling tape but took cover behind some bales
of straw. One of the cameramen pointed up by the cornfield where
they'd been camped out. The news crews still by the field began
rolling tape, taking cover themselves behind open van doors and
stacked-up coolers. Mr. Feirst looked at Ronald and me and said,
"You think your daddy got out again?"

We didn't answer him as all three of us peeked around the nose
of the tractor to the barn entrance. The two cameramen with equipment on their shoulders ran as if they were in a war zone, their
equipment flapping wildly. They sprinted back up to the edge of the
field to try and nab the footage the others were getting. We could
hear somebody from the other crews yelling, "Out there! Out there
in the corn! I can see it moving!"

Mr. Feirst and Ronald and I left the tractor, snaked around the
loose tires and bales in the barn. Ronald checked the boars quickly
and opened the gate to their pen to let them back inside. They were
fine and had apparently dismounted during the attack. A sense of

melodramatic panic overcame me. "Oh shit! Lucy!" I took off and ran to the house to check on her, leaving Ronald and Mr. Feirst behind me as they also ran toward the corn and crews. It was as if we were in some combat movie, hunkered down, racing as fast as possible to avoid friendly fire.

As I sprinted to the house, I could hear the newspeople yelling even more about how it had to be one of the church zealots. One of the reporters was hollering about getting exclusive coverage. He said, "Make sure the camera has plenty of tape. I'm goin' out!" He pointed to the field as he tied a rope attached to the bumper of the van around his waist.

Lucy stood at the backdoor as I ran up the steps, her hair in a ponytail and her lips glossy and pursed. "What the hell was that?"

I told her what had happened as I hugged her. "Stay inside. I'm going back out there with Ronald and Mr. Feirst." I felt manly and brave, about to ship out. I kissed her on the mouth and ran down the steps.

"Lance, do you think your dad would shoot at you guys?"

I called over my shoulder, "I don't know, but call the hospital. See if he's there."

Part

THREE

CHAPTER TWENTY

Six months after we found out that our mother and the Midwest's most prolific toolshed salesman were in fact swingers, I prodded Ronald to try one more time.

"Lance, she's into things you can't even imagine. Your mother's a sex fiend, face it." He was reading a book titled *Vet Care for the Rabied, Distempered, and Flu-Stricken.*

"That bitch is your mother, too," I told him. He tossed the book to the ground and took off out of our bedroom. I ran after him as he stomped down the stairs and out the backdoor. It was May, and everything was in bloom: the ditch mallow and wild poppies along the garage, the redbud tree towering next to Aunt Lee's garden, even the vast wild strawberry field Ronald rushed through to try and lose me. It was all blasted in color, scented like shampoo.

"Leave me alone, Lance. Go back in the house. For Christ's sake, give me a chance to breathe!"

I was annoying and relentless, running to catch up with him as he made his way toward the blackberry hideout. "What are you gonna do?" I asked, sniffling. I'd accepted that our mother was a tramp, but I couldn't stop believing that she still hid a litter of little brothers and sisters from me like a mother cat hides her kittens in a haymow.

Ronald flung open our makeshift door to the bramble den and stormed inside. We'd stashed a tin of cigars in the dirt and a women's underwear catalog behind a heavy log. For a while, all Ronald did was stomp around the interior of the hideout, the sparrow chicks in their nests overhead bleating for their mothers as bits of hay floated in a shaft of sun entering the brambles. It looked like a homemade church inside there, maroon and black, with just the right amount of filtered light to indicate salvation. Ronald kicked a stump we'd set up to play cards on, but it didn't budge. He hopped around angry, his toe jammed.

"She's just as sorry as he is, you know that?" screamed Ronald.

"That's why we got to go back and get Danny and any other ones that witch has made. We gotta save them." Ronald sat down in the black dirt and tucked his knees under his chin. He looked like he was freezing, and maybe that was it. The interior of our brambly cave was cool, and an early spring wind blew through the tangles, causing me to shiver. But he also shook with more than cold. He was passing through something, an acceptance and anger that would descend upon me much later. I walked to him and sat down so close that our shoulders rubbed as he rocked slightly. A cloud passed over outside, making our space temporarily darker.

"I'm just sick of it, Lance. Sorry. I shouldn't have yelled at you." He turned to me and pushed his forehead on mine, held the back of my head with his hand, as if he were trying to apply enough pressure to leave a print.

"Come on," he said, forcing a change of mood. "Let's have us a smoke and a pop." We always kept a six-pack of ultra-cheap sodas in a hole covered with peat. Ronald had read about how to keep things cold this way, and to my amazement it worked. He jumped up and removed the peat and plucked two black cherry colas from the hole. In a flash, he had two stogies lit, puffing mine to a nice glow before handing it over. We moved to our stump to play cards. The air smelled great; cigar smoke hung in little clouds above our heads as he let me cut the deck. "Aces are wild, bubby!" said Ronald, trying hard to sound upbeat, forcing himself to be happy to forget about being sad. He dealt the cards and warned me: "Don't smoke it too fast. Last time you puked a little."

"Screw you, you bastard shit," I said, knowing Ronald needed my profanity to help keep the mood light.

He rolled the Swisher Sweet to the side of his mouth and held it there loosely, smiling. "If Aunt Lee finds us out here drinking pop, smoking, gambling, and cussing, she's gonna cut a switch." It was a strategic taunt.

"Hell, that ole' damn lady can kiss my ass." Ronald burst out a shot of laughter, then told me to pick up my cards. My head started to feel logy, and something in my stomach churned.

"Ronald?"

"What?" he asked, splaying his cards, rearranging them.

"So we're not going to try again?"

"No. They don't have any other kids. And besides, the last Christmas cards she drew us didn't even have our names on them. You could tell she just slapped them together at the last minute."

I couldn't keep my cards from falling to the stump even using two hands. "Can I?"

"Yep, I won't look," said Ronald. I placed all my cards on the stump so I didn't have to struggle holding them.

"But maybe if we go one more time, we'll know for sure."

Ronald put his cards facedown and mashed out his cigar, motioned for me to do the same. In the failing light he appeared gray, weary, and much older, not a teenager but a middle-aged man on the ropes. "Look, Lance. She's a bad mother. Okay? I don't want to try anymore." He picked his cards back up. Light reappeared, shining between thousands of spaces in the thorny bushes.

"I'll go by myself then, dickhead."

"No you won't, and if you do, it will be a mistake," said Ronald, nodding for me to play a card. I tossed a queen of hearts on his jack and took the hand. "Good one," he said, calm and reassuring.

"Fuck you. And fuck everyone!" I yelled, throwing a tantrum. I stood up. "I'm going again, and when I see them goddamn kids of theirs, I'm going to tell him you're too big of a wussy face to come along." Snot clogged my speech, so I sounded like a troll.

Ronald was the one now to offer support. "Hey, it's okay. Just forget those people."

We might have gone on that way, each of us raring up, calming down, and starting all over again, but our dad had come back early from a seed show he'd been attending in Fort Wayne. When we heard his truck idling past us and down toward where the tractor and corn planter sat in a loamy field ready for seed, we peeked at him. As always, he returned home after some exhibit or training full of verve and prepared to change it all: his life, the farm, us, Aunt Lee, his methods, the land—all of what he'd been dealt—even nature itself. But inevitably the new energy wore off, and a day or two later we'd be right back where we'd started, floundering to stay afloat.

Dad pulled the truck up to the planter, the radio blaring the Culture Club's "I'll Tumble 4 Ya." He loved pop music, whatever the radio stations were playing to death at the moment, and he'd sing them off-key and without complete knowledge of the correct lyrics. We watched him through the thorny bushes, prying apart a little viewing hole by putting on our leather gloves. Spying on the tiny guy was something we practiced with glee. Most of my memories of him are from a distance, scouting him like a secret agent, Ronald by my side as our father made private missteps. It was comforting to watch him this way, knowing that whatever he did wouldn't end up being repeated all over the county.

"What's he doing?" I asked.

"Looks like he bought some of that special seed. A guy at school, his dad sells it. Just like Amway, a real big rip-off. That's what our

FFA sponsor says." Our dad struggled to lift a bag of it to the planter, slipping with every step, the seed nearly as heavy as he was.

"Why are the bags so girly?" I asked. They were baby blue with pink stripes.

"That's part of the deal. You get to pick the packaging. If you open them at the side, you can keep the bag as wallpaper. They're double-lined. You can peel the backing off, and there's glue on it just like wallpaper. Kinda like how they used to make cloth feed bags with flowers on them. Ladies used them to make dresses. The kid at school said that's what gets men to buy them, at least the suckers, that is. Dad probably thought getting that kind would make Aunt Lee happy. You know she's been wanting to redo her bathroom."

Dad fell to the ground with one bag but finally managed to get the seeder filled to the brim, all the while looking around, checking to see if Aunt Lee was about. He took out his knife and deftly cut the wallpaper bags right down the seams, placing them in a pile, smoothing out the crinkles. It was one of the few tasks I'd seen him perform with precision. He was so short that if he drove outside the county, he'd often be misjudged as a child driving illegally. And now, as we watched him from our hideout, his head seemed nearly even with the tailgate of the truck.

"Why's he so short?" I asked Ronald, never really thinking to ask before right then. Ronald loved biology, genetics, and nature, so he answered the question with a certain amount of delight.

"Oh, that's easy," he said, sounding like the teacher's pet. "See, our great-great-grandfather had a condition called Colye-Fyes syndrome. Aunt Lee has pictures of him with a team of mules. I'll show you if you want. He looks like a little boy in them, but they were taken when he was about fifty. Anyway, it's very rare and skips generations." He put his fingers on his chin and pondered his next bit of information. "I think it's a defect in a Y chromosome. I saw it in our biology book. Even though Dad's aren't this way, it can also produce bug-eyes, pigeon toes, and floppy ears—you know, big ears,

I mean." Ronald was pleased with himself and took a much needed deep breath.

Our dad pushed the tailgate up with an effort and placed a board across the wallpaper bags so they wouldn't blow away. He scuttled onto the tractor and started it, diesel fumes rising into the air. For a little while, he drove perfectly down the field, leaving his new Amway seed in the moist earth. Then, on his second time around, he pulled the tractor over and climbed down in a hurry, as if he had to pee.

"Now what?" said Ronald. Our dad was in a panic, searching for something, looking around, ducking first by a fencerow, then running to the planter and finally to the truck, where he promptly yanked down his pants with urgency. Irritable bowel syndrome wasn't a term that was used then, but that's what he had, whether it was from swallowing tobacco juice or eating too many sugary jelly beans.

"Gross," I said. "He's squirting from his butt right out there where anyone could see."

"I know. He could at least make it over to the tree line," said Ronald, always the pragmatist.

"That silly son of a bitch is gonna fall over," I said as our father teetered to and fro, his wee knees giving up.

"Look, those wallpaper bags are getting loose," said Ronald, as if providing the narration to a troubled sports scene on the radio.

"Uh-oh," I said as Dad pulled up his pants too soon, stuff still shooting out of his tiny rear. "He just pooped his pants, Ronald."

"You mean watered them."

Dad tried to run after Aunt Lee's wallpaper bags, but the breeze had lifted them over his head, and try as he might, they seemed determined to stay just out of his reach. A stronger May wind picked up and lifted the bags into the sky as if they were filled with helium. One by one, they drifted on airstreams, moving up and away, over the birch trees that lined the riverbank. Our dad stood with his hands on his slender hips and watched them like a child—that is, before another wave of intestinal distress hit him and he yanked down his pants, promptly falling over into the soft earth. "Uh-oh," said Ronald as he rushed to the door of our hut, "now the tractor is in gear." Ronald slipped out of the hideout and was on his way to help. I watched our dad thrash about and get to his feet. He ran after the tractor, his pants around his ankles, and a smattering of black topsoil stuck to his white, teeny ass.

I decided then that I'd go one more time to see our mother, with or without Ronald.

CHAPTER TWENTY·ONE

By lunchtime, the farm had once again become a swarm of activity, and now officials from the Indiana Bureau of Investigation, Malloy police department, and even more news crews joined them. A motorcade of law enforcement personnel proceeded through our yard and down toward the barn lot. A man in a dark suit handed Ronald a sheet of paper and told him, "Court order to set up surveillance. Make sure it gets to your parents." Ronald just stared at him and tucked the paper in his back pocket. The authorities set up outposts and tents and barricades without ever once asking if they could do so. Helicopters beat over the house, rattling our windowpanes, clinking the dishes in the cupboards. All we could do was watch the TV in the kitchen and try to get the story that the media was piping over the airwaves. The gist of it was this: some nuts from a conservative church had taken shots at the boars and had nearly killed one of us in the process. Whether it was in response to Mrs. Graves's blatant support of homosexuality or just some rogue individual who wanted to kill a gay pig, the hunt was on.

Every channel had video of the farm and the paddock televised live. The channel we watched highlighted the moulage an IBI agent prepped to pour into the footprints that had been left in the corn. The plaster of paris they stirred in a plastic tub looked like cake batter to Lucy.

We'd found out that our dad was, indeed, out of the hospital. Lucy said the nurse had told her that he'd contracted a staph infection and needed to stay another five days to make sure it didn't get into his bloodstream, but of course he didn't listen. He left, the nurse said, clad only in his hospital gown. Lucy looked like she was afraid she'd hurt our feelings when she spoke. "The nurse said two guys told him they were taking his clothes to get them dry-cleaned, but they never brought them back, including his boots." I said, ashamed, "Bill and Leroy."

As we sat around the table with Mr. Feirst, watching the TV intently, we heard a loud knock at the door. Ronald got up to answer it. A man with the IBI came into the kitchen holding a solid piece of what looked like the material the men on TV were mixing. He had on silver sunglasses and a wrinkled black suit with dandruff on the shoulders. "Ronald and Lance Bancroft?"

Ronald pointed to himself and then at me and said warily, "We're Ronald and Lance Bancroft."

The IBI man asked us, without any explanation, "What size of shoe does your father wear?" Without waiting for us to respond, he commanded, "Go get me a pair of his shoes." Ronald motioned with his head for me to go upstairs and get them out of my dad's closet. I ran up the stairs and grabbed the only other pair of shoes he owned besides the big boots he wore. They were a pair of loafers that actually fit him properly: men's size 6. Ronald and I had always had big feet, and as I carried the shoes back downstairs for the IBI man, they felt like a child's sneakers.

It was quiet in the kitchen. Obviously no one, including the IBI man, had spoken since I'd left to get the shoes. On the TV set, a newsman detailed the manhunt. It seemed funny to think of them hunting my father, and the term manhunt itself brought a smile to my face. But the news junkies and psychosocial pundits were about to get more material for use as tabloid fodder.

I handed the shoes to the IBI man who'd been joined by a second, smaller man with a clipboard and micro-cassette recorder. The IBI man took off his sunglasses and inspected the inside of each shoe. He turned them over and showed his helper. As I watched, I wondered why Ronald hadn't just told the men that our dad had twice in twenty-four hours escaped from the hospital and that for several weeks we'd been trying to keep him from maiming or killing the boars. But then he spoke up. "Sir, I'd like to know what this is all about. Is there something wrong with . . . that is, is our dad okay?"

"As you are aware, your father, Gerald Bancroft, aka Jerry Bancroft, was reported missing from the Malloy City Hospital at approximately 11:30 a.m. today. We have reason to suspect that he is aiding and abetting some of these religious nuts."

Ronald laughed out loud. It was one brief, completely free guffaw. The IBI man glared at him.

"Son, you think this is funny?" said the G-man, his beady eyes trained on my brother's heart.

Ronald answered, very sure of himself, "No, sir, I don't, but the only thing our dad could aid and abet is more ridicule, and if you'd spend any time around this county, you'd know that. He isn't tied up with anyone. He's just pissed off that a breeder sold him a pair of gay boars. And we're trying to keep him from killing them."

When Ronald was finished talking, he looked around at the rest of us. Mr. Feirst took his cue and introduced himself. "I gotta agree with the boy here, Mr. . . . . uh?" The IBI man did not offer his last name. Mr. Feirst went on, "Uh, anyway, these boys here have got it straight. Seems their father is a bit touchy, but . . ."

The IBI man cut him off. He held out the moulage and presented it to us all like it was a show-and-tell item. "This is the footprint we just took out there in the corn next to the empty casings of a .22-caliber rifle. As you can see," he pointed to the large red writing at the top, "this is the tiny, bare footprint of a small man, size 6." He put his sunglasses back on and handed the plaster form to his partner. As he turned to leave out the backdoor he said, "Your father is being added to an official most wanted list. We are considering him a danger on the undeniable fact that he has taken shots at two cameramen out here." I tried to speak up, to tell him that it was *a* shot (not shots) and that our dad was an embarrassment, a continual nuisance, but nothing else and certainly not clever enough to do anything except through fluke and happenstance, but he and his buddy were out the door before we knew it.

We were all dumbfounded when the smaller man poked his head back inside the door and said, "Agent Tost told me to let you know that your aunt Lee has been ordered to turn back. No one will be allowed to leave or enter the farm without permission. Anyone here when the shooting happened is to stay put, and no one is to enter the premises. Everyone is considered a subject of interest."

CHAPTER TWENTY·TWO

On the television, Mrs. Graves was now a national, staple figure, kind of an Aunt Bee to our Mayberry Malloy. She relayed her views on letting those who are gay live and let live so many times on air that home viewers probably even knew the spots when her teeth would most likely fall out. The footage the two cameramen took of our gay boars made the news, too. The headline and hyped-up promo read, "Artificial Insemination Keeps Gay Boars Alive Another Day!" It was used by nearly every network and newspaper throughout the Midwest and beyond. Talk show hosts of all kinds aired programs on our homosexual boars. Animal husbandry experts and sociologists alike debated the idea of gayness in the animal world. The shows always ended in fisticuffs. If it was one of the major "respectable" networks, the conclusion was littered with the experts shouting over each other, questioning their esteemed colleague's credentials, and bad-mouthing anyone who showed a hint of neutrality. At one point we counted at least fifteen church denominations represented on the television. Only the Quakers came out in complete support of homosexuality in both beast and man. Their national leader, a simple man dressed all in denim, calmly told an entire panel of religious leaders as the camera zoomed in on his face, "The Religious Society of Friends has been a witness for peace since 1660, and people who are gay are being treated like the supposed witches of Salem."

He was booed, and a female evangelist from the South named Donna Wisteria claimed, "Your church doesn't even have real pastors. Y'all just take turns. That's not a real church anyway!"

What had been a manhunt for the shooter now became a hunt of a different sort: a national controversy over whether a gay animal should be permitted to live and reproduce. People on the streets in major cities were polled and interviewed. One woman shown on the TV said, "If you ask me, they should put those pigs down for their own good. It's one thing to have to put up with gay rights in humans, but this is ridiculous. I'm thinking about not eating pork." A nut for Americans for Wholesome Virtues issued a proclamation to his members in our area: "I'll give anyone one thousand dollars who can successfully capture one or both of these hogs and bring them to Naperville, Illinois, for reparative therapy. It works; trust me. We abduct heterosexual teenagers with homosexual problems by the hundreds each year to make them into fine upstanding ex-gays."

Our phone had been tapped just in case our dad tried to call, but that didn't stop it from ringing off the hook. It hadn't been four hours since the beaker had been shot and blown to pieces, and now the news frenzy was at a feasting high point. The gunshot was the blood in the water that the news sharks craved.

Mr. Feirst and Ronald talked at the table while Lucy and I made a midafternoon meal; none of us had eaten a thing all day. We made a breakfast banquet of pancakes and sausage, two-dozen scrambled eggs, and a loaf of buttered toast with grape preserves, Aunt Lee– style. When we sat down at the table, Ronald was saying to Mr. Feirst, "I don't know if he'll try to get to them now or not. And if he does try, they'll catch him before he gets to the pen. I mean, there's gotta be forty cops out there."

The food sat steaming on the table. Mr. Feirst said, "Well, let's eat, and then we'll get back to all this. It pays to have a full stomach when under stress." The TV was on, of course, and we'd all grown accustomed to seeing the perimeter of the farm and house on the screen. Everything felt vaguely familiar, but strange, too, as if you'd changed bodies with someone but kept your mind. If one of us wanted to (and we did do it a couple times), we could go to the kitchen sink and see our figure in the window on TV if, that is, it was timed just right, during the sweeping panoramic views that included some live shots of the boars asleep in their pen. On a banner below the video footage of our house and farm, the producers had typed "Gay Boars Under Siege in Malloy, Indiana. Bancrofts Holed Up Inside!"

The coverage of our dad, as he was now the focus of the manhunt (a true contradiction in terms), had the media stalking our house like hungry bears in a national park. As we tried to eat, they pounded on the kitchen windows, mouthing requests for exclusive interviews. Their sweaty, broad faces had looks of ravenous desperation. Mr. Feirst said, with a full mouth of pancake, "Kids, I think you better see if that IBI fella will escort you all out of here. It could get pretty nasty before this thing is all over with."

Ronald almost bit Mr. Feirst's head off. "No! No fucking way are we leaving here!" Even Ronald was shocked by his own reaction. His eyes instantly became apologetic toward his mentor. Ronald regained some control. "I'm sorry, Mr. Feirst. But I'm not going anywhere. Those boars will be dead if I do." He addressed himself to me then. "Lance, you and Lucy should go, though. I'll be all right here. I can manage." Lucy looked at me.

"No. I'll stay right here," I said. We were quiet around the table. I began to have an odd feeling; however, I felt comforted, too. I had a hopeful belief as I looked around at the faces of Ronald and Lucy and even Mr. Feirst. They seemed like a family to me, and if Aunt Lee had been there, I'm sure I would've felt totally complete. The truth was, it was the first time I'd felt the possibility of a life separate from our dad. And the simple fact that I could begin and maintain relationships with other people who judged me not on the basis of being "one of Jerry Bancroft's boys," but instead saw me as an individual, was something I'd simply not thought of before. But my heartfelt philosophizing was interrupted by a news bulletin bleating over the TV's airwaves.

Another familiar sight to viewers everywhere was the town square in Malloy, and it now flashed on the screen while the view of our farm from a helicopter continued live in the top left hand corner. An official anchor, who was not pictured on camera, began to speak. "There is yet another new development in the case in Malloy, Indiana, dealing with the individual who has been added by the IBI to the manhunt. Apparently, there is a portion of a church congregation that is offering its support to this fugitive from the law, who is named Jerry Bancroft, whose hog farm you can see from the helicopter shot. The pastor from that church says he is willing to hide Mr. Bancroft out, believing he is doing the Lord's work. He believes, as we have been reporting here recently, that the so-called gay boars—or peculiar hogs as some have come to call them—do indeed need to be euthanized and put humanely to sleep, so that they do not pass on their defect to future generations of piglets. The pastor is offering protection to Mr. Bancroft. . . ."

The TV crackled, and for a moment the live shots were gone, but they reappeared in seconds. The anchor said, "Our apologies to our viewers. We were experiencing some technical difficulties. In any case, let's now go live to Lawrence Peacock, who is talking with two local newsmen on the town square in Malloy, along with the pastor. For those of you who don't know, the town of Malloy is approximately twelve miles from the Bancroft farm. Lawrence, what can you tell us?"

The vision of Lucy's father and her brother and the pastor who'd been praying over the old man who'd shared my dad's hospital room appeared on the screen. Lucy stopped eating, her eyes widening to take it all in. Here was her father, with her brother and the pastor, too, looking like starstruck tourists. Mr. Wolfrum had finally made the big time, even it wasn't as a professional but a local yahoo willing to be interviewed live on-air.

The remote newsman said, with one eyebrow raised, "Well, it would be an understatement to say that this manhunt following the developments today of a shooting at the Bancroft farm is anything but complete chaos. But we are joined here with a father-and-son team who knows a little bit about TV and has a personal interest in what has transpired out at the Bancroft home. These are the Wolfrums." The news guy introduced Lucy's dad and brother with a Vanna White, palm-up hand gesture. They seemed really excited to be on national news. Their faces were covered in poorly applied makeup, and they were beaming from ear to ear with dry-mouthed smiles and stiff necks. The reporter said, "Tell us, if you will, what this manhunt has done to your family."

Lucy's brother stepped forward and opened his piehole to speak. Behind him were vans parked everywhere, other news reporters interviewing other people. The streets looked as if they'd never be mundane again. The whole area had been roped off, sequestering Malloy's citizenry behind yellow tape. A view of the courthouse and its sprinkler-busy lawn was the backdrop for what the Wolfrum men had been waiting for all their lives: a spotlight on national TV.

I held my breath, thinking that Lucy's brother would berate our family for endangering her life. I thought her dad would step up to the mouthpiece and give us holy hell for simply being the Bancrofts. I feared that the pastor would point at the screen and say he'd seen the vile offspring of Mr. Bancroft and pitied him for his misfortune. And they might have all very well done just that, but before Lucy's brother even got a word out, a figure behind them on the courthouse lawn was caught immediately by the person operating the camera that was supposed to provide the Wolfrums the big break they'd been waiting for. There on the lawn, adorned in a dingy blue hospital gown, was our father, looking every bit the deranged Barney Fife that he was—barefoot, his bony shins smeared in mud, his hair standing on end. The ruckus outside our house went instantly silent. Several noisy helicopters overhead could be heard chopping off toward Malloy. In just a few seconds, the choppers, now in the airspace above Malloy's town square, could again be heard at full babble via the TV. The vehicles on our farm roared to life: sirens and bullhorns pierced the air as the motorcade of lawmen and the convoy of news vans tried to beat one another down the lane to get to Malloy.

On the TV, they zoomed in on our dad. His eyes were dark underneath, and he looked as sad as I'd ever seen him. "Holy shit," said Ronald, his voice monotone, eyes staring at the television set, afraid to blink.

My stomach hurt. Lucy let go of my hand and turned me by the shoulders to face her. "Oh no," she said, brushing my bangs from my eyes. I could see her father smile broadly, his profile at the corner of the screen, as our dad stumbled some, then pointed at the crowd.

The pastor, offscreen but easily heard, went into autopilot, quoting scripture. He chanted: *"Mark chapter four verse twenty-eight and twenty-nine. For the earth bringeth forth fruit of herself; first the blade, then the ear, after that the full corn in the ear. But when the fruit is brought forth, immediately he putteth in the sickle, because the harvest is come."* Something hit the ground with a dull thud. You could see the obese body of the pastor, or rather, the bottoms of his feet and flabby legs, in the lower corner of the TV screen. He'd passed out, but he was still breathing. Even his fat legs seemed to inhale and exhale. His Sansabelt slacks were too tight, unflattering at the crotch.

In a flash, as if another man had entered the hospital gown, our dad ran off behind the courthouse. Someone yelled in the background, "He's getting away! Hurry!" Tires squealed as the picture on the television bounced and jittered. A cameraman was running after him in vain, video camera on his shoulder, huffing and puffing. The reporter tried to speak. In the background, coming from the TV, we could hear the approaching sirens.

Mr. Feirst spoke up, a vacant expression on his face. "Well, kids, your dad doesn't look too good."

"He's really done it this time." I glanced at Lucy, then Ronald and Mr. Feirst.

"He looks like he's lost weight," said Ronald, widening his eyes in disbelief.

"Really?" asked Mr. Feirst. "I wouldn't think that possible."

We sat and watched as the television teemed with action and noise, none of it comprehensible. Anchors in studios everywhere scrambled onto the airwaves to add to the story. We couldn't believe our ears when finally we heard the on-air reporter saying, "He's gotten away. He's gotten away." More sirens squalled over the television. Malloy was the place to be.

CHAPTER TWENTY·THREE

After hours of exposure, our retinas ached. Before long, we all bedded down, except Ronald, who carried a sleeping bag to the barn, figuring he'd once again keep watch on the boars. He looked ridiculous with the sleeping bag. It was a smiley face design, the yellow round mugs beaming optimism against a solid white background. Ronald armed himself with an oversized pillow, our pellet gun, and a thermos of coffee. We tried to convince him otherwise, but it was no use.

"Good night," I called after him as he clutched everything in his arms, the sleeping bag trailing him like a tail on a costume. Without even looking back, he flipped me off over his shoulder. Seeing our dad on television had made our moods sour, and I wondered if Lucy thought less of me, but it was comforting to see her dad, too, in a less than favorable role on the news.

In the living room, finally alone together, Lucy and I kissed and made out. I needed to prove I was nothing like my father, and I was trying too hard, keeping up a carefree attitude even though I felt like running into the cornfields myself and throttling my father's neck, then running even farther until I found a plane to steal. "What about Mr. Feirst?" Lucy asked, clad in only her bra and panties, my underwear bunched at my feet as we groped and mashed on the couch.

"I prefer you," I whispered in her ear. She giggled as we nearly rolled off the rough cushions. The upholstery was a dark brown and similar to burlap. In the dim living room, a small amount of light from the TV spilled onto the carpet. We fumbled our way to the floor and made love there. This time, I was only slightly more prolonged, and the experience was more subtle, complete with moments of nonmovement when we stared into each other's eyes and listened to our breathing. When Lucy said sweetly, "More," and pushed into me, I believed the entire Midwest might buckle and disappear, return as only a blanket on which we rested our bodies. Sweaty and entwined, we sprawled out on the floor. In the blue light, Lucy said, "You really don't think your dad could've shot at you guys, do you?"

"No," I said, propping myself up on an elbow as she remained flat, her soft white stomach irresistible to stroke. "I don't think so, but maybe." The house creaked, and for a moment we thought we'd heard Mr. Feirst up and about, walking toward us.

"Shit," said Lucy as I reached for our crumpled clothes. The moment passed, however, and upon closer scrutiny, we realized it was only the foundation slightly shifting, planks slowly giving way. "It's not him. Listen, you can hear him snoring." We held our breath, but my heart was pounding too hard to catch much of the ag man's noisy sleep. I was sad to see Lucy put on her clothes. She was scared that he might actually walk in on us. Being the only one naked is even sadder, so I hopped into my jeans and pulled on a white T-shirt. We sat on the floor and kissed, sleepy but alert. Lucy's lips were moist and generous. She planted a kiss on my forehead and said, "Do you think he'll try to get here again tonight?"

"I don't know," I said, feeling embarrassed, even a little indicted. "Maybe he's sick. I hated seeing him on television, but I hope he's okay." Lucy took my hand in hers, and we just sat and thought.

"Lance?" she asked, a tender note in her hoarse voice. I turned toward her, expecting that she was about to say she loved me. I'd rehearsed the moment in my head and was completely prepared to give it back, pick her up, and swirl her around like a commercial for a cruise line.

"What is it?" I asked, waiting for her to become all mushy and sentimental.

"Don't you think we better go check on Ronald? He's got to be lonely out there, maybe even a little freaked out." She was right of course, but I'd wanted the moment to bring us closer, maybe even allow me to talk some more about my thoughts on our dad, in hopes that it would help us shuck our clothes off again.

"Let's go," I said, helping her to her feet. She grabbed me at the waist, and we kissed, long and slow, as my hands moved to touch her. Lucy backed up. "Come on," she said as she took me by the hand and led me out of the house.

Outside the sky was black and peppered with stars, the smell of fuel and trash lingering in the air. A light green band of aurora snapped across the horizon and disappeared like a snake down a hole. "Did you see that?" I asked Lucy.

"Yeah, they've thrown shit everywhere." It was true, even if we were talking about two very different things. The news crews had really torn the place up; litter tumbled over our feet as we trudged toward Ronald. There was a group of feral roadies standing around a weak fire, sipping beers and chatting, knowing their station in life was to guard any equipment left behind.

"Hi," I said as we passed them, Lucy and I still holding hands.

No one responded out of the sheer darkness, which seemed thick as ink, even though I could make out several forms against the orange glow of the fire.

I picked up the pace. Loose gravel crunched under our feet. We got to the paddock and stood still at the perimeter. I whispered, "Ronald?" We should've carried a flashlight. Everything seemed to blend into everything else, while the flames from the fire still danced in my vision. "Ronald!" I called louder.

"Maybe he's asleep," said Lucy, moving her hand from mine and up to clutch my elbow. Water trickled somewhere. A dark figure slid inside the barn, across the opening, methodical and strange. "What the crap was that?" whispered Lucy, her hold on my arm tightening. I felt the muscles in my neck turn into twisted roots. My scalp tingled. I assumed it was either our dad or Bill or Leroy.

"Stay here," I told her as I started toward the ghostly barn.

"Screw that," she said and clung to me so closely that our legs were Siamesed. Foot by foot we approached the area where Ronald should've been. I couldn't bring myself to call his name again. My hair was wet with sweat by the time we made it to the end of the fencerow. I swallowed hard and forced myself to call out my brother's name again. "Ronald?"

Something moved along the interior wall, scraping the boards as it went. "Holy crap," murmured Lucy, her body rigid. Even struck with fear, I couldn't help thinking what this might produce in her, a tension that would need releasing.

For a few moments I was struck with indecision. We stood together not moving while the barn seemed to be housing quiet, dark creatures that moved only slightly.

"Let's go back to the house and get a flashlight," I said. "You can stay up there." We started to back away when a muffled shout came from the dark insides of the barn. "Shit! Lucy, run to the house and get Feirst!" I said and started toward the barn. I felt her take off in the other direction at full speed as I plunged into the darkness.

"Ronald! It's Lance. Where are you?" I tripped over something and fell flat on my face, the air knocked out of me. I shot back up to my feet and pawed the wall for a weapon, anything. All I could manage to grab was the flimsy yardstick we used to measure hay bales. I swatted it in front of me, yelling for Ronald. The yardstick sliced through the air like a laser as I made it to the back of the barn, where a weak shaft of the utility light outside shot through a crack in the siding. I squinted at the area I'd just passed through, and the same dark figure hovered, then moved away again at a quicker pace than before.

"Lance!" I heard Lucy scream, and I turned around and took off back through the barn and toward the paddock. She'd obviously not made it to the house. I was at a full sprint, knocking my shins on every protruding piece of crap that our dad had kept over the years. Lucy's screaming was muffled now. I wielded the yardstick like a maniac, and several times it slapped me in the face. I was right back where I'd started, just outside the barn doors, and yet there was no sign of Ronald or Lucy.

"Goddamn it!" I yelled. "Where are you guys?" I sounded like the brat who gets mad when he can't find the other kids during hide-and-seek.

From out of nowhere, an arm clutched my neck, while another hand grabbed my yardstick and broke it in two as someone pulled me into their body. The person behind me was about my height and seemed jittery. He spit into my ear, "You've just been cap-thured by the Merthers Furniture Store Sympa-zizers."

I could tell the voice was young and that he was proud of whatever the hell affiliation he bragged about, even if he couldn't quite say the words right. In the dark, he marched me toward the barn again, a flashlight leading the way as he nearly drug me by the neck. I thought I could get loose from him, but since I hadn't had much success finding Ronald and Lucy on my own, I figured I'd let him show me the way. The guy had on an overabundance of knockoff Polo cologne. He smelled like a Christmas tree that had been sprayed with the stuff. If it hadn't been for the voice, the abduction had all the markings of something my dad would've managed to botch.

I was led along an old chute toward the back of the barn, around a large set of tires, and past a pallet of feed. Mice scrambled in all directions, their feet scratching the wood floors. There was an ancient cracked silo attached to the side of the barn, and it was accessed by a small door at the base. It was open, and as he shoved me forward, I could see light inside. "Get in, dumb assth," he said. As I crawled through the opening, he kicked me in the butt with his boot. Inside the silo, Ronald and Lucy sat cross-legged, another kid guarding them with a flashlight, shining it alternately in their faces.

"Stop that," said Ronald, as nonchalant as if he were reprimanding me. The other kid crawled in behind me and pushed me toward the dusty floor. "You sit down, too, you, you ass-thole."

The three of us sat in a circle, looking up at the two kidnappers. One had a severe case of acne, and the other, the one who'd captured me, was actually really young, maybe twelve, but big for his age and apparently in need of speech therapy. It was easy to tell they were brothers; they both had the same pointy noses and awful teeth, gapped and misshapen, growing wildly under their lips, too many of them to properly close their mouths. The boys were nearly the same age. The pimply one was only a year or so older, but he clearly wasn't the leader. He brandished the flashlight like it might be a pistol, training it on each of our faces, nervously switching from one to another. It just about blinded us. He had an anxious smile on his face, as if he wanted to make friends.

"You knows why we're here, ass-tholes?" said the leader. "We're the Merthers Furniture Store Sympa-zizers, and we're taking them fucking gays you're protecting."

Ronald seemed bored but patient. He asked, "Are you trying to say Mercer's? The furniture store off the square in Malloy?"

"No," the kid lisped, defensive. It was obvious they'd not thought through much of what was happening, but I had to give them credit for somehow catching Ronald off guard.

"Well," said Ronald, "there's not another Mercer store around that I know of."

The kid with the flashlight and festering skin piped up. "Uh-huh, we've got two stores: one on the square and another out by the bypass."

"Shut the fucks ups, numbs-nuts!" shouted his brother, extra saliva hanging at the corner of his mouth, his snaggle teeth gleaming.

They each wore Van Halen T-shirts, black and nearly falling apart. I'd guess they'd had to work for a year to afford concert tickets, moving dinette sets for their father, polishing fake brass and glass tables with Windex on Saturday mornings. They were as poor as us.

"Why do you want the boars?" asked Ronald, genuinely interested. The brothers looked at each other and seemed at a loss. Then they blurted out at the same time: "A thousand bucks!"

"Oh, you're going to take them to Naperville to that crazy guy with the Americans for Wholesome Virtues? So he can perform reparative therapy?" The boys were stunned. They cut their eyes toward each other and twitched.

"We don't know what that last part means, but we sure as hell want that money. Got an ATV all picked out already. It's a Kawasaki 415, and it can fly to beat all hell," said the boy with the flashlight, his face nearly as bright as the beam when he mentioned the ATV. "You guys can come to our house and ride it with us. We'll take turns."

"How many times I goths to tell you to shut up, Reggie!" demanded his brother.

Lucy stood up and turned toward him. "Nice to meet you, Reggie," she said.

"Sit the fucks backs down, lady!" commanded his brother, his speech impediment providing all the mercy we needed.

Lucy smiled at him. "Okay," she said as she walked over to him, "but first, what's your name?"

He stammered and gave in. "Wils-thon."

"Nice to meet you, too, Wilson," said Lucy. The poor kid had a name that actually accentuated his lisp.

Ronald leaned back against the silo bricks. "So, how do you guys plan on getting them all the way to Illinois?" He put his hands behind his head and interlocked his fingers, casual.

"We thought we'd take one of you as a hostage since we ain't got no driver's cards," said Reggie. He looked at Ronald directly. "Is it okay if we take you as our hostage? You look big enough to drive."

"You don't ask them, numbs-nuts!" said Wilson. "We just half-a take 'em."

"I can't go," said Ronald as he stood up, yawning and stretching. "When you snuck up on me, I was cleaning that one boar's eyes. I've got to stay here and take care of him."

Wilson looked like he was working on an algebra problem. "But if you was with us, you could stills takes care of 'em."

"Yeah," said his brother. "We could pull off at rest areas and shit like that. Get Hostess Pies for the road while you cleaned his peepers." Reggie liked ideas that gave him pictures in his head. He was beaming again, just like with the ATV, face jubilated, red and eager.

"That won't work," said Ronald as he walked around the silo in circles, the boys watching him like owls. "The boar can't travel. Besides, I won't let you take them anyway."

"Why not?" asked Reggie, totally into the reasoning.

"Because," said Ronald, "they're fine here. There's nothing wrong with them that I can't fix."

Wilson disagreed. "Excepts that those sons a bitches is as queers as three-dollar billths." He shook his flashlight at Ronald and lisped some more. "I think that manzs right. They should be made normals."

Lucy scooted next to me, and we held hands, watching as Ronald took control. "You mean make them straight?"

"Yep, theyths not righths," said Wilson, confident but backing away from Ronald.

"See, I disagree, Wilson. They're just the way nature made them. You could no more change them than you could a tree's curve or a crooked stream."

"Yeah," said Reggie, excited. "It's like our teeth and stuff. They're not straight, and they can't be fixed. God just made us this way, Wilson." He'd betrayed their mission, forgotten about his ATV.

"You're an idiots," said Wilson, losing his beliefs, body slumping from the inside.

Ronald, ever the biology enthusiast, corrected Reggie. "Not exactly, Reggie. You could have braces or some dental work, and your teeth could be straightened out. But with the boars, we're talking about fundamental, biological makeup, chromosomes and specific levels of intended hormones directed by brain chemistry."

The boys sat down on the silo floor and pulled their knees to their chins. Wilson said, "You guys ain't gonna tell on us, are yous?"

Reggie chimed in. "Yeah, that would suck if you big kids told on us. We won't tell if you don't." He picked at his elbow and offered us his most gnarly, submissive smile.

"Nope," said Ronald as Lucy smiled at the boys. "We'll keep it between us. But to tell you the truth, we sure could use some help out here guarding the boars. There are others who'd like that thousand bucks, too."

"Okay," said Wilson, resigned to his fate.

Reggie shook his head rapidly, excited to be hanging out in a silo with other kids. "It'll be cool," he said. "Besides, kids at school call us the piranha twins. You guys won't, will ya?" Reggie glanced at his brother, who now hung his head.

"Never," said Ronald, patting Reggie's, then Wilson's, back.

"No way," said Lucy. "You guys are cute."

I felt for them, too. "We're just here together helping one another out. No name calling at all."

Reggie grinned, exposing the many squiggly layers of teeth. "Good," he said, thinking a while as he watched Wilson, still hangdog, flashlight lying on the floor. "You know what," said Reggie, speaking confidentially. "I'd rather have that ATV than get our teeth fixed. We could ride that dern thing all the way across America. And if we wore helmets, they wouldn't see our mouths anyways." He nodded proudly, happy he'd been able to draw the conclusion.

One by one we crawled out of the silo, pants dirty with dead flies and the grimy powder of ancient silage. It made me sneeze. Wilson, too. In the dark, even his sneeze had a lisp. Back at the open front of the barn, we spread out the smiley face sleeping bag and used gunnysacks for pillows. The deal was we'd each take a turn watching out, but Ronald never went to sleep. All through the night I'd wake up and then fall right back into sleep. The boys' breathing over their twisted teeth made a whistling sound as they slept, providing flutelike music as our background. Lucy didn't move an inch. Deep in slumber, her back curved against me as we spooned. In fits of sweaty sleep, I was visited by our mother in a nightmare that had me perched on her shoulder, both my mother and me in parrot costumes. I partially woke and sat up, leaning against a bale. I couldn't tell if Ronald was around or not or if he was on patrol somewhere. The only sound was the boys, their raspy harmony.

I fell back to sleep as the controls in my hands felt powerful, solid. I drifted effortlessly above the farm, circled out over the vast cornfields, puttering along, flying low. I reached out and touched the tips of the corn, a Duran Duran song blasting. I tipped the left wing and looped back, and there it was: a crop circle, mashed down in a haphazard figure, certainly not created by anything with supernatural intelligence. A small fire burned in the center as Aunt Lee smoked a peace pipe on the back of a stuffed sow, and right there smack-dab in a colorful lawn chair was my father smiling broadly, his body of average size, and friends all around him, looking as normal in the corn hideaway as could be. A tall, round oak tree, one I recognized from a certain field, tinkled with wind chimes made of medals. Often you figure out some of life's most ridiculous mysteries by simply lying down and giving in to the human necessity to sleep, letting nature lead you to the river or, in this case, the cornfield.

CHAPTER TWENTY·FOUR

Near dawn, the diffused light making everything hazy and steel blue, something moved near the boars' pen. It didn't surprise me. With the thousand bucks bounty offered up, I'd started to think we'd be doing this forever—waking to shadowy movements, trying to keep our senses and our land.

Ronald poked my leg with a two-by-four and tipped his head toward the movement. We communicated using hand signals, mouthing words. The newsman up near the edge of the cornfield was passed out and dead to the world.

We rose slowly, careful not to wake the boys or disturb Lucy. Ronald and I crept along an old passageway that led to a defunct corncrib that would provide excellent cover and still offer a closer view of whoever was out there. We peered through the slats. It was difficult to see really, the sun not up yet and the murky paddock like a ship at sail, gloomy and overcast. Ronald poked me in the side, whispered, "Who is it? What are they doing?"

I made an exaggerated face and pantomimed, "I don't know." The slats blocked our view, so we skulked farther down until we reached an opening. If the person, who was now simply standing at the fence, looked up with any interest, they'd be able to spot us fairly easily.

Even from that distance, the boys whistled their tune, but most likely it sounded to the stranger like a sickly birdcall or a leak in a hose.

We remained on our haunches, like ducks, ready to take off if need be, but nothing seemed to be happening. My knees hurt as I propped myself against the jamb. The figure at the fence finally moved, climbed over the gate, and stood there without moving, just like it had on the other side. Ronald was tensed up, though, prepared to attack if the person tried anything on the boars. It wasn't Bill or Leroy—too skinny—and it was about two feet too tall to be our father. The sun rising finally turned the murky blue light into something clearer. Amber and yellow provided a better view. Still, the man was a mere outline as he moved farther into the pen. If he spooked the blind boar, it'd bring the boys and Lucy out of sleep. Ronald nodded at me, indicating that he was going in, and was I with him?

I nodded, legs almost numb. I was afraid I'd fall when we took off. Ronald counted, "One, two, three." We hopped up and shot forward about six feet and stopped. "Hold it, mister," said Ronald, as if he had a gun. The man held up his hands.

"I mean no harm," he said calmly, cloaked in the poor visibility. We took steps closer to him, and I felt a mist on my face, a light precipitation in the air. He was dressed in dark clothes and clutched a wide-brimmed hat under his arms. "I'm just here to say a prayer over you and these creatures. I'd like to minister to them. You, too, if you'd like." He kept his hands raised. He looked as if he were invoking the heavens.

"Who are you? How did you get past the IBI?" demanded Ronald. We were just a few feet in front of the man now, and it was easy to see that he was dressed in black, a cross around his neck. The boars began to stir, and I thought I heard Lucy and the boys scrambling awake in the barn.

"I'm just a concerned citizen out to help, and you'd be surprised how easily a man of the cloth can squeeze through roadblocks." The preacher inspected Ronald more closely, actually leaned in and squinted at him. "You must be the boy who's going to be a vet. My brother says you're quite talented, have a real caring way for God's creatures."

Ronald dismissed him with a scowl. "What are you trying to pull?"

"Not a thing, son," he said, contemplating something. "May I?" he asked, indicating with a shrug if he could lower his hands.

Ronald looked to me but didn't wait for agreement. "Okay, but keep your hands where we can see them."

"I'm Pastor Feirst. My brother's here about, isn't he?" Before we could answer, he pointed at me. "You must be the other boy, the one who's going to fly for a living." He made a motion with his hand, the space shuttle taking off straight to the moon. That's when I noticed that he had a severely lazy eye. It moved sluggishly about its socket, like a goldfish about to keel over.

"What kind of preacher are you? Presbyterian or Nazarene?" I asked. Pastor Feirst laughed out loud as Lucy and the boys appeared from the barn, yawning and sleepy-eyed.

"No special kind, I guess. Least not these days. I suppose you could say I was a crossbreed, mixed over and over again, not much left that's pure, if you know what I mean. I'm a mongrel, a feral dog of all denominations." He had to be a true man of God, knowing exactly which words to use, the analogy that would charm Ronald right off the bat. Lucy and Reggie and Wilson staggered to our sides.

Reggie said, "Why you big kids got a preacher out here for?" Reggie's hair stood on end just like his brother's, the static electricity rampant, made possible by gunnysack pillows.

Wilson pointed at the pastor. "Ain't no one thousand dollars out heres for the takings, misters. You can't change these boarsssss."

Pastor Feirst smiled at the boys and then looked past them at the boars. The blind one smelled his lover's rear end, about to mount. "What'd ya say we go wake up my brother and eat us a good breakfast?" He placed his large black hat on his head. "I can make one heck of an omelet."

Reggie brimmed with anticipation. "Dang," he said, his little wild teeth like miniature tusks in the better light. "I heard those things was real good." He turned to Wilson and said, "That's a folded-over egg that's scrambled!"

Ronald said, "You guys go ahead. I can't leave them." He pointed to the boars.

Pastor Feirst said, "Just like an apostle, huh?" He should've stuck with the biology comparisons. Ronald shrugged. "Then we'll make you some food and bring it out."

"Yeah!" said Reggie with gusto, spit flying from his awkward mouth.

The pastor became solemn and looked directly at me. "I think you're right about where to look." His unmoored eye struggled to find me. "Lance, is it?"

"Yes."

"I believe the cornfield might be right." He raised his eyebrows and addressed us all. "Come on. It'll make for good breakfast talk."

CHAPTER TWENTY·FIVE

My last attempt to visit our mother was, indeed, a solo trip, just six months after the previous try. "Here," said Ronald, miffed I was going after he'd insisted once again that he wasn't, "take this good thermos." For fifteen minutes he helped me pack and check and recheck my knowledge of the road. "Once you get down there, just call that number." He pointed to the index card I held in my hand. "That's the guy we met at the bus stop last year. He's an electrician, and he'll drive you from the bus to their house."

Ronald stood up from his single bed, his boots unlaced and the sleeves of his shirt rolled up. He'd started scrubbing his hands all the way to his elbows, like a doctor, and even used a bristle brush on his nails. It made him feel like a vet and caused him to smell like a box of detergent.

"You sure about this?" he asked. I nodded, and he grabbed me and hugged me tight.

"Lance, sometimes it doesn't matter who your mom or dad are. You know those runt pigs we have to give to other sows to mother?" I nodded. "Those mothers love and take care of them just like they're their own."

The phone rang downstairs, and Aunt Lee answered it. "Bancrofts'. Lee speaking." Her voice reminded Ronald of the plan.

He slipped a twenty-dollar bill into my shirt pocket and became conspiratorial, his loyalty stronger than his fear of what Aunt Lee might do to him if she knew that he was helping me. "Okay," he said softly, "she'll be busy with the chili until the fish fry tonight, so that should give you some time." The radio we shared was set on a classic rock station. "Free Bird" crackled from the busted speaker. For a few moments, my brother and I were stuck, confused about what to say to get out of the bedroom and make it to Malloy for the bus. Finally, Ronald smiled some and patted my back. "Let's go."

The bus ride went by so quickly, I could have sworn we'd only gone about thirty miles. I exited the bus and looked around, found the little storefront that read Captain Electro-Man! The electrician didn't recognize me until I introduced myself, so I figured the disguise worked pretty well. Of course, we'd only talked with him for about fifteen minutes at the bus stop, where his booth was set up next to an oily funnel cake stand. Now he was trying to sell franchises of his Captain Electro-Man! Company. For some reason (maybe it was the way he seemed to be on the verge of tears, eyes perpetually watery) I thought he was financially desperate, in over his head, about to put a shotgun into his mouth and commit himself to another world.

Now as I introduced myself, he still had those crybaby eyes when he shook my hand. "Looks like you've grown there, son," he said as he flipped the open sign over and turned out the light to his shop. "I don't quite recall you having such a beard. Must be you're a fast grower." He was dressed nicely, the little Captain Electro-Man on his shirt pocket in midflight, yellow cape trailing behind him, sparks flying.

We walked to his truck, and I hoped my beard wouldn't fall off en route. It'd been entirely my idea; Ronald didn't know anything about it. When I left the house, the beard shoved down the front of my boxers, it made the tip of my penis itch. I'd had just enough time at the bus stop bathroom in Malloy to apply it with the glue I'd stolen from our school's theater director. It had been in the same cabinet where the beards had been stored. There'd been a brown beard and one that would've been considered sandy, but I'd opted for the very black one, a decision I hoped didn't leave me looking incredibly obvious.

In a flash the electrician had me at the driveway that led to our mother's house. He said, "Here, take a few of these. Put them in your backpack. Never know when you'll need a good refrigerator magnet."

"Thank you," I said. "And thanks for the ride, too."

His eyes seeped as he gave me a thumbs-up. "Give 'em away, kid. I sure could use the sales."

With that, I climbed out of the truck and ducked behind a large oak as the electrician drove away. I'd stolen a compact of Aunt Lee's, and now I fished it out of my backpack. When I opened it, the mirror flashed in the sun, made a silver form dance over the base of the tree. I froze, thinking it'd given up my covert location. I clamped the compact shut and peered around the fat tree. The house was quiet this time, no loud music like there had been six months ago. The porch looked vacant, abandoned. In a grassy patch of fescue sat a lone car, a Ford Pinto with a license plate that read HOT LEGS. The toolshed salesman's truck wasn't around, and it looked as though his own toolshed was empty; the doors were wide open, and nothing but a skid of feed bags sat in the middle of the otherwise empty floor. Birds tweeted above me as I ducked behind the tree again, this time to really check my disguise. Aunt Lee's compact held some old blush, and a chunk of it fell out onto the ground where it lay like a potsherd. The beard looked fine, maybe a little off-kilter, but pretty believable. I tugged on it lightly at my chin and used the mirror to make sure the sideburns weren't lopsided. By now Ronald would've been back at the farm, pretending he knew exactly where I was if asked by Aunt Lee. Our dad would be busy fumbling with a barn addition he'd designed himself and cobbled together out of unclaimed plywood that had fallen off a truck near our lane. He'd called the sheriff and reported it. For an entire month he'd waited with bated breath until the official thirty days were up, pacing the kitchen and dreaming out loud of what he'd do with his grand fortune. He went to work wholeheartedly on something that ended up looking like part of a shantytown, complete with patched wiring he'd installed without even a rudimentary understanding of electricity. Ronald figured he could cover for me until midafternoon the next day, when Aunt Lee would have a nice Sunday meal made and all of us would be required to sit like a family at the kitchen table.

The driveway was noisy. Each step I took made a crunchy sound, and it seemed that the gritty stone was a siren announcing my approach. I slipped lightly into the patchy yard and crept toward the house. To my right, a For Sale sign shimmied in the breeze. My heart sank. They'd moved, I thought, or were in the process. Suddenly, even though I should've been in touch with the shame earlier, I was humiliated to be wearing the fake beard. I reached up and dug my fingertips under the top of a sideburn. I'd rip it off, hoping it'd burn like hell. The damn thing felt like a snake I wanted to be rid of instantly. I was about to yank it off when the front door opened. For a moment, nothing happened. Only the dark interior of the house could be seen in the frame. Keys jingled, and high heels scuffed the wood floor. Finally, our mother walked onto the porch, closing the door behind her. I stood ten feet in front of her, near the For Sale sign.

She startled some. "Oh my," she said, rubbing her lips together. "You scared me." I stood stupidly before her, feeling lost and hot. "What can I do for you, sir?" she asked, smiling, her torso twisting to and fro, as if she were on a slow spin cycle. I panicked and couldn't speak. Her hands were slender, and I stared at them. For nearly ten years those same fingers had drawn our Christmas cards, and now, as she left the porch and sashayed down the steps, I knew they'd be warm when she offered her hand. "Hello," she said as we shook hands. "Are you interested in the house?" She bit her lip, and I wondered why she seemed restless. She was dressed up, clad in a tight pantsuit, her top underneath the jacket splayed wide, freckles dotting her tanned skin.

I shook my head and managed to say, "Yes, yes I am. I'd sure like to see the inside, get a look at the rooms."

She peeked at the watch on her wrist and stalled, thinking it through. "I've got the time," she said, as if convincing herself. "Yes, come on in. I'll make us some coffee and tell you all about the home." She seemed to linger on my face, inspecting it.

The house was empty. The big stereo and many couches and chairs we'd seen during the swingers' party were gone. Only a lonely dinette set occupied the space; however, the walls had her drawings on them—self-portraits in onyx and intricate sceneries ranging from forests to cluttered downtown areas, all of them flawless and meticulously detailed. The sound of her heels on the floors echoed as my mother went to the kitchen. "Have a seat," she said over her shoulder. Then she called back, "Sorry there's not more appropriate decor. It's just that I'm recently divorced, and Mr. Teague took all his stuff with him." She didn't sound upset, but neither did she appear relieved. It was hard to tell if she cared at all about the toolshed salesman leaving her.

She clomped back into the room, and the sound reminded me of the Clydesdale horses during the street fair in Malloy. At the table, I sat slightly hunched over, head dipped, trying to conceal my eyes. I thought she might recognize me somehow. "Here," she said coolly, "watch it. It's pretty hot." She handed me a steaming teacup of coffee, black as my beard. "Didn't know how you liked it." When she sat down, too, a strong whiff of perfume rose up. Her nails were polished in red, lacquered as if perpetually wet. She squinted at me. "Do I know you from somewhere?" she asked, smiling. "Have we met before?"

"I don't think so, ma'am," I said, making my voice deeper. "I'm not from around here." That information intrigued her. She scooted to the edge of her chair and allowed her fingers to graze my arm. She uncrossed her legs and recrossed them, the swishing sound of her panty hose like fine grade sandpaper.

"Well, where on earth are you from, Mr. . . . ?"

"Just around," I said, not sure how much to divulge. Somewhere along the way, back when Ronald and I had fought in the blackberry hideout, I'd quietly given up on Danny or any other siblings. Now I just wanted to see if we were in her thoughts, if she wondered about us the way we did her.

"Around," she mimicked, "you can do better than that. Tell me where you've been."

I took a deep breath, the mustache tickling one nostril. For some reason, our mother's hairdo reminded me of Pat Benatar, even though it wasn't spiky at all. Maybe it was her eye makeup. "I've lived most of my life upstate, near Malloy." Something registered on her face. Nothing much, just a slight crinkle, a fleeting expression that meant she knew something about the place, but she held back, eager to sell the house, not spoil the opportunity—or that's what I thought, anyway.

"I see," she said softly, bracelets tinkling as she began to tickle my forearm, her long nails making my skin itch. "I think you could be very happy here, Mr. . . . ?" She pouted. "I've asked you twice now. What's your name?" I couldn't think of anything, then remembered the electrician's cards and magnets in my pockets. It was a risk, but I figured her toolshed salesman probably had done all the work around the place himself, and she'd likely not know Captain Electro-Man. I plucked the stuff from my pocket and handed it to her. She gave me a look of admiration. "A man who owns himself," she said. "Now, that's the way the world is supposed to work." She read the card and smelled the magnet. "I sure love the way new plastic smells." I felt something flapping at the right side of my head, as if someone were tickling me with a long feather. The detached sideburn caught my attention from the corner of my eye. I immediately grabbed for it and smashed it back in place, hoping the glue would hold.

I was nervous that the beard would fall off completely, so I asked to use the bathroom but moved too fast standing up from the table, spilling my coffee. The cup crashed to the floor, and coffee splattered slightly on my mother. She was talking, but I couldn't hear what she was saying. It was as if she were on mute. I struggled with my backpack, which was caught on the chair. After trying to free it, I simply yanked as hard as I could, toppling the chair and table and the other cup of coffee. My beard now dangled off the right side of my head, as if I'd been scalped. I didn't bother fixing it again.

"Are you okay?" Something about this stranger giving birth to me made me want to sprint away from her. I ran toward the door, her horseshoes clomping behind me, reverberating off the empty walls.

The front lawn was slick as I sprinted over it. Behind me, standing on the porch, she called out. "Hey, don't leave like this. Let me drive you." The world became silent except for her voice in my head. "Come back," she yelled.

I ran as hard as I could, losing the beard in a ditch after it blew right off my face. The sun kept flickering, getting lost behind cottony clouds as I tore down the five miles that led back to the bus stop. At one point, I saw her Pinto coming down the road, and I ducked into the ditch, hid there until it was quiet. It was a long way back, and I walked the last few blocks, finally arriving at the same benches Ronald and I'd slept on the year before. I plopped down, heart pounding in my chest, my breath short and painful, a stitch in my side. Some trucks clunked around the streets off the square, and a train ballyhooed along the tracks, clacking to beat all hell. It rushed past, the flashing red lights at the crossing vibrating from the speed. I caught my breath and checked the bus schedule. At this rate, I might even be back home before Aunt Lee ever noticed I was gone.

CHAPTER TWENTY SIX

Reggie and Wilson didn't so much chew their toast as masticate it. The boys used their molars to grind and crush, but the truly spectacular sight was how they had to utilize those same back teeth to take a first bite. Their pointy misaligned choppers at the front of their red mouths didn't allow for nibbling, so they pushed all their food to the back of their throats right off the bat, making them appear cartoonish, shoving whole slices of bread into their mouths without even so much as an introductory bite. After Reggie swallowed, his little face lit up again with enthusiasm. "You're a preacher," he said, pointing to Pastor Feirst. We were sitting very close together at the table. The boy's teeth were clotted with strawberry jam, and I'm ashamed to say I thought he might sink those vampire teeth into my neck.

"That's right," said the pastor, smiling at Reggie as if he were a Sally Struthers's kid knee-deep in garbage and filthy water. It was quiet around the table then. Mr. Feirst and his brother did have some vaguely similar facial features, but their lanky bodies were dead-on, exact replicas. They moved the same way and sat at the table upright, proper, and well-mannered. The television was muted, but the scene of the farm and a scrolling text about the latest developments in the manhunt for a shooter trailed along the bottom. Lucy sat on one side of me and Reggie on the other. Wilson was still disappointed that he'd not been able to abduct the boars, and it showed: his lower lip drooped, and he seemed to be mumbling to himself, face red and eyes somewhat wild. It was clear that Reggie had been born with the sweeter personality while his brother had inherited an angry worldview, but who could blame him. After all, his mouth was strange, and he was doomed to work the rest of his life at the furniture store. I couldn't look at him for fear that my heart would break.

Finally, after sipping a bit of coffee, Mr. Feirst spoke up. "You kids wouldn't know this, but my brother here was the state horseshoe champion from the years 1972–1977." The pastor's lazy eye swam farther to the side as he listened intently to his brother, a wry grin on his face. "He could toss a twelve pennyweight over fifty feet and still clink a ringer."

"Wow," said Lucy, her lack of interest very apparent. I felt her leg rub against mine as she reached for more bacon.

"These kids don't want to hear about some old fogy throwing horseshoes," said the pastor, patting his lips clean with a napkin.

"Thath for damn thure," sputtered Wilson, bits of toast and sausage flying toward Mr. Feirst, who politely wiped off his sleeve. The pastor grinned at his brother, a playful look similar to the ribbing Ronald and I were prone to give each other.

"I better get back out there," said Ronald as Lucy put her head on my shoulder. He'd given in and come to the house for some food but had never sat down. He just kept watching out the window toward the paddock, eating his food nearly as obscenely as the boys.

"**S**on, you think you might know where your daddy is holed up? Someplace near an old oak in the middle of a cornfield?" It was the second time the pastor had mentioned it, and I thought he was somehow tapped into my soul. The pastor noticed my quizzical expression and added, "You were muttering it in your sleep when I approached the barn at dawn." I felt put on the spot, mostly because his tone of voice quietly indicated that he believed me to be as crazy as our father.

I stammered and in the process spit a little fragment of food myself. Wilson of all people said, "Sthays its. Don't sprayths its." He continued shoving whole pieces of food into his mouth as Reggie smiled on, giving everyone all of his attention.

"I guess," I said, sounding weak. "I mean, it's possible he could be there. It was a field we used to farm. He has to be hiding somewhere," I added, not feeling the same resolution I'd experienced in my half-awake dream.

"Well," said Mr. Feirst, "that may well be. All things are possible."

The pastor chimed in sarcastically. "All things are possible for he that believes in the *Lord*."

Mr. Feirst cut his eyes toward his brother, kind of made a kissing sound in his direction. "As I was saying, stranger things have happened, but at this point, I think we've got all we can handle with keeping the boars alive. Although it would help if we knew just what your father had planned in terms of his actions." As soon as he'd referred to Dad, our farm showed up on the television screen, as if it had heard his comment. It was a replay of the "Artificial Insemination Keeps Gay Boars Alive Another Day!" story. But it was interrupted by a late breaking newscast.

"Better turn that up," said Mr. Feirst, his back erect in the chair. Wilson moped to the TV and cranked it too loud, but no one had the heart to correct him. Reggie beamed, clapped his hands. The kid was having the time of his life. Maybe it was his first sleepover ever.

A highly polished newscaster touched his earpiece and nodded. "This just in: we are being told by our affiliate in South Bend that a new piece of video footage has just arrived." He pressed his fingers tighter against his ear and listened intently, and for a moment—for once in a really long time—there was silence on the TV. The newscaster tilted his head and nodded, making certain to get the information being piped into his shiny earpiece exactly right. He took a deep breath and sat back in his swivel chair. Behind him was a puzzle of TVs, each with a different scene playing silently. "Malloy!" was plastered on every one of them.

"Apparently," said the newscaster, "the new video we are about to show our viewers is footage of one Jerry Bancroft on the courthouse lawn. We'll take you there with our own Flip Riceland." The newscaster whipped around in his chair to address a large screen to his right, where Flip and a college student stood shoulder to shoulder, bright green tree leaves fluttering around them.

"That's right, Gus. I'm here with Randy Southwell, a junior here at Midland majoring in communications." Flip held the microphone in the student's face. "Tell us what you've discovered, son." In the background, news vans raced onto the campus sidewalks, yanking equipment out and maneuvering for the next shot with Randy. Some of the faces were familiar, and I recognized them as men who'd been camping out near our cornfield for days.

"Well," said Randy, his Midland U. T-shirt ragged and stained with pizza sauce—the kid looked hung over and crusty—"I watched that footage over two hundred times and kept pausing it, but I couldn't catch what I thought I saw." Randy itched his nose and looked around. Maybe he needed some kind of fix. The more I watched him, the more it seemed that the guy was on something.

"And?" asked Flip intensely. The concern that the kid was going to end up a dud, a lame-duck interview, entered his eyes. I was pretty sure that if Randy were pulling his leg, he'd end up with a punch to the gut from Flip.

"And, well, I sorta broke into the communications lab. . . ." He paused and whispered, as if it would be just between him and Flip, "Is there some way we can edit this part out?"

Flip lied to the kid. "Yes, yes. Just go ahead, please."

"I broke in there and used the high-tech equipment and slowed the frames way down, man. I'm talking like super slow-mo, dude."

Flip pursed his lips, barely able to hold back his frustration. He said, very slowly, articulating each word distinctly, "And what did you see, Randy?"

"What I saw, man, was the little dude had a handgun tucked in his underwear waistband." He looked straight into the camera and became the expert. "Roll tape!"

"Well, I'll be damned," said Mr. Feirst, as if he finally understood what it was like to live with our father.

"That's not a good thing," said the pastor, looking at his brother. Ronald marched from his lookout post by the window back to the television, nervous and yet engrossed in the story, like the rest of us.

The boys left their chairs and plopped down on the floor, legs crossed, as if watching Saturday morning cartoons, heads cocked at steep angles to see the TV. The tape rolled as the newscaster in the studio did a voice-over. "This is pretty tricky to catch if you don't know what you're looking for. We've invited Dr. Kramer Cantrell from the Digi-Telecom Institute in Chicago to give us a play-by-play of what you're seeing. We'll be looping the split-second shot so our viewers can really get their bearings. Welcome, Dr. Cantrell."

The video was slowed down so much that it looked blurry, and our dad's hospital gown over a pair of underwear seemed to pulse on the screen. On the first through fifth replay, I couldn't catch anything, but on the sixth we all seemed to witness it at the same time. "I see the gun!" yelled Reggie, just as Dr. Cantrell said, "There. I think that's your best shot of it. Freeze the frame."

"Shit!" said Ronald, running to the backdoor, slipping on his boots.

"What is it, son?" asked the pastor, already on his feet, prepared to follow Ronald like a disciple.

Ronald held the door open, about to leave. "We got protesters out there by the boars." He squinted toward the barn. "They've got signs, about ten of them." His face lost some color as he turned toward the pastor. Despondent, Ronald repeated out loud what he read on one of the signs, "'Gay Swine? Let's Dine!'"

The pastor held back a smirk, then said, "Come on. I'll go with you. I've got a bit of experience with these sorts of things. I protested 'Nam peacefully." He looked back at us and said, "You gotta watch it though. These things can turn deadly in a heartbeat." With that, he and Ronald were out the door.

The air shifted in the room. Lucy lit up a cigarette and blew smoke toward the ceiling. The boys became antsy. "Shhhh!" said Wilson to no one, a sound that he could make perfectly.

On the TV Dr. Cantrell continued to talk about lighting, digital nanoseconds, and tape speeds. The newscaster gave Randy his due. "Flip, please give our thanks to the young man who took his own time to discover what we'd missed. This shows the IBI's manhunt is dead-on." A brief shot of Randy and Flip shaking hands blipped from the screen. Back in the studio, the image of our father was blown up, the pixels growing and enlarging, until the butt of the pistol stood out like a tumor. A cold and angry disappointment settled over me.

Mr. Feirst rose to help his brother and Ronald. Lucy rolled her eyes as a chant started outside by the paddock. I got up and looked through the window. The group had formed a circle and were marching, hoisting their hand-painted signs. "Hell no. We won't eat homo! Hell no. We won't eat homo!" they repeated with real rhythm, a singsong quality that brought our fanged boys to their feet, shimmying their asses to the beat.

CHAPTER TWENTY·SEVEN

Three agents from the Indiana Bureau of Investigation returned shortly after the chant had started at the paddock. The IBI guys looked genuinely dismayed at the spectacle of a lazy-eyed pastor praying for peace with one of the protesters, a yellow-haired woman wearing an abundance of blue eye shadow, who'd jumped ship to our side. She and the pastor were in a counseling session, using gunnies spread out on a tarp to rap, sitting with their legs crossed. Ronald and I and Lucy sat on bales of straw and answered the agents' questions.

"So, you're saying you've not seen your father in the last twenty-four hours?" asked one, directing himself to Lucy.

She blew smoke from the side of her mouth and said, "He's not my dad, dumb ass." The young agent, surely a farm boy before this gig, looked to us to answer the question.

"No," said Ronald, watching the protesters go round and round like a carousel. "But it's like we told the other IBI men: he's not going to give up. He's mad about the boars and all." The three agents ignored him and kept on.

"Has he set foot on the property since the shooting?"

Ronald couldn't take it anymore. He jumped up from the bale and headed to the paddock, where Mr. Feirst was doctoring the blind boar, but the older agent grabbed him by the arm and shoved him back down.

"Sit the fuck down, hayseed. I'll tell you when you can motherfucking leave." Ronald lay sprawled out on the bale, dust circling him. The pastor saw the whole thing and approached us with confidence, leaving his client meditating, her eyes closed, head tipped to the sky.

"Is there a problem here?" he asked, clutching his Bible. The old agent, red-eyed, his neck as flaccid as a turkey's, must've been a churchgoer. He caught a glimpse of the thick good book in the pastor's hand and calmed down. "No, pastor," he said, puffing, "just a disagreement in point of view. We're fine."

We answered more questions until late afternoon. Finally, the old agent told Pastor Feirst, "We're aware that Gerald Bancroft was not initially part of the shooting. We've got a punk in custody who may have fired the shot. Still, with his footprints in the cornfield and the fact that he was seen on tape with a pistol, we're considering Mr. Bancroft armed and dangerous."

Ronald laughed. "Well, he's got arms, and I won't debate that he's dangerous, but only to himself—and whoever he accidentally hurts along the way." The agents all acted as if we were not there anymore. The pastor shook their hands, and they were off. A lone news van came blasting in from the lane, forcing the IBI men to swerve to avoid hitting them. They honked. Then the news van honked, and it went on like that, volleying longer and longer horn blasts until the IBI men slowly drove out of sight.

The local newsmen set up a shot using the protesters as the background. Ronald and I slipped away toward the back of the farm after he'd secretly motioned for me to follow. The sun was lower in the sky, and the smell of burnt rubber from the old tire heap lingered in the air. It seemed implausible that we'd ever perform the chore again.

"Do you think he's going to use that handgun?" asked Ronald as he stood turned away from me like an informant. I felt like I had in the kitchen, cold and tired, ready for it all to stop. I kept looking around to make sure no one was filming us. The last thing I wanted was for some station to run our faces alongside our father's, showing the world that our eyes, maybe even our noses, favored our father's.

"No," I said, trying to think it through. "I don't think so, anyway. I don't think he'd try and hurt us, even if it was by accident."

Ronald contemplated it all. "Yeah, you're probably right," he said, looking toward the barn. I watched, too, as Lucy talked with a long-haired boy grip wearing acid-washed jeans and a muscle shirt. I wanted to take off toward him and fetch my gal, but I kept thinking about the dream in the barn, the view from above of the intricate crop circle.

"Well," said Ronald, "the good news is Aunt Lee's on her way back." He rubbed his wrist. "She called during breakfast, but I forgot to tell you." He seemed weary. "How in the hell are we going to explain all this?" he asked, motioning toward the barn. It was true: we had quite the menagerie formed. I had a Wolfrum girl staying over, and Ronald had managed to keep an expert boar whacker and his wild-eyed pastor brother on the farm, not to mention the toothy boys and our religious protesters who were now in a heady frenzy, trying in vain to get the convert back from Pastor Feirst.

"I don't know." I watched my brother as he cracked the bones in his neck, then all of his knuckles. I kept seeing the crop circle like a vision; it swirled in my head. Even the sight of Lucy now sitting with the grungy boy grip couldn't make it go away.

"Ronald?" I said, taking a leap of faith.

"Yeah," he muttered without much thought, cracking his neck again.

"Do you think he could be using a hideout? You know, like our old blackberry one?"

"I guess, but what's that got to do with anything? There's only been a complete manhunt going on. Don't you think they'd have found it by now?"

"No one knows about ours, and it's only forty feet from where we're standing. Besides, they don't know these fields, and they've spent most of their time posing for the video cameras. Not to mention there's thousands of square acres of corn in the county."

"So what?" said Ronald, looking toward the barn and his boars. I knew I'd not get much more of his time.

"Well, I think I could find him, maybe keep things from getting any worse. Besides, he's probably sick. I had a dream in the barn. I saw it like I was in a plane." The protesters retrieved their lost sheep and stuck a sign back in her hand as they pushed her to march, and the pastor made the sign of the cross.

To my surprise Ronald said, "How are you going to get in the sky?"

"I figure I'll lie and tell one of the news crews that I know where he's hiding out. They'd water at the mouth for a chance like that. They'd take me up in one of their helicopters."

"Any idea about where this mythical hideout is?" he asked playfully.

"Yeah. You know that field with the old oak? They haven't searched those fields west of town. Most of the looking has been done farther east and then out here."

"Well," said Ronald, "you better do two things: one, go get your girlfriend before that news creep gets down her pants; and two, get a move on before Aunt Lee makes it back." He patted my upper back, and before he could catch himself, Ronald leaned in and kissed me on the cheek. It embarrassed us both, but luckily the walk toward the barn provided some emotional cover. Lucy was holding a boom for the news guy as the Feirst brothers and our little boys with the unsightly choppers tried to hide, huddling together to avoid an interview. Smart farm boys, they were.

CHAPTER TWENTY·EIGHT

Even after reading about flight for over three years, whether in a commercial airliner or a small twin-engine, I wasn't prepared for the helicopter experience. My knuckles were white as I clenched the seat.

I'd used the business card that the helicopter pilot had given me when we'd met on the farm, back when Ronald had made a big deal out of introducing me as his brother who wanted to fly. When I'd phoned him up, he said he remembered me perfectly well, and now was as good a time as any for me to decide if I wanted to pursue that career in aviation. He had orange-colored hair, which once had been red and had lightened to its current tone by age. He dipped the copter toward the west, forcing me toward him, the air whipping wildly. With only half doors, the contraption felt like a Ferris wheel with too much power about to fly off its axis and throw our bodies into the deep green of the cornfields. The pilot wore the obligatory dark shades and a bomber jacket, lightweight, but it still had to be torturous in such heat. I'd made it into the air and was saddened by my lack of thrill, sickened more by how my stomach seemed to writhe below my rib cage.

"Hang on," he yelled, his headset wobbling some as we took a wide turn, flew out over yet another identical-looking hundred

acres of corn. It was hard not to think of *M*A*S*H,* how I might
have to bundle my frail father in a blanket and load his light body
into hyaline bubbles on the side of the helicopter, even though this
particular model, owned by TNC News Corporation, didn't come
with the capability of carrying wounded bodies.

"You're lucky you came clean," said the pilot, whose hair had
mussed up, giving him the look of Mr. Heat Miser from *The Year
Without a Santa Claus.*

I nodded. "Yep," I shouted over the noise, my stomach tossing. "I
appreciate the lift out here. Who knows, maybe the dream was just a
crock." He gave me the thumbs-up.

After Ronald and I'd made it back to the barn, I'd fessed up to
Mr. Feirst and the pastor. Lucy, too. "I don't know," I'd said, miffed
at Lucy for talking with the news kid, not really making eye contact
with her. "It's probably only a stupid dream, but I've got to see."

Mr. Feirst was the one to suggest trying TNC. He'd caught a
ride into town with my pilot on that first day of teaching us AI and
thought it might be my best chance. He was right. At first, I'd tried
fibbing to the man, but he stopped me. "That Feirst fella's already
called me on his CB. I'll take you up but not in the airspace over
Malloy. That'd be like flying in Da Nang. There's enough activity
over that town to call in the National Guard."

We took a wide orbit around a field near Shanty Falls, a two-
hundred-acre area grown high with a hybrid called Yellow-Sister-
Twisted. A high school dropout named Sanders McCoy owned
the field. He'd spent three solid years developing crossbred seeds in
his barn at night, employing the same hydroponics system he used
to grow and smoke weed. Sanders, it had been said, made a pretty
penny off the sale of his hybrid and now stayed stoned day and night,
waking and baking, doing things the way he wanted, which included
walking nude all over his land. That's why, when the pilot sped up,
the blades whacking the graying sky, I first thought Sanders's pale
white ass was my father's as he darted from one row to the next and

finally took off running. As we lowered over him, still not sure who we had in our sights, it was like I was Jim on Mutual of Omaha's *Wild Kingdom,* and my job was to shoot a dart into the beast before he managed to get away. Sanders craned his neck to look up at the belly of the helicopter, his mop of brown hair damp. He flipped us off, then stopped dead in his tracks at the edge of the field, his house only a few feet away. He bent over and splayed his buttocks wide, exposing a hairy ass crack as we elevated and shot off toward the stormy horizon.

"That was not called for," said the pilot, his voice sounding as if he were delivering a radio broadcast. I felt disappointment wash over me—not so much because of the mooning we'd gotten but because I was still afraid. It was my first time in the air. I'd never flown in anything before, and as much as I tried, I couldn't shake the feeling of dread in the pit of my stomach. How was I going to become a pilot myself if I couldn't even ride in a news chopper? For the next half hour we flew farther and farther away from Malloy, almost out to the county line. The pilot handed me a pair of binoculars and said, "These might help. This corn is thick as all hell." I didn't want to use both hands, which I'd have to do if I let go of the edge of the seat, but the damn things were so heavy, I thought I might flop right out the door, so I scooted back toward the interior of the loud helicopter.

"We're gonna go back real slow," said the pilot, who I'd heard over his radio was nicknamed Red. Other pilots kept talking to him on the news frequency as we zigzagged at a lower speed over the fields we'd crossed earlier. The sky was getting darker, and some heat lightning flashed way off in the distance. I was drenched with sweat as I tried to get the binoculars into focus. More activity popped from the pilot's headset as he talked in alphanumerical code. I almost dropped the binoculars and felt heat redden my face when the pilot tapped me on the shoulder. "Use the lanyard," he said, a word I assumed meant the rope attached to the binoculars. I pulled it over my head and quickly started looking again. Through the lenses, the fields were blurry patches of green, and the rigidity with which I sat in the seat didn't provide for a very good inspection. Soon I was feeling stupid for wasting the pilot's time. He was clearly a decent guy, and I'd taken him on the proverbial wild-goose chase.

"Look there," he said, pointing toward a large, flattened-down circle ahead of us, a depression in the sea of green that appeared as though a spaceship had landed there. "Might be the source of your dreaming," he quipped, his orange hair starting to curl some with the humidity. We flew faster, and I could feel the excitement building in me. The pilot lowered us farther, letting up on the speed as we passed over the edge of the circle. Dark clouds churned in the distance, avoiding Malloy. Some wayward raindrops began to pelt the high corn as we crisscrossed the mowed-down area. Nothing was there. It wasn't a hideout at all.

"I think this is a low spot," said the pilot, watching the ground below intensely as we hovered just a few feet above. It was definitely a patch of corn that'd drowned in too much rain. The stalks were all yellow, and the entire area was swampy. I realized I'd also wanted to see my father, to make sure he was okay, maybe even see if his eyes would tell me whom he'd really intended on hurting—the boars, us, himself.

A call came over the radio, more cryptic talk that left me bewildered. "Ten-four," said the pilot, adjusting his seat. "I've got to get you back home, son. They've got some sort of riot happening in town. And they've found the handgun your daddy . . ." He trailed off, kind of shrugged. I nodded, accepting that I'd failed. He sensed it and said, "Hey, what the hell. Let's fly you over the town on the way back to your farm. That'll cheer you up. It's a freaking madhouse."

The rain increased a little, and the corn steamed from the water falling on it in large drops. The pilot looked out his door and said, "Now that really looks like Vietnam. That's just the way the jungle steams." We flew faster than I'd ever believed you could in a helicopter, and when we reached the city limits, I thought the pilot would say the same thing about Malloy looking like 'Nam, because there were no fewer than twenty helicopters in the air, and all the ground below us was covered in refugees from the countryside, looking wild and hungry and desperate—protesters marching in circles, and a group of transsexuals carrying signs with Mrs. Graves's face plastered on them. But he didn't. All he said was, "Look, you're not scared anymore." And I realized I was nearly hanging out the side of the door, the power of being above it all as intoxicating as Lucy's kisses.

CHAPTER TWENTY·NINE

I'd gotten so sick of the news that I couldn't take even a second more of it. The footage of our father, the experts on animal sexuality, and the older story of Mrs. Graves taking a stand against bigots were shown hundreds of times per hour. To break the monotony, some channels aired the protesters around our paddock, but that was done more or less as mockery, highlighting how truly stupid and out of touch Midwesterners really are. After all, the only thing more despicable than dumb farmers was their lame attempt at protecting the gay rights of pigs. It had finally happened: our father had taken his fumbled life and made national news with it. Ronald had suspected it all along, and here it was in perfect cable glory.

"I'm getting out of here," I said, agitated. The rest of the group sat around the kitchen table, devouring a roast the pastor had made with rosemary and apricots. It was delicious, but I only nibbled a small piece. Ronald was eating his on a paper plate out by the boars.

"Where ya goin'?" asked Reggie, as chipper as a little sprite. He had a stem of rosemary lodged between his little daggers and looked as though he might ribbit like a frog.

Lucy got up. "I'll go with you." I stomped out the backdoor and toward the backside of the farm. I didn't slow down for her as my feet brushed through blooming hawk's-beard and billowy dandelions. It had only sprinkled where we were, the tall grass damp but still sharp. A blade sliced my forearm as Lucy called after me.

"Hey," she said, "wait up. Jesus, you going to a fucking fire or what, Lance?"

Like an immature punk, I wheeled on her and shouted, "Why don't you get your hippie boy grip to go on a walk with you? I'm sure he's got what you're looking for!"

"Don't be an ass, Lance. He was just showing me how the equipment works." Nothing came to me as I sat down in a patch of soft heather and turned my back on her. I could hear her footsteps brushing through the undergrowth. She plopped down next to me and lit us both a cigarette. She was four years older than me, and I'd proved it by acting the fool.

"Here," she said, handing me a smoking Salem Light. As the sun glowed, we sat quietly and smoked. Mourning doves purred nearby. My back ached, and all I wanted to do was get back up in the air, find a point of view that was distant and removed.

"Lance, I'm sorry if I gave you the wrong impression. It's all been a little fucking wacko around here. But I'd like us to always know each other, maybe even go on dates after this is over. Still, what I'm doing is wrong even if we're only a few years apart."

"I hate this place," I said, looking around, trying to sound as cool as Mellencamp. Lucy didn't respond, except to move closer to me and snuggle up. "Come on. I want to show you something." We got up and brushed each other off. Lucy followed me around the backside of the property, holding hands like we'd not fought at all, but something was fading, a space growing between us.

I yanked the plywood from the opening and helped her crawl inside after me, offering my hand. The blackberry hideout was mostly dark, but some sunlight filtered in, too, giving the space an impermanent feeling, as if it were about to ignite. "This is cool," said Lucy, looking around. "You guys even have a little table in here."

"Yeah, but it's old. We don't use it anymore now." I took a burlap sack and spread it out on the ground. Lucy sat down with me as we fell into an awkward silence. I dabbed at the grass cut on my arm. Lucy kissed it. Before long, we were groping and shucking off our clothes, the hideout becoming more stifling. Her skin was as soft as the loam beneath us. I was overzealous and banged my teeth into hers during a kiss, and my mind held onto the vision of Reggie and Wilson. How would they ever be able to kiss with mouths like that? I shook the images, though, and before long it was over, and we lay heaving next to each other, our sweat having made a pasty clay with the dirt.

"Crap," said Lucy, looking at her own body, then mine. The paste clung to our pubic hair and rubbed into our skin like taupe bruises. "We look like we're made of clay." I surveyed her body, too. She picked a mud goober from her belly button. "Gross," she said, flicking it off. "How the hell are we going to get cleaned up before your aunt gets home?" I'd forgotten, and the idea socked the air out of me.

"Shit," I said, reluctantly. "That's right—she'll be back anytime."

I reached for another burlap sack and tried to wipe the mud off Lucy's stomach. "Ouch," she said, "that hurts." I let up on the pressure and began to swab her more gently, first along her arms and hands and then down to her feet, where inch by inch I dabbed softly at her skin, moving up her calf and onto the soft inside of her thighs. "Hmm," she moaned, and it shocked me. I'd really thought I was just being gentle, helping her clean up, but I welcomed the surprise. I used the rough burlap to touch lightly her erect nipples, brushing over them, cleaning the light daubs of mud. She pulled me to her, and in our attempt to get clean our bodies became dirtier.

Afterwards I pulled on my clothes and told her to stay put. At the spigot I filled a bucket with water and toted it back to the hideout. I undressed again, and we took turns washing each other off. And it was in that moment, with her back to me and the soft curve of her spine slightly off center, I realized it was over. Lucy and I got dressed and kissed, but I knew we were nearing the end of what had been between us. I'd be lying if I didn't say it was a relief—sad, yes, but surely a reprieve, too. I wasn't ready to be someone's man. I wasn't even my own yet.

"Come on," she said. "I sure could go for some of that pastor's roast right about now." On the way back toward the house, we passed the paddock, where the protesters, now just a handful, were reading their Bibles.

"Sinners!" yelled the woman with yellow hair stacked high and feathered. Lucy smiled at her, then flipped them all off. Ronald stood inside the boar pen, cleaning the boar not unlike I had Lucy.

CHAPTER THIRTY

It was a very weird thing to see Aunt Lee flying into the yard driving a yellow GTO with Cragars. It was jacked up so high in the back that its nose scraped the sod as she tried to stop but couldn't. Aunt Lee coasted the car into the corner of the house. It made a loud smack when the bumper hit the cornice of the foundation. And that's what made the others, still at the table watching the TV as Malloy went under siege, leap up and join me at the living room window. Ronald, bewildered, said, "Is that Aunt Lee? What the hell?"

She had someone with her whose hair was like a beehive. The woman got out of the car as calmly as if they'd pulled into a parallel spot. She looked about six feet tall, not including her wall of black hair, and her bare arms and shoulders were long and muscular. She went around to open Aunt Lee's door, carrying herself in a formal manner that seemed to indicate she was somehow paid to be doing it, like an indebted assistant or well-tipped chauffeur. The woman had on a gaudy outfit of lime green, sequined stretch pants, and an untucked, sleeveless silk blouse of the same color. She'd donned a lot of turquoise jewelry on her wrists and long fingers, along with several strands of colorful beads around her neck. It was then that I recognized her. I looked to Ronald, but he didn't seem to understand what he was seeing. When the woman opened the car door, she stooped and took Aunt Lee's hand, pulling her out like she was a Raggedy Ann doll. The woman escorted Aunt Lee but was having trouble keeping up with her. Aunt Lee was making for the house at a clip reminiscent of an enraged elephant on the loose. When we could no longer see them from the window, I led the group back through the kitchen and to the porch door.

Aunt Lee was inside and hugging and kissing Ronald and me before we could even get a word out. She said, "Oh, boys, my wonderful boys," as she pinched our cheeks and absentmindedly tried to fix our hair, stopping short of spitting in her palm and flattening our cowlicks like she'd done when we were kids. Aunt Lee pulled away from us and said, "Ronald, Lance. I should've never left. I swear to high heavens I don't know what your aunt Lee was thinking."

She dabbed at her eyes and nose with a raggedy, crumpled pink tissue. Ronald could think of nothing else but seeing her driving the souped-up car. He was amazed. "Aunt Lee, I thought you couldn't drive?"

"Oh, there's a lot of things you boys don't know about ole' Aunt Lee. It's Mr. Dickers's car, a hobby I can't understand," she said, as if she'd gotten to know him better. "Anyway, I want you to meet somebody." She motioned for the woman standing behind her to come forward. I saw the woman's strong features, the way her eyebrows arched and her red lips appeared plump and soft as pillows.

Aunt Lee stopped before she introduced the woman, noticing for the first time the other people gathered in the room. She gave Ronald and me a look meant to convey that we were being rude for not dealing with the formalities right off the bat, even if she had been too busy fussing over us to notice the young woman and older, dignified men. Ronald spoke up. "Aunt Lee, this is Mr. Feirst. He's the man from Midland University who . . ."

Aunt Lee cut Ronald off. She finished his sentence. "Who is teaching you boys how to do that awful thing they talked about on the TV. I know."

She shook Mr. Feirst's hand. He said, tipping his hat toward her, "Ma'am."

Aunt Lee said, "Mr. Feirst, you and Aunt Lee will need to talk later." She was pleased to meet the pastor. "That's all that kept Aunt Lee going, once a man of the cloth appeared on the scene." She kind of curtsied when they shook hands.

Ronald looked at me then to introduce Lucy. I stepped up and did it.

Aunt Lee took Lucy's face in her hands and kissed her forehead. Lucy looked more beautiful than I could remember seeing her. Aunt Lee said, "Honey, Aunt Lee knew your momma when she was no bigger than a pumpkin. You and Aunt Lee are also gonna have a little talk. Okay?" Aunt Lee let loose of Lucy's head. Lucy looked away, slid off behind the group, and began removing the plates from the table, trying to hide the cigarette butts piled in a saucer. Reggie hugged Aunt Lee like she was his while Wilson tipped his cap to her and grunted.

Aunt Lee cleared her throat and again motioned for the woman to come forward. "Now, boys, this isn't the way Aunt Lee wanted to do this, but with your daddy plum nuts now, she has no choice." She pulled the woman next to her, then gave her a little shove toward us. The woman smiled awkwardly, revealing a beautiful set of perfect white teeth. "Boys, this woman here is your momma." She'd grayed some, and a mild tick affected her right cheek, but it was our mother, older looking, but still pretty.

The TV was turned up real loud. It sounded like the end of the earth: reporters bellowed over the masses now gathered on Malloy's town square, and the emergency alert system was in full use as Shriners performed figure eights around the crowd, taunting the amassed gay and lesbian activists. My senses were becoming frizzled. The prolonged views on the TV of our farm deep in live coverage, our lost mother standing in the kitchen, and our fugitive dad with his face plastered on the national news—it all made me feel detached from myself, as if I would not have to wait to learn to fly. I might merely rise up from the kitchen floor and disappear like a vapor through the ceiling, take off into the hot sky like a wayward helium balloon.

Our newly arrived mother held out her arms and tried to latch onto us like she'd seen her ex-sister-in-law do, but she didn't want to get her clothes dirty, so the maneuver ended up looking like a do-si-do. I wondered if she'd ever figured out that I had been at her home, trying to buy it. She was going to say something—what, I could not imagine—but Mr. Feirst beat her to the punch, though not on purpose. He blurted out, after seeing the two sides of the gay boars' debate commence to be a full and outright brawl, "Looky there, folks, that's turning into a public emergency!"

As we all watched the TV, Malloy's town square became a boil. The people and the newsmen were its whitehead about to pop under the heat and force of friction. People clamored together. I imagined the smell of body odor and foul boots laced with hog manure churning low to the ground to form a knee-high fog. Everywhere voices all spoke at once—the fury of the repeated, of the echoed, of the recapitulated—they all buzzed like a swarm keyed up for attack. Some of the transsexuals grabbed ahold of old men and kissed their bald heads. Mrs. Graves's face popped up and down on signs in the hands of protesters on each side. Some overweight church ladies fainted and were caught and drug off to side streets by lesbians with crew cuts wearing T-shirts with two pigs kissing. A toothless farmer threw a clawhammer at the windshield of one of the news vans. Electricity surged, popped, made people jittery enough to shove for the pure release of ending the exposure. Now an official for the town tried to speak through a bullhorn. The crowd booed and hissed at him. Stones were thrown at his feet while a gang of cops tried with all their might to make it through the thick sea of brow-creased men and women. Teenagers and town outcasts clung to the branches of trees. A shirtless newsman who seemed as if he might be losing his mind oinked into the camera.

Our mother laughed out loud at the newsman's oinks. She said, as we all stood glued to the TV, "Isn't he a clever man. And I'll be damned if I've ever seen a man as muscular as him." Aunt Lee glared at her. Our mother didn't seem to mind our aunt's disapproval. "I mean that man is a little crazy and all, but I wouldn't kick him outta my bed for eatin' crackers, that's for sure."

Aunt Lee had had enough. "Now, missy, you clean up that trap right quick, or I'll take you right back where I found you, and I mean like pronto."

Our mother didn't seem to hear Aunt Lee. I wanted to look at her but didn't feel right doing it directly. I peered at her out of the corner of my eye. She was biting her lip as she watched the muscular, crazed newsman on TV. I thought I saw Mr. Feirst's face blush as our mother stared at the TV.

"I tell you what, I'd make that man see stars if I ever got ahold of him."

Aunt Lee stepped forward automatically and slapped her across the face. The sound beat off the kitchen walls as if we were a clan in a cave.

"Uh-oh," said Reggie, looking around in vain to find someone to tattle to. Wilson smiled so large that his inflamed gums showed. Our mother was barely able to register what had happened. She brought her hand to her red cheek and patted it as Aunt Lee took a step back to the spot where she'd been, reoccupying the space like she might lose her place in line.

No one looked as our mother went to the freezer to get a piece of ice for her face and gingerly returned to stand in front of the TV with the rest of us. Aunt Lee straightened the creases on her dress. She cleared her throat slightly and stood more upright. On the TV, some kids wearing John Deere T-shirts could be seen flipping off the camera as it again panned over the crowd. Several groups of farmers huddled separately. The town seemed to erupt with activity as more cars and trucks rushed in to the side streets. I wondered if the panoramic view we were now seeing was being shot from Red's helicopter. Sirens and flashing blue and red lights twinkled over the television screen. A news reporter in New York stated, "This is the scene in Malloy, Indiana, where a pair of gay boars has given way to a full-out demonstration, drawing hundreds of people to the town square from both sides of the debate while the manhunt for a man suspected of trying to kill his own is still the focus of the authorities."

Aunt Lee put her arm around my back and pulled me to her for my mother to see. It was strange, but I hoped Aunt Lee's attention was producing a pang of jealousy in my retrieved mother. But when I again cautiously looked in her direction, she was entranced in using her thumb to rub circles over her index finger, testing the paste her makeup had made from the melting ice.

On the TV, several storefront windows out of focus in the background could be faintly heard crashing as a few of Malloy's hungry and homeless did what was natural. More newspeople poured into the crowd. The man I'd seen in the cornfield back when it all started, the churchgoer in his Sunday clothes, had somehow gotten a portion of the mob's attention. Over a bullhorn of his own he said in a low voice, "Heed these words, my lost flock. We all pay the price for the wages of sin." He brought his voice back up to the level of a scream as he looked straight into the camera and pointed to the audience at home. "God does not indulge in the unnatural, you guys!" With that he tried to look for a route of escape, but the crowed roiled this way and that, like a mechanized sea wave, the agile movements not of nature's design but man's invention. He was trapped by members of the other side of the debate, and they swarmed him, screaming into his face like barracks sergeants, trying to scare him into converting to their side, right on the courthouse lawn.

Clinging to a boom, a familiar anchorman was lowered out of the sky in a cherry picker. He had a mic in hand, his toupee flapping ever so gently in the exhaling exhaust of the crowd. Lucy sort of forced down a burp at the sight of her father getting his chance at real reporting. From a helicopter, a cameraman also descended and was dangling over the crowd, filming it all. Corn silk twisted in conical swirls of forced air. In the distance, away from the town square, the paradropping of the National Guard commenced from bulky planes. The riot raged on the television as we stood and watched it in the house on the Bancroft farm.

CHAPTER THIRTY·ONE

As we stood in the kitchen watching the National Guard swoop in on Malloy and try to restore some semblance of peace, you could feel our old group wanting to get the hell out of Dodge. The violence on the television made us all reflective. The first to speak up was Mr. Feirst. "I hate to do this to you boys, but I best get back up to Midland U. while the getting is good." He grabbed Ronald's hand and pumped it furiously. He said, "Ronald, you're gonna be just fine. If you need any help or if you run into trouble with collecting the boars, don't hesitate to call. I can talk you through most of the problems right over the phone. I hope we see you in the near future on campus. Good luck."

He shook my hand, too, and simply said, as if he'd just remembered my name, "Lance." He hugged Lucy, tipped his hat to Aunt Lee and our mom. "I'd like to volunteer to get these young fellas home," he said, rubbing Reggie's head but not daring to touch Wilson. The boys pouted but didn't resist. "I assume you boys can show me the way," he said.

His pastor brother added, "I'll go with you. I'd like to talk with the boys' parents about a fund they can access." With that, they were out the door. We watched them as they climbed into the university truck, now considerably banged up, and drove out of the yard and over the first hill of the lane. It was quiet in the kitchen then.

I can't say I was shocked to hear Lucy speak. I guess at those times when it appears a family is about to do some thinning of its herd—and with Aunt Lee having belted our mother—those without familial ties sense they are in danger themselves. They might think, "God, if they'll do that to their own kin, how safe am I?" Lucy said, in an apologetic tone, "You guys, I'm going to get going. My mother is probably going nuts at the house worrying about my dad and brother and me." Lucy gave Aunt Lee a hug and kissed Ronald on the cheek, something Aunt Lee normally would've frowned upon. I walked Lucy to her truck. Outside, Mr. Dickers's cornfields and the yard were torn to pieces. A few helicopters, ones that couldn't find any room over Malloy, made passes above our farm. Ronald said when I kissed Lucy good-bye, it was on the same channel her father worked for, shot from one of those helicopters, I guess. When Lucy drove away, I turned and started back to the house, feeling homesickness like a tight knot in my chest but liberation as well. For the first time since it'd all started, I was as tired as hell and couldn't care less if I'd made it onto the news. As I walked toward the house, I tripped on one of the many piles of trash that the TV crews had left behind and scraped my shin on a concrete slab. As I pulled up my jeans to look at the blood already seeping through my pant leg, I heard an unearthly bawling coming from the barn. Before I could even glance up, Ronald was blasting out of the house, looking at me quizzically, as if I'd been the thing making the noise. To him it seemed like I was making a big deal over a little scrape. Ronald's face had the look of a person who feels guilty for something they could've never stopped anyway. Aunt Lee and our mother quickly moved across the yard toward the barn, too. The cry came again, this time sounding much more like a high-pitched wail.

Ronald was off like a rocket toward the barn, barefoot over the old garage foundation as if the spiked shards of cement were not even there. He shot across a volunteer patch of potatoes and into the paddock. I followed him, already sensing something was there I didn't want to see, but I couldn't stand hearing anymore either.

Ronald hopped the fence ahead of me. He immediately disappeared from view. I was almost to the fence myself, about ten yards away, when he rose back up holding something limp in his arms. It was bloody and shrouded in some torn and soiled powder blue cloth—a hospital gown. Ronald's face was white. His features, though, were as dark as I'd ever seen them. When he climbed the fence without any difficulty with the weight he now cradled in his arms, I knew it was our dad. Ronald told me to get away, don't look. He added calmly, "He tried to castrate them. The blind one has taken some pretty big bites out of him." He walked past me and commanded, "Just don't look," as he carried our dad toward the house.

I ran to the pen and found the floor soupy with blood. The blind boar stood over the other one, sniffing him, his eyes and snout covered in blood. The boar lying on the ground was in shock, dying, one of his testicles hanging out of a jagged slit that gushed forth blood onto the concrete with every beat of his heart. A rope was tied around his neck, and baler twine cinched his hind feet. I turned and ran toward the house. Ronald was coming back out in a hurry and met me halfway. His arms were empty but smeared with mud and blood.

"Aunt Lee is calling 911, but he's dead, Lance. He's dead," he said, his eyes watery, his hands shaking. A stone-cold blast of hurt hit me in the throat. For a moment, we stood still next to each other, Ronald's right hand slightly grazing mine in a quick grasp that reminded me of when we had been little boys holding hands at night, walking in the dusk from the barn to the house after the late night chores were done. Ronald looked up as some more news helicopters, after hearing the 911 call bleat over their scanners, flooded into the sky overhead. He took me by the arm and said, "Come on. I need your help to get the bleeding stopped on the boar." He knew it was useless, but it was something to do, and working on something was all we'd ever known.

We rushed together toward the boars' pen as the extreme air pushing down on us from the helicopters parted our hair. I could see Ronald's white scalp along his natural part so clearly that I thought for a minute it was a healed scar I'd never known about. The helicopters landed in Dickers's trashed cornfield. I turned and looked back over my shoulder as the cameramen came running. When one of them tripped and fell, I had to bite the inside of my lip to keep from becoming hysterical. I didn't know what I was feeling, but I could always watch the video on the six o'clock news, watch it real close and see. Maybe they didn't get a good zoom-in on my face. Maybe they wouldn't compare our faces side by side with our father's, the image on the television for the whole world to see. I closed my eyes and thought of the gunmetal gray B-52 bird that had plagued my dreams for months. In my dizzy head I saw it land smoothly on its belly in the pasture, the clamshell doors opening up like heaven's fulgurant gates, taking Ronald and me away to another place, where our dad was competent and strong, alive, too, and our mother was kind and stable, not lascivious, and had never left us.

I felt Aunt Lee at my side, trying to get me to breathe deeply as the sirens howled from somewhere at the end of our long lane. My mother jockeyed for position as the crews charged us. The last thing I remember before passing out was the way the glassy eye of the camera looked just inches in front of my face, my mother posing by my crumpling body and bragging to the world while she primped.

I went face-first into the polyester cleavage of her lap as she knelt reluctantly by my limp body. Before going completely out, I heard her say to the camera, "This is my boy here." She looked at me with a sympathetic frown, like a farmer might look at a runt or a newborn hydrocephalic calf. She wrinkled her nose and said, softer, "He's one of 'em, at least."

EPILOGUE

I've lived in Indiana all my life. Today is a special day. They call it a "Year-to-the-Day Exposé." And when they say it, they sing it like a song. It has a ring to it, I guess. The TV anchors, now mostly women, have been stalking me for three days, begging for my story and demanding one-on-one interviews Barbara Walters–style. Even the Wolfrum men, parlaying their exposure during the Tragedy into jobs at a TNC affiliate in Fort Wayne, have sent me hams with kind notes, basically trying to convey that they'd treat us fairly if they obtained the exclusive right to interview our whole family. None of the notes attached to the hams ever mentioned Lucy.

I've gotten e-mails, phone messages, and Federal Express packages from twenty stations trying to lure me in. One even suggested that my story would make a fine movie. The polite voice on my answering machine said, "People love pigs, Mr. Bancroft, and homosexuality is very hot these days. It could even make a good sitcom. Call me!" Apparently they've been searching for everybody, including Bill and Leroy, who disappeared after our dad died. Ronald believes that Aunt Lee had something to do with their disappearance, that she more than likely told them to leave and never come back.

I belly crawl out my backdoor to the little silver hangar where I house my beautiful two-seater. You'd think that people who make a living violating the privacy of others would be more devious in their methods than a Midwestern crop duster, but I've gotten away with the belly-crawl deal now ever since they've been trying to get me to talk about the Malloy Gay Boar Tragedy. Lucy, who is a nurse in Fort Wayne and is married to a podiatrist with three kids, was on the TV just a few days ago, pushing back the cameras as they tried to get her to talk about it as she left the hospital. It was nice to see that she'd not changed. Sometimes I wonder if I should have dated her more, even proposed, but she seems happy, the head of a fine family, and, besides, I'm best when left alone.

As strange as it seems to me, Pastor Feirst and I have stayed in touch. Years later, when I was leaving the practice hangar and trying hard to figure out how to scrape together some money to start the crop dusting business, I was met at the chain-link gate by a man dressed in shorts and a Hawaiian shirt. At first, I thought it was his brother.

"Hey, Mr. Feirst." I was actually excited to see him.

He removed a cabana-style hat and bowed. "Nope, it's me, the pastor." He smiled benevolently and offered his hand. "I've called your brother and told him. He said you were out here, so I thought I'd see how you were and tell you, too." He patted me on the back. "My brother passed away yesterday. Liver cancer." We walked, and I tried to tell him how sorry I was, but he seemed as positive as ever. We strolled toward his station wagon, and I noticed it had an insignia on the side: "The Pastures of Forgiveness Foundation."

"Who's that in your car?" I asked.

He beamed. "Well, that's kind of a surprise for you," he said warmly. The car door opened and out stepped a tall young man with broad shoulders. As we approached him, the pastor said, "You know, there's a lot to be said for investing in our youth, don't you think?" I nodded.

At the car, the rugged guy looked at me as if I should've known him.

"You don't remember, I guess," he said, thrusting his big hand out. "Reggie Mercer." I was floored. He'd grown nearly two feet, but the biggest change was his mouth. He had a perfect set of wonderfully aligned teeth.

"Reggie and I work together on the Foundation, seeding money to young people to pursue their dreams," said the pastor. "After Reg had his braces off, he came to work with me. He's also going to school to become a dentist." The sun was warm on our skin, and for a moment, all I could think of was how it must've taken a real miracle to fix those teeth.

"How's your brother?" I asked him. He didn't pause or look wary when he said, "Fine, but doing time at Pendleton. But the pastor and I are putting in place a transition plan for him after his release next year." He'd caught the pastor's can-do attitude, and I was happy for him. I was due at a banker's office to try and get a loan, a prospect the banker had told me was highly unlikely, but I figured I'd give it a shot anyway.

"Well," I said, looking at my watch, "it's sure been nice seeing you both again, and, again, I'm sorry to hear about your brothers." The pastor and Reggie smiled at each other.

"Thank you, son," said the pastor, his white chest hair at the collar of his shirt waving in the breeze. He turned to Reggie. "Why don't you do the honors, Reg."

Reggie stepped forward and handed me an envelope. "On behalf of the Pastures of Forgiveness Foundation, we'd like to offer this token of our belief in your abilities to help nurture our Midwestern way of life through your business and dream. Should you ever have the opportunity to help another young person in a similar manner, we ask that you consider sowing this same type of seed." The envelope was thick. It contained five thousand dollars. I handed it back to the pastor, who stood meekly by.

"Nope," he said. I started to argue, but he drowned me out. "And I'll tell you why. Lance, I knew you boys would never do it, so I gave an exclusive interview at a news studio in Indy for the anniversary of that thing. Well, one of those tabloids saw it and said they'd pay me five g's if I let them take pictures of me and Reggie and the Foundation and talk some about what happened back then. I figured it was a good trade-off—exposure for the Foundation and money for you. Ronald was all set up, so he told me about your crop dusting business and the loan problems."

I was embarrassed and grateful. "Thank you." It didn't feel like enough, so I hugged them both, Reggie towering over me. In an instant they were off as I stood watching their station wagon kick up dust, the money heavy in my hand.

Since then, I've seen Reggie and the pastor at their Foundation events. I've not been able to give much, but Ronald and I offer free training to kids interested in flying or veterinarian science. The pastor was even kind enough to name our work with the kids after our dad—"The Gerald Bancroft Fellowships." A nice gesture, one that he commented on after one of the banquets, saying, "Most of us have our weaknesses. Your father's may have been having too big of dreams, but he fathered you fine young men, so in my book that should get your name put on something more than a gravestone." That pastor, he's a helluva guy.

On the one-year anniversary of our mutual exposure, our mother had soaked it all up, allowing interviews from nearly every network. She spent weeks after the death of our dad sketching coffins and pictures of her crying, a red rose in her mouth like a Spanish dancer. She tried over and over to send some of her drawings to the newsman she fancied so much, but to no avail. The envelopes just kept coming back to her marked "Return to Sender." Finally one day she left town after the toolshed salesman came back to her, suffering from hepatitis and needing her love. We see her more often now, at potlucks and the occasional family get-together. She's tired most of the time but by all appearances somehow more normal now. We talk about our dad sometimes, and even she seems to forgive him for his ways. It's a relief to grow older in the Midwest: things seem to change, then turn back on themselves, and everything—the landscape, the people, our families—are similar yet somehow altered, like a field of corn, identical but vastly different if you spend much time in it.

There's always been a yearly commemoration of that summer, but this is the biggie, the one that the cable channels count on for high ratings and increased profits from hawking pop, Fords, erectile dysfunction meds, and beer.

Ronald called last night from his vet clinic in Richvalley. He said, "I told them to kiss my ass when they wanted footage of you and me and Mom by the boar. Do you know they asked me if we'd be willing to put a leash on him and do a live thing with Mom and you and me at Dad's grave? They said they had people talking to Mr. Wolfrum about it, too. Can you believe that?" We laughed until I lost my breath. He was talking about the blind boar he still keeps in a ten-acre field of sweet alfalfa and has specially housed during the winter in an old heated basketball gymnasium along with the twenty or so other barn animals from his practice he refuses to put down. On the phone, once I could breathe again, Ronald said, "Are they hounding you more this year, too?" It was true—the anniversary coverage in the media seemed to have gotten more and more intense over the years. He laughed as hard as I did when I told him about crawling out to the hangar on my stomach at four thirty in the morning for a couple days running. We reminisced some more, even telling the funniest stories we could remember of our dad, which was a cinch. In the end, we stayed on the phone for over an hour.

Before we hung up, I said, "Aunt Lee asked me if I'd fly her and Dickers to Florida for their tenth wedding anniversary. You want me to swing by and pick you up?"

Ronald said that wouldn't be necessary. "I'm all caught up on her lectures about finding a nice girl to marry, but thanks for asking."

After I hung up, I sat in the darkness of my apartment and replayed it all in my head—Lucy, Dad's lifeless body in Ronald's arms, the way the sky seemed overtaken with helicopters—and I wonder how things might have turned out if Dad had lived. One of the stranger parts of the event was how a small offshoot of one of the protesting groups took to making our dad a hero. It didn't last long—just a couple of years or so, thank goodness—but still, it's one of my life's greatest mysteries to think that Dad could've been someone others aspired to.

Now as I finish my belly crawl out to the hangar, I have dirt on my jacket and some pieces of grass wedged into the zipper, but other than that I've made it for the third day in a row to the plane without the news freaks seeing me. They shake their fists at me as I circle out over a field and head back at them like I'm going to do a kamikaze number. I smile as I feel the air lift the wings up a couple of notches. When I rise fully above their vans and upright antennas and radiant pole lights, I toss the sheets of paper out the window, the same ones I'll have to pick up when I return home. I cut a path over a clump of pine and oak and come again at them as they read the fliers: NO COMMENT. Some of the news ladies hold up the sheets of paper and report on them, live on the air. But one guy who bears a striking resemblance to a monkey gives me the up-yours fist. I cruise away from them and don't look back, the quiet early morning only broken by an accompanying air rushing over my wings. Outside the windshield, there's a full, eager moon in front of me, prettier than anything they could show on TV.